ROSE'S FIGHT

BOOK THREE IN THE TRENWITH TRILOGY

ROSIE CLARKE

Boldwood

First published in 2008 as *Forbidden Love*. This edition first published in Great Britain in 2024 by Boldwood Books Ltd.

Cover Design by Colin Thomas

Cover Photography: Colin Thomas and Unsplash

A CIP catalogue record for this book is available from the British Library.

Paperback ISBN 978-1-83518-190-4

Large Print ISBN 978-1-83518-191-1

Hardback ISBN 978-1-83518-189-8

Ebook ISBN 978-1-83518-192-8

Kindle ISBN 978-1-83518-193-5

Audio CD ISBN 978-1-83518-184-3

MP3 CD ISBN 978-1-83518-185-0

Digital audio download ISBN 978-1-83518-188-1

Boldwood Books Ltd
23 Bowerdean Street
London SW6 3TN
www.boldwoodbooks.com

1

Rose stood in the ancient church listening as the vicar baptised Lucy's son, John Arthur Pelham. She smiled inwardly, her gaze moving over the happy faces of the assembled company. Lucy was clearly delighted with her beautiful, healthy son, as was her husband, Andrew Pelham. The boy was Lucy's first child. Sarah, standing next to her, was Lucy's cousin and sister-in-law and the two were very fond of each other. Sarah was also Rose's friend. She had recently given birth to a daughter. Mary Anne Pelham was considered too young to be christened just yet and was at home with her older brother being cared for by their nurse.

Rose had seen Sarah's youngest child for the first time the previous evening when she'd arrived to stay for the christening. She still felt slightly stunned by Lucy's invitation to become John Arthur's godmother.

It could not have happened before the war. Although Rose had left service at the start of the war, she knew that Sarah's mother, Lady Trenwith, would always see her as the servant she had been. Here at Pelham she was treated as a guest, warmly welcomed by Sarah, Troy and even Lord Pelham, who always seemed glad to see her on her visits. Lucy had followed her cousin's lead in asking Rose to be godmother because, like Sarah, she believed that the war had changed everything.

'All that servant stuff and showing respect is nonsense,' she said when Rose asked if she was sure she wanted her to be John Arthur's godmother. 'Andrew spent five months in hospital after he was wounded in the leg. He says the VADs were absolutely marvellous. I really admire what you did during the war, Rose. I helped out by raising funds and rolling bandages, things of that sort – but I could never have done all the work you did.'

'I am sure you would if you'd had the chance,' Rose told her. 'We did our bit but the doctors and nurses were the people I admired. Sometimes they performed miracles. We had our failures, but time after time they brought young men back to life when all hope seemed lost.'

'Yes, I know. Andrew was so ill at first we thought he might die. You wanted to be a nurse, didn't you?' Lucy looked at her curiously.

'Unfortunately, it didn't work out. For one thing I got married without asking permission – and I refused an interview because I'd promised to go away with Rod. Matron could have dismissed me when she discovered I had married, but I think she felt sorry for me because I lost my husband so soon afterwards. I suppose the fact that I married might be the reason I was passed over for nursing training. In the end I was doing most of the things the nurses did anyway.'

'What will you do now the war is over?'

'I'm not sure. I don't intend to return to service. With my father and brother gone, and my mother living by the sea with her cousin Myrtle, there's nothing for me at Trenwith.'

Lucy gave her a sympathetic look. 'It was awful your brother Jack going missing the way he did and never knowing what happened to him – and then losing your husband and your father. I think you have been so brave, Rose. I'm really proud of you and I shall be honoured if you will stand as John Arthur's godmother.'

Lucy had been so sincere that Rose had agreed at once. Other guests might think it odd that a girl of Rose's class had been chosen, but Lucy and Sarah were true friends, and it was them she cared about above most others.

Rose's wandering thoughts were recalled as she was required to give her responses as John Arthur's godmother. His uncles, Troy Pelham and Luke Trenwith, were his godfathers.

Her part in the ceremony over, Rose glanced at Luke. He had been injured once or twice during his time with the Royal Flying Corps, receiving several medals for gallantry. She thought the war had changed him a lot. His profile seemed that of a stern, unsmiling man. She remembered him before the war as being gentle, almost diffident at times. He certainly gave off different signals these days, but then the war had changed all of them.

Her thoughtful gaze moved to Troy. One side of his face still bore the horrific scars of the burns that had threatened his life. The fact that he now lived an almost normal life was in large part due to his wife's courage. Sarah had refused to let go when he'd pushed her away. Her unflinching love had helped Troy through the months of pain and despair, forcing him to realise that his scars did not matter because she never saw them. Troy was the man she loved and always would. Rose thought they were lucky to have such a wonderful marriage.

Rose's husband had not survived the war. Rod had died in the flames of his crashed aeroplane. Rose had mourned him sincerely, but they'd had such a short time together that it was hard sometimes to remember his face. She had a slightly blurred photograph taken after their wedding, but it didn't do Rod justice. He had been warm and loving, so vital and alive. Her grief was still sharp when she thought about him, but there were days when the memories seemed so far away.

Luke glanced at her as they all prepared to leave the church. She smiled a little tentatively. Luke had sent her some diamond earrings one Christmas. She'd wondered why, but he hadn't written or sent her anything else since. It had been the year her father died; the year she became a wife and then a widow in the space of a few weeks. She supposed that Luke had felt sorry for her and had wanted to show his sympathy.

* * *

God, she was lovely! Luke was finding it a struggle to keep his eyes from straying to Rose the whole time the service was taking place. He hadn't seen her since that day at Trenwith just after her father's funeral. He'd wanted her then as he wanted her now. Luke couldn't remember a time when he hadn't wanted to make love to Rose Barlow. Of course, her name wasn't Barlow now; she'd married that Canadian Royal Flying Corps officer, Rod Carne. Luke had been sick with jealousy when he first saw them together, and angry too, feeling as if she had betrayed him.

He was rueful because he knew there was a time when he might have had a chance with her. It had been impossible then because she was a servant at Trenwith and his parents would have been horrified at the idea. She wasn't a servant any more and yet nothing had truly changed.

Luke thought the war years had been good for Rose despite all she had lost. She'd been a girl before she left Trenwith to join the VADs; she was a woman now – beautiful, confident and extremely desirable as far as he was concerned. He wanted her but marriage was still out of the question. Luke owed it to his father to marry the right kind of girl. Sir James expected it and Luke had always known his duty. He'd done his duty to his country for the past four years and more. Now he was home again and his father was making it pretty clear that he wanted his son to take over the estate and settle down.

Luke frowned as he thought about his recent interview with Sir James.

'My health isn't what it should be, Luke. I am grateful I was spared long enough to see you come home. You know as well as I do that things can never be the same. This war has swept away the old lines between the classes. Your mother believes we shall gradually get back to what we were before the war. I do not think it, Luke. I shan't be here to see the new order when it finally takes shape, but you must hold the estate together for as long as you can. A good marriage to the right sort of girl will help.'

'I am afraid Mother will be disappointed, sir. I can't see that we can go on as we were – and I'm in no hurry to marry. I should like a chance to enjoy life for a while, take a breather...'

Sir James looked displeased. 'I know you had a hard time over there, Luke – all of you suffered. It was a wretched war and it claimed too many lives, on both sides no doubt, but it is over now and you must move on. You do not have to rush into anything – but I should like to see your son before I die.'

'Give me a little time, sir. I have no idea who would make me a suitable wife. A lot of the young women I knew before the war are married.'

'I should not dream of dictating to you in this matter,' Sir James said. 'However, I think Amanda Rawlings an excellent girl.'

'Amanda?' Luke was shocked. 'Surely she is still in the schoolroom?'

His father laughed. 'It is four, perhaps five years since you saw her, Luke. I assure you she is a young woman now and quite beautiful. Her father and I go back a long way and the family has money. I don't mean old money or land. Rawlings invested in munitions at the start of the war. I daresay he made a small fortune. Whereas we...'

'Have stagnated,' Luke agreed and looked grim. 'I know I shall have my work cut out finding ways to make the estate prosper. I wondered if you and Mother would agree to open the grounds to the public a couple of days a week. Not the house, of course, but the gardens. We might turn a part of the old stable block into a smart café and souvenir shop...' He saw his father's frown and smothered a sigh. 'Well, I daresay there are other things we can do to improve the family fortunes.'

'We may be forced to invest in some sort of trade,' Sir James agreed heavily. 'However, I will not have Trenwith turned into a fairground.'

A tea shop and paying visitors to the gardens was hardly a fairground, but Luke had known there was no point in arguing with his father. Sir James had been born to another time and was entrenched in the old ways. Though he was sensible enough to understand that they must move on, he would cling to his pride for as long as he could. Luke knew that his mother would never accept the need for change. She had hated the move into the dower house when they were forced to it by lack of servants and had insisted that the house be opened up again almost immediately after the war ended. For the moment they were struggling with a handful of servants, most of whom had remained loyal because they were too elderly to look for new ways.

Still bothered by the talk with his father, Luke climbed into his car for the short drive back to the Pelhams' house. Seeing Rose standing with Sarah, he opened his window and leaned out to call her.

'Rose... may I give you a lift?' She turned her head, seemed to hesitate and then said something to Sarah before coming to him.

'You may as well ride with me – if you are going straight back to the house?'

'Yes, I am, thank you,' Rose said, and she slid into the front passenger seat. 'You have a different car. I remember the last time you offered me a lift you were driving a little roadster?'

'I still have it at Trenwith,' Luke said with a smile. 'This saloon is more comfortable for a longer drive, though I zip about the estate in the roadster.'

'Has Lady Trenwith got used to the automobile age?' Rose asked, remembering that her one-time employer had been a stickler for her carriage and horses. 'Jack thought she would never give up her carriages for a car.'

'It was a case of necessity. Father had to get rid of the horses towards the end of the war. He couldn't find enough men to look after them, and there was a shortage of oats. We have a chauffeur now. Hadleigh is a decent mechanic – though not as good as Jack might have been, given a chance.' Luke glanced at her as he released the brake and the car moved away from the church. He drove slowly through the quiet village, aware that dogs, children and the occasional goose or duck might consider the road their personal territory. 'How is your mother?' He steered the conversation away from her brother, because he was uncomfortable with the subject. Rose and everyone else believed that Jack Barlow had died a hero in France. Luke had made the decision after Rose's father had died that it would do more harm than good to tell her the truth, which was complicated. Jack was alive and living under an assumed name in France. Technically speaking, he had deserted his post during the war, though there were mitigating circumstances.

'Mother is doing fine. She enjoys baking and helping to run the hotel. It's a shame that my father never got to own the little board-ing-house he fancied.'

'Your father's death was unexpected, Rose.'

'I think he broke his heart over Jack.'

'Yes, perhaps...' Luke frowned. It was just over a month earlier
that he'd received a letter from a certain Monsieur Georges Marly
and his wife Louise. They had moved to Paris just before the end of
the war and were now running a small café. Georges had plans for
the garage he wanted to own one day. Luke knew that Jack hoped he
might have told Rose her brother's story, but it hadn't been the right
time after her father died, and Luke hadn't got around to it since. He
didn't know why but he was reluctant to tell Rose that the brother
she thought dead had been alive all this time. Jack was a hero in his
way, because he'd worked with a group of French freedom fighters
after he recovered his memory. However, his duty had been to make
his way back through enemy lines. He had saved Luke's life and
Luke would have helped Jack if he'd chosen to come back with him,
but Jack had wanted to stay on the farm with Louise. He'd known
that he might never be able to return to his home, but he'd asked
Luke to tell Rose that he was still alive.

Luke glanced at Rose as he brought the car to a standstill in the
courtyard at the back of the house. 'You are all right, aren't you,
Rose? It must be difficult for you now that you've been discharged
from the VADs.'

'I'm fine,' Rose told him. 'I miss them... Rod, my father and Jack.
Jack the most, I think, because he always understood me. I've been
working in a draper's shop but I just handed my notice in so I'll
soon be out of a job, though I can afford to look around. My father
left some money and Ma shared it between us. I'm not sure what I
want to do now.'

'You might get taken on as a nurse now that all the volunteers
have gone home.'

'Perhaps...' Rose screwed up her mouth. 'I'm not sure I want to
any more. I've had some other ideas... Something very different.'

'Do you want to tell me? I might be able to help... A reference from the family or something...' Luke said and then wished he hadn't, because it sounded patronising. 'Of course, you will have all the references you need from your time in the VADs.'

'Yes, I do, but thank you for the offer. I shan't be going into service again. I might do shop work for a while, but it isn't what I want.'

'What do you want?' Luke asked, lifting his brows.

'You would laugh if I told you.' Rose shook her head as he opened the car door for her. 'Sarah knows. I'll tell her if it happens and she will tell you.'

'Rose Carne, you are a tease,' Luke said and made a rueful face. 'Now I shall be kept awake at night wondering what you're up to.'

Rose hesitated, then said, 'All right. I've been taking singing lessons for a while now. I'm going to start auditioning soon.'

'Sing on the stage?' Luke stared. He wasn't sure he approved. Singing on stage wasn't the life for a girl like Rose. He didn't want to think of her at the mercy of predatory men who waited at the theatre door for girls who sang for their supper, and who were often expected to do more. 'Somehow I don't think Barlow would have approved of that...'

'My mother doesn't like the idea and Father would have worried,' Rose told him with a little frown. 'Jack would have understood. I've done my duty and now I want some fun. I may not make a success of it, and I may end up working in a café between shows, but it is something I need to try. I suppose I'm just looking for something different before I settle down.'

'You deserve some fun out of life after what we've all been through,' Luke agreed. 'I feel much the same way – but be careful, Rose. The kind of men that hang around outside the stage door hoping to take the girls out aren't the sort you're used to.' Luke knew he sounded pompous even as he spoke. Rose was a woman, not a child, and she had a right to choose her own life. 'I'm sorry, I have no right to preach to you.'

'No, you don't,' Rose said, but she wasn't offended.

She smiled at him, making his heart jerk and his stomach clench with longing. He wanted her so badly, but he could only offer her an affair. If she had been short of money and alone he might have made the offer, but she was now John Arthur's godmother and she was his sister's valued friend. She would be insulted if he suggested making her his mistress, and he couldn't blame her. If he followed his heart he would offer her marriage, but the sense of duty was too deeply entrenched. He owed a certain consideration to his parents.

'Perhaps I shall see you on the stage in the West End of London,' he said, trying to recover. 'I wish you the best of luck, Rose.'

'Thank you.' Rose looked at him thoughtfully. 'I know you are right. I shall be very careful who I go out to supper with – and thank you for caring.'

Luke watched as she walked on ahead of him into the house. He wanted to run after her and tell her that he loved her, had loved her for years, but something held him back. He owed it to his father to at least try to find a suitable wife.

* * *

'You will visit again soon?' Sarah asked the next morning as Rose prepared to leave. 'I wish you could stay longer. The house is full of people at the moment. Please come another time so that I can have you to myself.'

'Yes, I shall,' Rose promised and kissed her cheek. 'If you want me to – when I'm on the stage?'

'Rose!' Sarah threw her a look of mock outrage. 'You will always be welcome here and you know it. Besides, if you're famous I can boast about you to all my friends.'

Rose went into a peal of laughter. 'Pigs might fly, as Ma says! I don't expect to be famous, Sarah. I'll be content if I get a job in the chorus, as long as I can earn enough to pay the rent and keep myself decent.'

'You have a lovely voice,' Sarah said. 'I could listen to your singing for hours. I am sure you will do well, though I suppose it won't be easy at first. You have to get through the auditions.'

'I'm going to one tomorrow,' Rose told her. 'It is the reason I can't stay longer this time. My teacher says it's time and I want to try. I can always work part-time in a shop or something until I'm successful.'

'Good luck,' Sarah said. 'Who is taking you to the station?'

'Barney offered,' Rose said. 'Your sister's husband is always considerate and helpful, Sarah. Marianne is lucky to have him, though I'm not sure she appreciates him.'

'Marianne is used to having her own way. Barney has always spoiled her. He thinks he was lucky to get her and he lets her do much as she likes – though he can put his foot down occasionally.'

'Yes, I daresay he can,' Rose agreed. She kissed Sarah's cheek as she saw Barney coming towards them. 'Goodbye and take care, love.'

'You too, Rose. You know, don't you, there is always a place for you here? Father Pelham is keeping the convalescent home going for a few years. You could help to run it and live in one of the estate cottages if you wanted.'

'Thank you. If I didn't want to try singing I might have taken you up on that,' Rose said. 'I'll keep in touch whatever happens.'

'Yes, you must,' Sarah told her and hugged her. 'Life has to be better now the war is over, don't you think?'

'Yes, I'm sure of it,' Rose said. 'Barney is waiting. I must go.'

Rose turned away, got into the car and waved to Sarah as Barney drove her away from the house.

'This is very good of you, Mr Hale.'

'Not at all, Rose,' he said. 'And you really must start calling me Barney. You are one of the family, you know. You've done sterling work for this family and others. I think we as a country owe a great deal to our volunteers.'

'It wasn't really that much,' Rose said, her cheeks faintly pink. 'I enjoyed my work. I missed it a lot in the first couple of weeks after my discharge. I've been working in a draper's shop but I don't like it much. I gave my notice in a couple of weeks ago so now I shall have time on my hands.'

'A little bird told me you want to sing. I heard you in church and I think you have a good chance of being a success.'

'You are being kind,' Rose said. 'You're such a nice man, Barney.'

'Substitute dull for nice and you're getting there,' Barney said, pulling a rueful face. 'I sometimes wish I'd been allowed to join the glamour boys and fight for my country. Sitting at a desk wasn't my idea of the perfect way to see out the war.'

'You did an important job. Someone had to make sense of all the regulations.'

'Yes, and it suited Marianne to have me home.' Barney sighed. 'I wish you lots of luck in your career, Rose. Let us know when you're in a show and we'll all come to see you – send you flowers, too.'

'I said you were nice. I should have said generous,' Rose said. 'You shouldn't put yourself down, Barney.'

'Oh, I don't. My wife manages that very well,' he replied with an odd smile.

Rose sensed that he was keeping something inside but she wasn't sure what. She didn't like to ask questions, and soon he was pulling up at the station and parking the car. He helped her carry her suitcase, saw to her ticket and bought her some magazines and a packet of toffee for the journey.

'I meant it when I said I would come to your shows,' he told her as he saw her on to the train. 'Let us know how you get on, Rose.'

Rose thanked him again and settled in her seat. He was one of the kindest men she'd ever met and she thought it was a shame that Marianne took him so much for granted. He deserved to be loved.

Sitting back in her seat, Rose thought about the christening and the brief drive with Luke. For a moment she had thought Luke was interested in more than giving her a lift, but he had suddenly put up the barriers. She wasn't sure why it happened, but he'd done it before. Sarah, Troy, Lucy, Andrew and Barney all treated her with an open affection, but Luke was different. There was a kind of wariness about him, as if he were afraid of saying – or feeling – too much.

Rose sighed, because she liked Luke Trenwith. At one time she had liked him more than she ought. She sometimes thought she'd been attracted to Rod because he reminded her of Luke. Rod had been gentle, good mannered and considerate. Luke had seemed that way before the war but now she wasn't certain. She thought he was harder than he'd once been and she sensed he was hiding something, though she couldn't for the life of her imagine what it was. Unless it had something to do with Jack... Did Luke know something about her brother he wasn't telling her?

Since the end of the war a lot of awful stories had started to come out: stories about the way men died, about men being shot for cowardice because they refused to go over the top when commanded. Was it possible that Luke knew something like that about her brother but hadn't told her?

No, *her* Jack wasn't a coward and he certainly wasn't a fool. She wished that she knew exactly how he'd died, because then she might be able to accept that he was dead and move on. It was strange how she'd found it easy to accept the fact of Rod's death. She had grieved dreadfully for a long time and then moved on, but somehow Jack wouldn't let go. She sometimes had the feeling that he was alive and thinking of her, of his home – and yet that was stupid. Jack would have come home to them if he could.

Rose pushed the foolish longing to see him to the back of her mind. She must let the past go and think of the future.

* * *

Jack had finished sweeping the yard at the back of the café some time ago. He leaned on his broom, enjoying the feel of the sun on his face even while his spirit rebelled against the life he found boring. Louise was in her element running the café she had always wanted, but he knew that someone else could do the jobs he did for her. She was the one who made the café successful; she was the one who brought the customers in with her wonderful food. He had found life at the farm satisfying; the routine of the hard manual work and the dangerous ventures he undertook with the French freedom fighters fulfilled his restless nature. It was only when they had sold the farm and come to Paris that Jack had begun to think about the life that might have been his had he risked all and taken Louise to England when Luke begged him to return to his unit.

He'd had money saved, money he had willed to Rose. She must be certain he was dead by now. She would use the money for herself and he was glad, but if he had it here he could set up the garage he wanted for himself. He had given up everything when he chose to stay with Louise, and most of the time he didn't regret it, but sometimes he longed for a cool, green English day. He wanted to see his mother and Rose, but he knew it was foolish to dwell on such things. He was French now. His life was here and he must make the best of it.

'Jack...' Louise came to the kitchen door and gazed out at him. 'Is something the matter?' She looked anxious and he knew she sensed his moods. He walked towards her, stashing the outside broom under a lean-to at the back of the kitchen. 'I wanted to tell you... there is a job going at the garage in the Avenue Lombard. They need a mechanic...'

Jack's spirits leaped as he saw the smile on her lips. Louise understood that it wasn't enough for him doing the odd jobs at the café.

'When did you hear that?' he asked, keeping his voice light. He'd known about it for a day or so. It wasn't exactly what he wanted because he had plans for a garage where he could restore and sell vehicles he had rescued from rusting in barns, but working for someone else would be better than sweeping the yard twice a day.

'I heard customers talking just now.' Louise's greenish-blue eyes lingered on his face. She seemed to grow more beautiful every day. His stomach clenched with desire and he was reminded of all the reasons he'd decided to stay in France throughout the war. 'Why didn't you tell me? You must have known.'

'I did know. I thought you needed me here.'

'I can get someone to help me.'

'I can do most of it before I go in the mornings – if you're sure you don't mind?'

'Of course I shall miss having you here all day,' Louise said. 'But it isn't like it was at the farm, Jack. I was always afraid then that the Germans would come – or Jacques – but the war is over and Jacques is dead. I am not afraid of being alone in Paris. Besides, I never am alone.'

'You should call me Georges, even in private,' Jack said. 'We don't want anyone to hear you use my real name. It is a secret we must keep for the rest of our lives.'

Louise's eyes were on his face. 'You regret it, don't you?' she asked softly. 'I know you love me, but sometimes you regret that you can't go back to England.'

'That part of my life is over,' Jack said. 'I made my choice. I don't regret what I did, Louise. You needed me so I stayed.'

'You weren't a coward. You were commended for your bravery and given a medal by the local mayor,' Louise said. 'We could go to England and pretend that your memory has only just returned.'

'You are happy here,' Jack said. 'You always wanted your own café and now you have it. I admit that I haven't had enough to do. If I start work at the garage I shall be busy. We can't go back, Louise. We could risk everything.' He moved towards her, pulling her into his arms and looking hungrily into her eyes. 'You are my wife. I love you and I want to be with you. I shall take the job and everything will be all right. I promise you, I regret nothing.'

'If things go well you could have your own garage soon,' Louise said. 'We bought the café first but there is a little money left. In another year or so we should have enough for you to set up on your own.'

'Yes, I know, and what I earn working in the garage will help,' Jack said. He bent his head and kissed her, feeling the surge of desire as she arched into him. 'I love you, Louise. Never think that I might leave you or risk what we have.'

'I love you, Jack. Go and tell them you want the job.'

Louise watched as Jack took off the white apron he wore while helping her in the café. He was striding confidently as he walked away and she knew that he would be happier working in a job that suited him. However, despite the love between them, she understood that sometimes he was sad. She had seen him looking at the picture of his sister Rose and she knew he thought of her and of his mother.

Of late she had been afraid that he might leave her. She was no longer vulnerable; she could manage the café with the help of a girl called Marie. She had worried that Jack would go home for a visit and never return.

* * *

'You look a proper treat,' Mrs Hall said as Rose came downstairs that morning. 'I reckon they will take you like a shot, especially when they hear you sing.'

'I hope so,' Rose said, feeling a flutter of nerves in her stomach. 'This is the third audition I've been to in as many weeks. At the first one I didn't get to sing and at the second they told me to wait until the end but then I didn't get in.'

'Well, you said there were a lot of girls there. You can't expect to win straight off, Rose, but that new dress is very smart, and I like what you've done to your hair.'

'I've had the ends trimmed,' Rose said. 'I thought about having it cut shorter but decided against it.' She touched her chestnut locks and smiled. 'I think it looks better.'

'It will make all the difference,' Mrs Hall assured her. 'You'll get a job this time, trust me.'

Rose laughed. She liked her landlady. Over the years they had become good friends. She could have moved somewhere else now that she was no longer a VAD, but she stayed because she was comfortable. Mrs Hall was a good-hearted woman. She'd taken Sarah in when she had come to them in distress during the war, even though she might have been in trouble for it because Sarah, although unmarried, was expecting Troy's child. Rose might have been forced to move somewhere else and Mrs Hall could have been taken off the list of approved landladies, but thankfully none of this had happened.

Rose left the house and started walking. It was some six months now since the war had ended in victory for the Allies. Spring was here and this was the first day she'd felt warm enough to go out without a coat. She did feel smart in her new dress and black shoes with an ankle strap. She had bought herself a cloche hat, but after having her hair cut she'd decided not to wear it. Mrs Hall's words of encouragement had made her feel better. Perhaps this time she would be lucky.

She was auditioning for a chance to sing in the chorus of a musical show that would be put on at a theatre in the Haymarket later this year. Rose's pulse raced with excitement. She had found herself part-time work with an understanding shop owner who was prepared to allow time off for auditions, but the more auditions she attended the more Rose longed to be a part of the world she had found. The girls seemed friendly, most of them, like her, with good voices but no experience. She'd caught sight of one or two of the leading artistes as they swept in or out of the theatres. Rose didn't expect to become famous or make a fortune; she just hoped to find a job that would allow her to sing. So far she hadn't had much luck, but she'd made one or two friends. She saw Janice and Sally as she approached the stage door. Sally gave a whoop and ran to greet her.

'You look fantastic,' she cried. 'I love your hair! What have you done to it?'

'I just had the ends trimmed and then washed it.' Rose looked at Janice who was the quieter of the two. 'I hoped you two would be here. If we get turned down we can go out somewhere later and drown our sorrows.'

'I think we might be lucky today,' Janice said. 'I've heard they are looking for twenty female singers for the chorus and there are still a couple of solo acts open.'

'I just want a chance at the chorus,' Sally said. 'You could do a solo, Rose. I've heard you sing. You've got a lovely voice. I thought you would get in last time.'

'I hoped I might, but they said the other girl was more experienced.'

'They always say that.' Janice pulled a face. 'How do you get experience if they won't give you a chance?'

'I suppose you just have to keep on trying,' Sally said. 'I really want to sing on stage. If I don't get something soon I shall have to find a job. I'm working part-time at the moment, but it doesn't pay the rent and I've had to borrow from my sister. I can't go on doing that for much longer.'

Janice nodded her agreement. Rose was aware that she was luckier than the other girls because she had some savings. Of course, there was always the money Jack had left her. She had never been able to bring herself to touch it and she knew the interest was slowly building up. It was stupid not to use the money but she felt it belonged to Jack, and if she didn't spend it maybe one day he would come and claim it.

'I'm lucky with my landlady,' she said. 'Mrs Hall has never raised my rent, though I give her a bit extra when I can.'

'I've often thought I should like to share a flat,' Sally said. 'I need a decent job for that – and a couple of friends.' She looked at Janice and Rose, but they had reached the room where the other girls had gathered and joined the line to add their names to the list of hopefuls.

Rose could hear a girl singing on stage. She sounded good. It was no surprise when the girl came off stage smiling and calling to a friend with glee. She had been taken on, which meant that the places had begun to disappear...

It was Rose's turn to audition. To her dismay, it didn't last long. 'Thank you, Miss Barlow,' the producer said from out front. Rose stared down at him, her heart sinking. She'd only sung a few lines. 'Please speak to Miss Johnson as you leave. I think we can use you.'

A wave of euphoria swept over Rose. She thanked him, feeling dazed as she left the stage and was pounced on by her friends.

'I told you,' Janice said triumphantly. 'I felt lucky today, and we're all in so that makes it even better.'

'He only said he thought they could use me,' Rose pointed out, her stomach clenching with excitement. 'I'm not sure what that means...'

'It means that you will be given further trials, and if we are satisfied you will have a solo spot as well as being in the chorus.' A woman dressed in a smart black costume smiled at her. Miss Johnson was tall and thin, her dark hair marcel-waved neatly into her nape. She was holding a clipboard, on which she was writing busily. 'If you would give me your details, Miss Barlow... Is there a telephone where you live?'

'No, I'm afraid there isn't,' Rose told her. 'I can phone in from the corner Post Office...'

'It doesn't matter, though it is useful. You might consider finding lodgings at one of our recommended lodging-houses. The landladies cater for girls in show business and always have the telephone. I am giving addresses to anyone who wants them.'

'I've been with my landlady for ages,' Rose said. 'She is like family – is it compulsory?'

'No, but it is recommended.'

'If three of us rented a flat together we could have a telephone,' Sally said. 'I'm in a theatrical lodging-house and the rules are awfully strict.'

'And that is a good thing,' Miss Johnson said, giving her a hard look. 'We prefer our girls not to live in their own flats. In this business there is a lot of temptation. You will have frequent invitations to dine out or visit nightclubs. The rules are there for a purpose and sometimes they help girls to resist temptations that could lead them into trouble.'

Sally pulled a face as Miss Johnson moved away. 'Silly old trout,' she whispered behind the woman's back. 'We could have more fun in our own place, give parties and things...'

'It's a lovely idea,' Rose said. 'I'm going to stay where I am for the moment because I like it – but if I had to move I think I would go into one of those lodging-houses she recommended. She's right, Sally. It would be easy to fall in with the wrong company.'

Janice nodded her head in agreement. 'I'm going to move as soon as I can fix it up,' she said. 'I know a girl who got into trouble because she went to some private parties and ended up in bed with a man she didn't even know. I want to sing. If I wanted to be a call girl I could have done that a long time ago.'

Sally looked a bit aggrieved but said no more. After a few minutes she wandered off to talk to some of the other successful girls. It didn't surprise Rose a bit when she reported that she had joined forces with three others to rent their own flat. Some of the girls were as interested in the perks that might come through the men they would meet as in being in the show. Two of the girls Sally was going to live with were noticeably better dressed than the others and wore good jewellery. As they left the theatre, Rose saw the girl called Jennie get into a car with a man. In itself that meant nothing, but Rose couldn't help wondering if Sally had got herself into more than she realised.

Hugging her pleasure at getting the chance to sing on stage, Rose took a tram back to her lodgings. She was singing to herself as she ran the last few hundred yards to her landlady's house.

Mrs Hall grinned as she went into the kitchen. 'You got in then, lass. I thought you would.'

'Janice and Sally were there – you remember, I told you about them? They got into the chorus and so did I, but... the people auditioning us said I may get a solo spot if they are pleased with me.'

'That's grand, Rose. I'm really glad for you,' Mrs Hall said. 'By the way, did anyone come to the theatre?'

'No.' Rose frowned. 'What do you mean?'

'A gentleman came to see you,' Mrs Hall told her. 'Mr Luke Trenwith – he said he was in town just for the day. I think he was going to ask you to lunch, but perhaps I was wrong. I told him where you were.'

'Luke was here?' Rose felt vaguely disappointed. 'Oh... I'm sorry to have missed him. He didn't say if there was any news? Sarah isn't ill, or one of the children?'

'I'm sure he would have said.' Mrs Hall frowned. 'He asked if we were on the telephone. I had to tell him no. He seemed to think that was a disadvantage. You might need it when you start work – in case they want to call you in for some reason.'

'Janice has access to a telephone, or she will have. She says she'll let me know if I'm needed urgently.'

'That isn't very convenient for you.' Mrs Hall looked thoughtful. 'I shan't be offended if you decide to move, Rose. You might like to be nearer your work – or in one of them theatrical boarding-houses.'

'It was suggested, but I thought I'd wait and see how I get on. I like living here.'

'And I've liked having you,' Mrs Hall replied. 'But Milly is getting wed at last and her husband wants to move in. There will be more children, I daresay. I didn't want to ask you to leave – but now you've got this job you might enjoy being with other girls.'

'Oh – well, in that case I might take a look at the house Janice is going to stay at,' Rose said. 'I shall miss you though. You and Milly and the children are like family.'

'You can visit whenever you like. You will always be welcome.'

Rose felt a little sad as she walked upstairs. It was the end of an era. She knew that Mrs Hall would never have asked her to leave if she hadn't got the job she was after, and she almost wished she'd found work in a shop. It would be a big wrench to move on, and for some reason she felt nervous of the change.

But she was being silly. Rose knew her nerves were getting to her. She had been offered a wonderful chance that could be very exciting, but she would have to prove herself or she would soon be out of a job. She wouldn't let that happen. Rose felt a surge of confidence. She might be an amateur, but she had a good voice. She was able to hold her own with the other girls and she would learn all she could. If she were lucky, she might even get that promised solo spot.

2

Luke watched as the girls trouped out of the stage door. They were talking and laughing, clearly excited. Rose looked beautiful. She had a new dress on and her hair looked different. He liked it but he was glad she hadn't had it cut as short as some of the other girls' hair. If she had left the theatre alone he would have made himself known. He had planned on taking her somewhere nice for a meal; he'd even had ideas of asking her to move into his London apartment. It was just a small flat, somewhere to escape when he wanted to paint.

Luke had all his war pictures at the flat. He hadn't wanted to keep them at home, nor had he felt able to show them to his family. He believed they were good, a record of all he'd seen out there – a vivid portrayal of what war was really about. He was in London now to make an appointment for a gallery owner to see them. He had been thinking about putting on an exhibition since he left the Royal Flying Officer Corps and now he'd taken the first step. Sir James would think it was a waste of time, of course, but Luke had developed a stubborn streak these past few years. His duty was to the estate, naturally, but that didn't stop him having a life of his own. He had already drawn up a business plan for his father to approve and now he intended to take a few days off for himself.

He turned away as Rose boarded a tram. It was just as well he hadn't spoken; she wouldn't be interested in having an affair with him – why should she? A girl who looked like that would not be short of offers, and some of them might be for marriage. Luke's father had arranged a house party for the following week. Luke knew that Amanda Rawlings and her father would be a part of it. It would be wrong of him to court Amanda while he was having an affair.

Luke swore as he hailed a taxi. He didn't know why he couldn't just put Rose out of his mind. Damn it! He'd been trying for the past four years. He smiled ruefully. He would have thought he would have learned by now that she wasn't for him.

* * *

'I'm glad you came here,' Janice said as she and Rose went into the dining parlour for breakfast a week later. 'Sally should have come with us. I don't think the rules are so strict, do you?'

'No,' Rose agreed as she helped herself to some scrambled egg and toast. 'I don't want to bring gentlemen back here, so it doesn't bother me that we aren't allowed to have callers. Mrs Hall was strict about that sort of thing too.'

'Sally said they are having a party at her place this evening. She's invited us both. I'll go if you want to, Rose, but otherwise I'll give it a miss. I'm usually tired by the time we finish rehearsals. I keep wondering what it will be like once we're doing two shows a night.'

'And a matinée three times a week,' Rose reminded her. 'It will be hard work but I'm loving it – aren't you?'

Janice nodded, but her expression was odd as she spread butter and marmalade on her toast. 'Yes – but it is harder than I expected.'

Rose was thoughtful. In a way she had been working harder than Janice because she was doing a solo spot and all the chorus work. However, she had been used to harder work than singing and dancing, even though the dancing bit was awkward. She hadn't realised the girls needed to learn to tap dance as well as sing, and in the first few days she'd found it difficult to keep up with some of the more experienced girls. It was getting easier though, and the previous day she'd been praised for the first time.

'Yes, it is hard,' she agreed. 'But I want to do well. This means a lot to me, Janice. I thought it did to you too.'

'It does,' Janice said quickly, but she wasn't entirely convincing. Rose wondered if she would stay the course. She supposed that was why a lot of producers insisted on experience. Some of the other girls had told her about friends who had wanted to sing but couldn't stand the pace of rehearsals. Their producer made them go over the routines again and again until they were perfect, and not all the girls made it through. Rose would be sorry if Janice fell by the wayside because they got on so well together. 'It's just that...' Janice sighed and shook her head. 'It doesn't matter. I have to make up my own mind.'

Something was troubling her. Rose didn't push it, because she felt that Janice would tell her if she wanted her to know. They were good friends, but they didn't tell each other everything and it was best that way.

'I think I might go to the party,' Rose said as she finished eating her toast. 'It would seem as if we didn't care about Sally if we turned her down. If we don't like the way things are going we can leave early.'

'Yes, all right,' Janice agreed and smiled. 'I don't mind going with you.'

* * *

Rose looked around the sitting-room, which was heaving. There was a piano in the corner, and the girls and some of the men were taking turns to play and sing to entertain the company. Everyone was drinking, and there were a lot of couples entwined in corners. Rose had seen a couple of the girls disappear with men, and she guessed that they were headed for the bedrooms.

She frowned, because a large flat like this was too expensive for girls on the wages the theatre paid them for chorus work, even if four of them were living together. She was fairly sure that some of the men here were rich. Their accents were definitely not working class and their clothes were out of the top drawer, hand-made for them by the best tailors. She had seen enough men like this while she was in service. Some of them had tried it on with her, but she'd been adept at avoiding their groping hands.

She would have left the party before now, but surprisingly Janice seemed to be enjoying herself. She had thought the other girl would be begging her to leave by now, but she had been talking to one of the men for the past ten minutes and was laughing at something he said. Rose didn't like to interrupt, and she couldn't abandon her. She would wait for a while before suggesting they should go home.

'You're the new sensation, I gather... The beautiful Rose Barlow.'

Rose turned to look at the man who was standing just behind her. He was good-looking in a dark, roguish way, his hair the colour of coal and his eyes a piercing blue. She thought his mouth was sensuous, but the expression in his eyes was strange and she couldn't quite work out what he was thinking. He wasn't giving off the signals most men gave when they came on to her.

'You have the advantage of me,' she said. 'I don't think we've met before.'

'We haven't.' He grinned at her. She saw that he had a gold tooth on the right side of his upper jaw and somehow it made him seem like a pirate. 'But we can soon rectify that.' He held out his hand. She ignored it. He looked surprised, slightly annoyed. 'I'm Jason Brent and I could be useful to you, Rose. I'm an entrepreneur and I invest in theatrical shows. I'm looking for a new star, and you could be her.'

Rose instinctively distrusted him. He was too smooth, too sure of himself – and too damned good-looking! He might be all that he said, but there was sure to be a price to pay. Something about him made her wary.

'I have a job, thank you,' she said. 'I don't think I'm your new star, Mr Brent.'

'I'm sorry you feel like that,' he said. 'You may change your mind – here's my card.'

He held out his card to her. When Rose didn't take it, he thrust it into her hand. She hesitated and then put it into her purse. He smiled and moved away. Rose drew a breath of relief. Her instincts told her that Jason Brent was a man to stay away from, though she couldn't have said why.

'You made a mistake there.' Rose heard Sally's voice and turned to look at her. 'Turning Jason down was daft if you ask me. Most of the girls would die for the chance to go to dinner with him, let alone be his mistress.'

'I'm not interested,' Rose told her. 'I'm happy where I am – and I'm certainly not going to sleep with anyone to get a better job.'

'It's all right for you,' Sally said, looking annoyed. 'You have real talent, Rose. You were chosen for a solo spot and you'll probably make it anyway, but a lot of us will never get further than the chorus. If we're lucky and we take our chances, we can put a bit of money away for later – and sometimes we strike really lucky. One of my flatmates is getting married soon. Her fiancé has pots of money.'

'She is lucky,' Rose said. 'He must be in love with her – but a lot of these men are only after one thing. You must know that, Sally.'

'As long as I get what I want I don't care,' Sally said. 'If someone with money asked me to be his mistress I'd make sure I got enough to keep me in comfort for the rest of my life. A lot of the girls feel the same.'

'Well, I hope it happens for you,' Rose said, and Sally walked away. Her gaze followed Jason Brent. He was talking to two pretty girls who seemed to be lapping up his every word. His bright blue eyes met hers and the amused look in them made her blush. What was so funny?

Sally had joined them. Rose looked around the room. She saw that a member of the cast from the show was staring at her. Harry Rhonda did a star turn singing and dancing. He had the reputation of being a womaniser and of having a bit of a temper. A couple of the girls had warned her against him. She didn't much like the way he was staring at her. She turned her head and walked over to Janice, who was now alone.

'I'm thinking of leaving,' she said. 'What about you?'

'Oh, no,' Janice said. 'Mike is just getting me a drink. He has offered to take me to supper at an expensive hotel. You go if you want, Rose. Don't feel you need to wait for me.'

'Be careful, Janice. You were doubtful about coming, remember?'

'Oh, I thought it would be all horrible old men groping us,' Janice said. 'Mike is really nice. I like him.' She gave Rose an oddly defiant look.

'If that is how you feel, it's fine with me. I'll see you later.'

Rose went to fetch her coat. She left the party without saying goodbye to anyone. It wasn't her sort of thing, and she knew what her mother and Mrs Hall would say about the girls who had slipped off to the bedrooms or nightclubs with various men. It would be a long while before she accepted an invitation to one of Sally's parties again.

She had been walking for a couple of minutes when she became aware that someone was behind her. She looked over her shoulder just as Harry Rhonda caught up with her.

'You're leaving early,' he said.

'I have to be up early. I need my sleep. I have a lot to learn.'

'It's a waste having you in the chorus. I could have a word if you like, wangle another solo spot for you. You would find it a lot easier.'

'Thanks, but I enjoy what I'm doing,' Rose told him. 'I have to learn to walk before I can run. I'm not ready for two solo spots yet – and I like being in the chorus.'

'You're too modest,' Harry said, his grin so cocky that she was tempted to wipe it from his face. Something made her careful in her answer.

'You're one of the stars, Harry. I have a lot to learn.'

'I could teach you how to be a star,' Harry said, moving in closer. She could feel his warm breath on her face as he touched her. 'If you are nice to me, Rose, the sky is the limit. I know a lot of important people.'

'I am sure you do,' Rose said. 'I'm not interested, Harry. Excuse me, I have to catch my tram.'

She ran a few steps and jumped on a tram, even though she knew it wasn't the right one for her. She would have to get off at the next stop and go back the other way. The look in Harry's eyes had given her the shivers. She was afraid that she might have antagonised him. She would have to stay out of his way as much as she could, because men like that didn't like being turned down.

Jason Brent had seemed amused when she'd rebuffed him, but somehow she had an idea that Harry would find a way to get his own back.

* * *

'My father tells me that you are a clever artist,' Amanda said as Luke brought her a glass of champagne. The large room was full of guests, talking and laughing. 'And you won several medals in the war, didn't you?'

'Most of us got a few gongs,' Luke said in a dismissive tone. She was a pretty girl, but she didn't have much in the way of conversation, just social chit-chat. 'I did my duty, nothing more. I am having a show of my work in London in a couple of months. Perhaps you would like to come along – bring a few friends? I could do with all the support I can get.'

'Oh, I should love that,' Amanda said and giggled. 'It will be fun telling everyone I know a famous artist.'

'I'm not famous,' Luke said, squashing the desire to flatten her with a sarcastic remark. It wasn't her fault that he found her young and foolish. She was certainly lovely to look at and her father was the richest man he knew, but she didn't make his loins ache with the longing to make love to her. 'I'm not even sure I can truly claim to be an artist yet, though I've recently been led to believe that I might be quite good.'

'Daddy says you are, and he is usually right,' Amanda said. 'He says that the war may be a bit too recent for the paintings to be commercially viable, but in time they will be. He thinks you should paint something else – landscapes or portraits. People like a picture of their house or themselves – Daddy says that is what sells.'

Luke wished Daddy to hell, but obviously couldn't say so. He wasn't in the least interested in painting pretty pictures of country houses and the ugly daughters and wives of rich men. And that sentiment was priggish and uncalled for, he reflected ruefully. Amanda was trying to make conversation on his level. He thought he might like it better if she simply chattered away about her clothes and her friends as usual.

'I'm not too bothered about making a living from my work at the moment,' he told her, keeping his voice light. He ran a hand over his dark blond hair. Since leaving the RFC he had shaved off his moustache and he thought he preferred to be clean-shaven, though perhaps he'd looked more dashing with the moustache, especially in uniform. He couldn't think what Amanda would see in him. He wasn't much of a catch for a girl like her. He was older and sometimes moody, and she was bright, full of life. He carried too much baggage from the war to think everything was fun, as she did. 'I have some ideas for business that my father is looking at, though some of them may not appeal to him. I should like to turn Trenwith into a hotel, but I am certain that idea will be thrown out.'

'Daddy loves Trenwith,' Amanda said. 'You wouldn't really turn that beautiful house into a hotel?' She looked shocked at the idea, and Luke laughed.

'No, I'm certain neither my father nor my mother would hear of it,' he said. 'However, we do have other properties that we could sell and invest the funds in a hotel at the sea. I am certain it is the thing of the future. People want to enjoy themselves; they've had enough of war and being deprived. I am sure seaside holidays are the coming thing. I think we should get in on the ground floor.'

Luke felt it a pity that his parents were determined to cling to the past. Trenwith could have been a money-spinner if they had been prepared to make changes. A part of it might have been used as an exclusive guest house, and they could have had all kinds of things going on to attract paying visitors, but Sir James had vetoed that idea instantly. However, he must see that there was no point in keeping all the other properties they owned. None of the houses were suitable for use as a commercial enterprise, but if they were sold, a decent hotel could be purchased at the coast. Luke would quite enjoy overseeing something like that if his father could be persuaded. He wasn't quite sure where the idea had come from... unless it was from speaking to Rose. She'd talked about her father's idea for a guest house, and it had taken root.

Luke listened to Amanda chattering on. She had gone back to her usual stories about friends and the places they liked to spend their time. She was talking about going to the south of France later that year and then Switzerland. Luke knew that if he married her he would be expected to escort her to all the fashionable parties she attended. He found the idea boring and wasn't sure he could bring himself to the point of asking her to be his wife.

If he married Amanda, her father would probably give him shares in his business empire as a wedding settlement. The income, coupled with a few ideas of his own for the estate, would eliminate the need for him to open his hotel. Mr Rawlings liked the prestige of Trenwith and would probably help finance it so that his daughter could live there for a few weeks when she wished. Luke would be a kept man. Sir James seemed to think it an excellent idea, but Luke felt as if he were being asked to accept handcuffs; they might be made of gold and lined with silk, but he would be tied to his pretty little wife hand and foot.

Amanda's perfume smelled expensive and it tickled his nose. Rose always smelled of flowers, a light refreshing scent that appealed to Luke far more. His conscience smote him. It wasn't right to be contemplating a proposal to Amanda when the woman he wanted was Rose. He would be in London again soon for a meeting with the gallery owner. Perhaps he would take the time to see Rose in that show. It would be open by then. He might even wait at the stage door and ask her out to dinner.

He struggled to bring his mind back to Amanda and what she

was saying. He sensed that she was aware his mind had been wandering. His lack of attention had clearly annoyed her, but she seemed to be trying to hide her irritation. He wondered why she was even interested. Perhaps it had something to do with the fact that he was the son of a baronet and would inherit the title in time – and Trenwith. Her father could buy a dozen similar estates if he chose, but he couldn't buy the tradition that went with it. It seemed that Luke's parents were not the only ones who still believed that the old values counted for something. Perhaps he was wrong to want to sweep it all away.

He smiled at Amanda. 'This is a bit dull for you, Mandy. Would you like to go for a spin in the moonlight? It's a warm night and the roadster is fun when you can have the top down.'

'Oh, yes,' Amanda responded with evident pleasure.

Luke wondered if she was under instruction to capture his interest. He cursed her father and his for interfering. It was all very well pushing Amanda and him into a marriage for the sake of property and a title – but what happened later on if they couldn't stand each other?

'Come on then,' Luke said, giving her his hand. The least he could do was pay some attention to her. If he allowed his thoughts of Rose to get in the way, he would be a damned fool.

* * *

Rose looked at the bouquets of flowers in the dressing-room she shared with the other girls. They had been arriving nightly since the show opened and several of them were for her. A particularly large basket of red roses had arrived for her earlier that evening. She had looked for a card, feeling oddly troubled when she couldn't find one. She hoped they hadn't come from Harry. He had been haunting her for weeks. She tried to avoid him as much as she could, but he was clever at catching her in dark corners. He had made her squeeze past him in a narrow corridor twice, and once his hand had touched her breast. She disliked him, but he was the star of the show. His spots had been increased since opening night because he was so popular. He threw red roses to the ladies at the end of his last song each night and the papers had been intrigued. He was riding the crest of a wave at the moment. Rose knew it would be a waste of time to complain of him to the producer.

Rose wasn't the only girl who had to put up with his wandering hands. A couple of others had complained that he'd grabbed them when he got the chance, but most of them seemed to think it was good fun and liked being taken out to dinner by Harry.

'He is a star,' Sally told her. 'If you're seen out with Harry Rhonda, people want to know your name – besides, I like him a lot.'

'Harry only cares for himself,' Rose warned, but she knew that Sally wasn't listening. It was her choice. Rose just wished he would leave her alone, but she knew that his attentions to her were malicious. He was trying to provoke her into retaliating. If she lost her temper and hit him he would probably have her dismissed from the show.

Rose was doing well. She got warm applause when she did her solo spot, but she hadn't been asked to do another. She wasn't sure whether Harry had anything to do with that, but it didn't matter. She wasn't ready to be a star just yet. She wanted to learn from the others, and she enjoyed being one of the girls.

Janice had kept going despite her complaints. She'd seemed happier since the party at Sally's, and Rose knew she was seeing Mike regularly. She didn't stay out later than allowed at nights, and she kept to the rules, but Rose suspected they were having an affair.

It was none of her business what her friends did, Rose thought.

She went home alone after each show and sometimes she envied her friends their brighter lives, but she didn't want to sleep around. To be honest, she didn't know what she wanted, but she was certain it wasn't that.

It was a beautiful warm evening when Rose left the theatre. She paused for a moment, deciding whether to catch a tram or walk home. As a dark shadow loomed up, she jumped, her pulse racing. For a moment she thought it was Harry, and then she saw the man's face and relaxed.

'You made me jump,' she said.

'I am sorry,' Luke replied. 'I wasn't sure what to do. I saw the show and wanted to tell you how much I enjoyed your performance. Did you get the roses I sent?'

'They were from you?' Rose's heart jerked and started to race with excitement. 'I couldn't find a card. Thank you, Luke. They are beautiful. I would have taken them home if I'd known you sent them.'

'I sent a card. It must have got lost,' Luke told her. 'I wondered if you would have dinner with me this evening.'

'Thank you – but I'm not dressed for a nightclub or a posh restaurant. I seldom accept invitations, you see.'

'I know somewhere quiet by the river,' Luke said. 'I'm not wearing evening dress either.'

'Yes, all right then,' Rose said, feeling pleased. 'I should like that – if you're sure?'

'I wouldn't ask if I weren't,' Luke told her, and he offered his arm. 'You must know that I admire you, Rose. I always have. You've done so well for yourself. Are you happy where you are?'

'Yes, I think so,' Rose told him and took his arm. She liked the feeling, enjoyed having him close. He smelled nice; clean and sort of woody. 'The girls are all friendly. There's one person I don't like much, but I stay out of his way as much as I can.'

'Like that, is he?'

Rose nodded. 'I said no and it hurt his vanity. He has been punishing me for it ever since. He is the star of the show and thinks it entitles him to do what he likes with the girls.'

'Ignore him,' Luke advised. 'Some chaps are like that, Rose. They can't stand being turned down. It brings out the hunter, I imagine. Just be careful of him. I've met a few like him; they come in all walks of life.'

Rose nodded. It was what she intended to do, but it wasn't always easy. 'How are your father and Lady Trenwith?'

'Struggling to come to terms with life,' Luke said and grinned. 'I think Mother is beginning to realise that she can't carry on as she once did – the days of pulling your cap to the lady of the manor have gone. She has managed to find enough maids and "ladies that come in" to run the house, but they are different from your day, Rose. They come and go as they please and I think she finds them difficult, but she refuses to give up.'

'I think I rather admire that,' Rose said and laughed softly as Luke raised his brows. 'Yes, I do, Luke. Your mother is clinging to her beliefs. She may be out of step with the way things are going, but there is nothing wrong with holding on to what you believe in.'

'Even if everyone else is abandoning ship?'

'I'm not saying she is right, but she is entitled to live as she sees fit, Luke.'

'Yes, I suppose so...'

'You don't sound convinced. Is it difficult for you at home, Luke? I've seen notices about your paintings going on show. I thought perhaps you had more freedom these days?'

She would never have dared to say something like that to him before the war. Rose knew that somewhere along the way they had crossed over the line. It wasn't that she no longer respected him, just that it was easy to talk to him these days. She didn't see him as being her employer and far above her. He was just a friend... Perhaps he might even become more. A tingle of something she suspected was desire ran down her spine as she looked into his eyes. She had suspected that Luke had strong feelings for her some years ago, and now she was certain.

Rose hugged his arm. She had always liked Luke Trenwith. It hadn't been possible to think of him as anything but her employer before the war but now things were different. He was simply a man and she was a woman.

The restaurant was exclusive but not particularly busy that evening. They were shown to a discreet table that overlooked the river. Each table had little screens so that they were private, and the lighting was subtle. The cloths were red, and every table had a little oil lamp which gave off a faint perfume. Rose thought it was the kind of place where men took their lovers or mistresses when they didn't wish to be seen. However, it was just right because neither of them was dressed for a more elegant occasion, and when the food came it was melt-on-the-tongue delicious.

'This is nice,' Rose said, savouring the wine. 'I don't like some wines because they are so dry, but this has a lovely nutty flavour.'

'It is medium to sweet,' Luke said. 'Dry wine isn't really to my taste either, though my father will have nothing else at table, at least until the pudding course.'

'You didn't tell me what it was like at home now,' Rose said. 'Are you living at Trenwith or do you have somewhere in London?'

'I do have a place of my own,' Luke told her. 'It isn't far from here, actually, which is how I came to find this place. I have a studio and one bedroom, also a cubby-hole for a kitchen and a bathroom. It is all I need when I'm in town.'

'A little different to Trenwith,' Rose said and smiled. 'I hope you are a bit tidier than you used to be at home. Otherwise it must be difficult to get into the bedroom.'

Luke stared at her over the rim of his glass. 'You could find out if you like... if you want to come back with me...'

Rose drew a deep breath. She knew what he was asking her. Her heart skipped a beat. She had been right! Luke did have strong feelings for her.

She was silent for a moment, her thoughts chasing round and round as she tried to come to terms with her own feelings.

'I have to be in by ten thirty,' she said. She hadn't meant to say that – there were so many questions in her mind.

'This evening, yes,' Luke said, his voice deep and heavy with emotion. 'But you could move in with me. I shan't be there all the time and you would have it to yourself when I'm away...'

Rose swallowed hard. 'What are you asking me, Luke?'

'I'm asking you to live with me,' he said. 'For the present, that is all I can offer. You know anything more would be difficult...'

Rose nodded. She still wasn't sure what he meant. He hadn't said he was in love with her... That he wanted them to be together for ever. Her mother would tell her to refuse his offer, but Rose wasn't listening to the wise words in her head. She was listening to her heart.

'Yes,' she said. 'I should like to see where you live – for the moment, that's all I'm saying...'

Luke reached for her hand. He smiled at her and her heart jerked.

'I care for you, Rose. I'll never hurt you – you must know I wouldn't do anything to harm you?'

Rose nodded. She wanted him to declare undying love, to tell her that they would be married one day, but in her heart she knew it was impossible. His parents and her mother – even Sarah and Lucy – might be shocked. They were her friends, but marriage to Luke might be a step too far.

For a moment she thought about jumping up and running away,

but then she realised how foolish that would be. She had been married. She wasn't an innocent virgin. She had enjoyed making love with Rod, and her heart was telling her that Luke had always been special to her.

'I've had enough to eat,' she said. 'Shall we go?'

'You're sure?'

Luke's expression was so uncertain that Rose smiled. He seemed more like the man she had known – and loved, she could admit it now – before the war.

'Yes, I'm sure.'

Luke summoned the waiter and paid their bill. The air was cooler when they emerged from the snug warmth of the restaurant but still nice enough to enjoy the walk to Luke's flat. They walked side by side, not touching and yet in tune with each other. Luke's flat was part of a bigger house set in gardens close to the river. It had a separate entrance, which they accessed by wooden steps. Once inside, Rose could see why he had chosen it because the large windows overlooked the river and the gardens leading down to it.

He obviously spent more time in his studio than anywhere else, because the room had two easels and stacks of canvases piled up against the walls. Some used mugs and glasses were left lying around on the windowsill, the floor and various pieces of furniture. Rose smiled because he had always been untidy. She wouldn't have expected anything else.

'I'll get us a glass of wine,' Luke said. 'There's isn't much to see, but explore for yourself.'

Rose walked through to what was obviously his bedroom. This, apart from a discarded shirt lying on a chair, was surprisingly tidy. She had a feeling Luke had made an effort. She thought he might have changed the sheets because there was the scent of clean linen in the air. Had he been certain of her or just hopeful?

She decided on the latter as she went back into the studio and saw that he had brought wine and glasses. His expression was a little odd, almost nervous – as if this meant more to him than she might have imagined.

He poured wine and offered a glass. Rose sipped it once and smiled. She put the glass down on the nearest table, moving closer.

'You don't know how often I've thought of you being here with me,' Luke said, his voice deep with emotion. 'I wanted to tell you how I felt... such a long time ago. It was impossible, Rose. Your family had always been so loyal. If I'd asked you to be my mistress then...'

'Is that what you are asking me now?' Rose asked, feeling cold. 'I know there is a social divide between us, Luke...'

'Shush...' He touched his fingers to her lips. 'It isn't what I feel, Rose. It is my father... my mother...' He shook his head. 'I love you, Rose. I have for a long time, but... it would be hard for them to accept anything else.'

'Yes, I know. Ma would think it wrong too,' she said. 'Either I say goodbye now or we have to accept that we keep this secret – at least for a while.' Her eyes met his with a question. 'Tell me this isn't just an affair, Luke. Tell me it will be a for ever sort of thing – that I really mean something to you. We may not be able to marry, but we are together – not just two ships passing in the night. Tell me you care for me...'

'You know I do!' Luke said, his face twisted with passion. 'I want you – love you – so much!'

'Then we won't think of anything else,' Rose said, and she lifted her face for his kiss. 'Because I love you...'

Luke lowered his head to kiss her, his mouth soft at first, almost pleading. And then, as he felt her response, he deepened the kiss, becoming demanding.

'I'll look after you,' he promised huskily. 'If anything happens...'

'Just kiss me,' Rose whispered. She leaned into him, surrendering herself to his embrace, her body melting in the heat of the passion that had begun to rage inside her. Desire pooled low in her stomach as he swept her up in his arms and carried her close to his chest. When he placed her tenderly on the covers, she smiled up at him, her mouth slightly open, breathing hard. 'I think I have been waiting for this for such a long time...'

'I thought about you all through the war,' Luke said, bending over her. 'I was so jealous when I saw you with him... Your husband.'

'I thought you were angry!'

'With myself for allowing you to slip away from me. I always wanted you, Rose... I swear I'll be good to you...'

Rose pulled him down to her, kissing him with such a fierce hunger that the need for words disappeared. Luke fumbled with the fastenings of her dress. She undid the buttons of his shirt, slipping her hands inside to stroke the satin smoothness of his chest, discovering a sprinkling of fine hair, her fingers pushing through it. Luke shuddered, ripping his shirt off as she wriggled free of him for long enough to throw off her dress. Then they were lying close, flesh to flesh, the heat searing them as they kissed and touched. Rose trembled as his hand moved between her thighs, stroking and caressing, seeking out her wetness. His lips and tongue followed as he lavished attention on her inner thigh and then her feminine nub, his tongue stroking, arousing such strange new sensations. It was the first time Rose had felt quite this way, and her body arched beneath his, crying out for him to enter her. She gave a scream of pleasure as he did so at last.

Their loving the first time was fast and furious and ended too soon. For a while they lay panting, just holding each other, and then Luke reached out for her again. This time their bodies moved slowly, sensuously, savouring each touch, each movement, as he took her to a place she had never been. When the climax broke slowly over her again and again, her fingers dug into his shoulders, the nails raking his flesh, her legs curling around him. They clung together and then Luke rolled away, laughing as he lay back against the pillows.

'I always knew you were something special, Rose,' he told her. He turned his face towards her, stroking her cheek with his fingertips. 'We'll be together always. I promise you. It's going to be so good for us. I'll give you clothes, diamonds... Whatever you want. A house with a garden if you like.'

'I'm happy as we are for the moment,' Rose told him and smiled. 'You don't need to promise me the earth, Luke. I just want you to love me. Don't hurt me, please. If you ever want to leave me, please be honest...'

'I shall never want to leave you,' Luke said and kissed her. 'I shall buy you presents, Rose, because I've wanted to give you things for years.'

'You sent me some diamond earrings once. My landlady told me you were only after one thing.'

'She was wrong,' Luke said. 'I adore you, Rose. I may not be able to offer you marriage, at least for a while – but I shall give you everything else.'

'Just love me,' Rose whispered as he gathered her close. 'All I ask is that you keep your promise to love me for ever...'

Rose didn't make it back to the boarding-house that night. She knew that she could be asked to leave because she had broken the rules, but she didn't mind; she was leaving anyway. Luke drove her back in his car the next morning and she went straight up to fetch her things. The landlady was standing in the hall when she came back downstairs. Rose handed her an envelope.

'That is what I owe you plus one week's notice.'

'I hope you know what you are doing, Miss Barlow.'

'Thank you for your concern but, yes, I do know exactly what I'm doing.'

'I thought you had more sense than some of the others, but it seems you girls are all the same...'

'Yes, perhaps we are when we fall in love,' Rose agreed. 'I've been married; it's not as if I'm an innocent virgin. I'll be just fine, thank you.'

She went outside to Luke. He took her suitcases and put them in the boot of the car.

'Everything all right?'

'I got a lecture from Mrs Spencer but that's all right,' she said. She hesitated, then continued. 'I don't care what she thinks of me – and the girls at the show won't be bothered, because they all have friends or lovers – but Sarah and Lucy can't know about this, Luke.'

'My parents and your mother are the ones that we have to worry about,' he said with a slight frown. 'I think Sarah would understand. In fact, I'm sure she would.'

'I don't want her to know. At least, not yet,' Rose said. 'She is my friend. If she knew...' Her cheeks flushed. 'I'm not ashamed of what we've done – what we are doing, Luke – but I would rather Sarah didn't know for the time being.'

'I suppose it is for the best for the moment,' he agreed. 'I want it to be good between us, Rose. Perhaps one day we can get married...'

'Don't promise too much,' Rose warned. 'We both know there are too many obstacles in the way. I went into this with my eyes open, Luke. If you keep your word to me, I don't mind about the rest.'

Luke nodded. He wasn't sure that Rose had thought things through yet. How would she feel about visiting Sarah knowing that she was living with her friend's brother? She wanted to keep it a secret, but it meant they would be lying to the people they cared for most. Luke knew he had to keep this from his parents for as long as he could, but he would have been more comfortable if they had told Sarah, and perhaps Lucy, the truth.

'Will the flat do for the moment?' he asked. 'I meant what I said about looking for a house with a garden. It has to have a room I can use as a studio – but when I find it I'm going to put it into your name. It will always be yours, Rose – and there will be money too.'

'I don't need that...' Rose began, but he hushed her with a brief kiss.

'It's just in case something happens to me,' he said. 'If I were to die suddenly, or...'

'Stop it!' Rose silenced him. 'You're not going to die. You came through the war, why should you die now?'

'I don't expect to,' he said and laughed. 'I just want to make sure that you would be all right. We might have a child, Rose. You wouldn't be able to work and you would need money.'

'Yes... but don't talk about dying,' Rose said, feeling cold and shivery. 'I couldn't bear to lose you, Luke.'

'You won't,' he promised. 'I'm sorry, darling. Forgive me.'

He gave her an apologetic look as he steered the car away from the kerb and out into the traffic. He would find a house and he would make certain that Rose was secure for the future, but he would keep the details to himself for the time being.

Luke forced himself to forget the things he hadn't told Rose. He had never meant to ask her out for dinner, and he certainly hadn't intended what had happened afterwards, though it was what he wanted more than anything else in the world.

If only he hadn't taken Amanda Rawlings for that spin in the roadster. He tried to lock the memory from his mind, because he did not want to remember kissing her in the moonlight. It had been a spur of the moment thing and he was very much afraid that Amanda now considered herself engaged to him.

Luke wasn't sure what he'd said to her. He couldn't remember actually asking her to marry him, but he supposed he must have said something, because the next morning his father had congratulated him on making a splendid choice.

He would have to wriggle out of it somehow. He had no idea how, because he would feel all kinds of a heel for letting Amanda down. His father would be outraged, of course – and Luke couldn't blame him. He wasn't sure how he'd managed to land himself in this mess.

He'd been feeling trapped when he decided to send Rose the flowers and then visit the theatre. Seeing her singing on stage had made him ache with the need to be close to her and he'd ended up waiting outside the theatre. It wasn't the first time he'd done it, but this time he'd been lucky and she was alone when she came out.

He had made a commitment to Rose. He couldn't marry Amanda now. He couldn't marry anyone because Rose was the wife he wanted. One day he would find a way for them to marry, but for the moment he had to be careful. He had to think of a way to explain to Amanda that she had taken his kiss for a proposal when it was merely an impulse.

Luke cursed himself for being a weak fool. He should never have let his father talk him into paying Amanda attention in the first place. Perhaps it was best that Rose was determined that Sarah shouldn't be told, because she would have insisted that he tell his father and Amanda immediately.

Luke certainly wasn't a coward, but the thought of letting both Amanda – who was a nice, decent girl – and his father down in this way was disturbing. He knew exactly what Sir James would say, the look on his face. Luke had always tried to do his duty, but he had Rose to think of now. He couldn't expect her to be his mistress if he went ahead and married Amanda.

It wasn't going to happen! He would be attending a ball given by Barney and Marianne in a couple of weeks. Rose would not be invited because although Barney always treated her as one of the family, Marianne did not and she would not send an invitation. Amanda would be one of the guests. Sir James and Lady Trenwith would also be present. It would have been an ideal occasion to make the engagement public, but it would serve just as well for Luke to call it off.

It would be most unpleasant, but he had no choice.

3

Rose came off stage some weeks later. She had just finished her solo spot and had received prolonged applause. She was feeling pleased because the producer had been hinting at increasing her solo to include another song, which would also mean more money. It hadn't been made official yet, but she thought it might happen and she was looking forward to telling Luke when he came back from a visit to his sister's home.

'I can't get out of it,' Luke had told her the previous evening. 'I wish you could come, Rose – but you know what Marianne is. She would probably be rude and snub you.'

'You don't have to apologise for Marianne,' Rose said. 'She barely tolerates me when I visit Sarah. I know she would be angry if you took me – and she would guess why. I don't mind that you have to visit your family, Luke. I shan't go home until the show ends, but when I do I shan't be able to invite you to come with me.'

'I'm a selfish brute,' Luke apologised, running his fingers through his hair. 'I only thought about how much I loved and wanted you... Now you have to lie to everyone.'

'It doesn't matter.' Rose hushed him with a kiss. 'As long as we're together and you love me, the rest isn't important.'

She was smiling at the memory of Luke's reaction to her words. He had made love to her so passionately, and afterwards he had given her a beautiful diamond ring.

'This is instead of an engagement ring,' he told her. 'One day I shall buy you one of those, but until then...'

Rose had kissed him and then taken him back to the tangled sheets. She had no reason to doubt the strength of Luke's feelings for her and she was happy despite the fact that they were living in sin.

'Thinking about your lover? You little tramp! You act holier than thou but you're a tramp like the rest of them!'

The spiteful words cut into Rose's thoughts, making her aware of Harry Rhonda. She had been lost in her reverie and hadn't noticed him coming towards her. The corridor was narrow and at this moment deserted, because most of the others were getting ready for the finale. He stood there, deliberately blocking her path.

'Please let me pass,' she said, trying to hold her temper. His behaviour was getting worse and she'd had enough of his spite and his pinches. 'It isn't any of your business what I do in my own time, Harry.'

'Bitch.' He loomed closer and she could smell the spirits on his breath. He had been drinking more and more recently. 'I wasn't good enough for you, was I? You wanted a gentleman – well, he is just using you, bitch. He'll throw you out when he's finished with you. Don't come crawling to me then.'

'I wouldn't come to you if you were the last man on earth...' Rose began, and she screamed as he grabbed her. He slammed her against the wall and started fumbling with her dress, trying to pull it up so that he could touch her. He had never gone this far before and Rose lost her temper. She lashed out with her nails, scoring his cheek so deeply that it bled. 'Get away from me!' She brought her knee up sharply, hitting him where it hurt the most. He let go of her and yelled in pain. 'I'm sorry, but it was your own fault.'

'You filthy little whore!' Harry shouted after her as she ran towards the safety of the dressing-room. 'You'll be sorry for this, bitch. You've ruined my face.'

Rose let herself into the dressing-room. She was breathing hard and her heart raced with fear. Harry was a bad enemy. She knew that he would never forgive her for what she had done.

Sally looked at her curiously. 'Is something wrong?'

'Just Harry up to his usual tricks,' Rose said. 'I scratched his face and it bled, and then I kneed him where it hurts.'

'He will never forgive you for scratching his face,' Janice said, looking at her in concern. 'You shouldn't have done it, Rose. He's the star of the show. If he goes to the producer you've had it.'

'Too bad,' Rose said and shrugged, though she didn't really feel so unconcerned. She liked her job, and even though Luke had said she could give it up if she liked, she didn't want to rely on him for everything. She didn't earn much and Luke paid all their bills, but she had taken wine and food home and that made her feel better. Without a job she would be a kept woman. 'I expect there are other jobs going.'

'Not many at this time,' Sally told her. 'I know of one special production being put on, but you wouldn't get in there – they are only hiring big names.'

'Well, I could always work in a shop or wait tables, but I don't think they can sack me for defending myself. Harry attacked me.'

Sally looked dubious. 'You're new to this business,' she said. 'We have to put up with creeps like Harry groping us all the time. It's either that or we don't work. If they decide you are trouble, you won't get another job in a theatre anywhere.'

'Well, it is too late now,' Rose said and started to change for the finale. 'I can't believe that I could lose my job just for that.'

Rose was one of the last to leave the dressing-room that evening. She was just putting her coat on when the door opened and the producer entered. One look at his face told her she was in trouble.

'Harry said you attacked him for no good reason. He was just having a laugh and you went for him like a wildcat.'

'That isn't true,' Rose said, defending herself. 'You know what he is like – always groping the girls. He threw me against the wall. I think he meant to rape me.'

'He says he just kissed you.'

'He is lying.'

'Maybe.' The producer looked at her. 'I like you, Rose. I thought you had a future here with us, but after this... I have no choice but to let you go.'

'That's not fair! What happens to Harry?'

'Nothing. We can't afford to lose him. He will need extra make-up to hide those marks. You shouldn't have left a mark, Rose. If you'd just kicked him you might have got away with it. I'm sorry but when it's a choice between the two of you, Harry wins every time. He wants you gone tonight. I'll see you get a month's wages but that's all I can do.'

'It doesn't matter,' Rose lied. She was angry and hurt but she wasn't going to let him see how she felt.

'Someone was asking about your contract,' the producer said. 'Jason Brent. I told him it was watertight and we wouldn't let you go. He might offer you something if you ask.'

'Thank you,' Rose said. 'It was good of you to give me a chance when you did. I'm sorry it had to end this way.'

'No hard feelings. Maybe in the future...' He shrugged his shoulders. 'We all know what Harry is – but he pulls in the customers.'

'Yes, I understand. Thank you for the extra money.' Rose

accepted it even though she was angry. She had learned to appreciate money when she was a servant. Pride didn't come into it, even though she knew Luke would tell her to throw it back at them. She wouldn't tell him. It might be best if he thought she had left of her own accord. 'I'll clear my things out and go.'

'I've called a cab, Rose. I don't think you should walk to the tram stop alone this evening.'

Rose nodded. She knew that she had made an enemy in Harry Rhonda. He wouldn't be satisfied with getting her thrown off the show. In future she would have to be careful she didn't walk alone in dark places.

* * *

Rose bought a paper from the news-stand. It was three days since she'd left the show and they had been three of the longest days of her life. She wished that Luke was with her but he hadn't returned from his sister's home yet. She knew that he had planned a stay of a few days, because he couldn't rush away as soon as the ball was over; Barney and Marianne would be offended. Rose understood, but that didn't stop her feeling lonely and a bit miserable.

Was this the way it was going to be in future? Luke would attend family affairs to which she wasn't invited and she would remain at home alone. Rose didn't much like the feeling this thought gave her. She was Luke's mistress and as such she had only a small part to play in his life. She had agreed to the arrangement the night Luke first made love to her, and most of the time she'd been happy. While she was working in the show she hadn't minded if Luke wasn't always there. She had accepted that he had business and family matters that took up a lot of his time; she had been busy, absorbed in the life that went on backstage. Now, suddenly, her days were empty.

She went shopping for a few items for the flat, arranging new cushions, a couple of ornaments and flowers to give it a more homely feel. However, that took only a few hours and afterwards she became aware of the silence in the flat. It was the first time she'd lived completely alone, and she didn't much like it.

She wandered into the studio and looked at Luke's paintings. The stuff he'd done in the war was wonderful, some of it heart-rending. She found one or two portraits of herself and thought he had made her look too pretty. He had been working on a painting of Trenwith recently which she found most impressive. It deserved to be hung in the house, but she wasn't sure that Sir James would appreciate it.

Rose wondered where Luke was going with his life. Both his sisters were settled; Sarah was happy and Marianne made the best of what she had, even though she led Barney a dance when she was in a bad mood.

Sir James must want his son to settle down. He must be hoping that Luke would marry and provide an heir for the family – a legitimate heir. If Rose were to have a child, it would be a bastard and would not be acknowledged by the Trenwith family.

Rose felt her stomach churning as she thought about this. She had let her heart rule her head. She ought to have held out for marriage even though she knew it would cause so much trouble. She sighed and pushed the regrets away. Luke loved her. As long as he stayed true to his promise to love her and be faithful, she wouldn't ask for the rest.

* * *

Luke looked around the crowded ballroom. It was just like Marianne to invite too many people, making it almost impossible to move through the crush. She probably only knew about half of her guests as friends; the others would be acquaintances or friends of friends. More than half had titles or were the heirs to titles. His sister was such a snob! Troy was lucky he had escaped and married Sarah instead.

Luke had thought Troy and Sarah might be here, but they had sent their excuses. Troy had written to say that the children were down with measles and naturally Sarah wouldn't think of leaving them while they were ill, even though they had nurses. Luke didn't blame Sarah. Measles was a most unpleasant and potentially dangerous illness. He'd had it himself when he was about nine and he remembered it had been a horrible experience.

Marianne would have had no qualms about leaving her three children. They had all been born within the first two years of her marriage. Since then there had been no more, and Luke suspected that his sister's marriage was far from happy. Marianne seemed content this evening among her friends, but there was a look in Barney's eyes that told Luke he was a disappointed man. He had been very much in love with Marianne when they married, but the expression of adoration which had once been permanently directed towards his wife had long since disappeared. When he looked at her now it was with a sullen anger.

'Aren't you going to ask me to dance, Luke?'

He turned round as Amanda's voice broke into his thoughts. She was looking lovely this evening, her eyes bright with excitement. He sensed that she was expecting an engagement ring. She believed – as his father did – that he would make the announcement this evening. Luke wondered how soon he could get her alone so that he could tell her it was a mistake.

'Of course,' he replied. There was no harm in dancing with her. 'You look very pretty, Amanda.'

'Thank you. I bought this dress especially because I know you like me in green. You said so that night... in the moonlight...' Her look was inviting, a little coy. Luke knew it was his cue to produce the ring and tell her he was going to announce their engagement. He ignored it, taking her arm to steer her into the throng of dancers. He felt relieved as he discovered the dance was a progressive. He wouldn't have to make conversation with her all through it.

After the dance he took Amanda to where his sister was standing and then excused himself. 'I must speak to Pilkington,' he said. 'It's business but I daresay he won't mind.'

Luke was aware of Amanda's gaze following him. She was angry that he had abandoned her without giving her the ring. He couldn't blame her, because he supposed he had behaved badly. He must have said enough to make her feel they were engaged, though he still couldn't remember his precise words. It would be too cruel to disillusion her this evening. He would find her alone the next day and break it to her gently.

He had a brief conversation with General Pilkington, who was their closest neighbour at Trenwith. The man wanted to buy a meadow that backed on to his land and was at the far end of Trenwith Park. Luke thought it would be a good idea, but as yet he had been unable to persuade Sir James to sell. He apologised to the general for the delay in their decision.

'I expected my father to be here this evening,' he said. 'I had hoped we might settle things, sir – but he hasn't arrived. I don't know why. Marianne hasn't received a letter cancelling.'

'I'd be glad of an answer as soon as you can manage it,' General Pilkington said. 'I might ride over next week and have a word with Sir James.'

'I should like to speak to him myself first,' Luke said. 'I think you can leave it to me, sir. If he doesn't arrive by the morning I'll take a run down there myself and see what's going on.'

After leaving Pilkington, Luke went outside. The grounds were beautiful in the moonlight. Barney's father was fortunate in having the right kind of groundsmen to look after his estate. He ran it as a business and hired a large staff to care for the house and the grounds, but then he had a thriving business in trade. He had none of the reservations that made Sir James hang back and cling to the old ways.

'Luke...' Marianne's voice recalled Luke's wandering thoughts. He turned as his sister came up to him, sensing at once that something was wrong. She was looking anxious and he felt a cold shiver down his spine. 'What is it – Father?'

'Yes. I've had a telephone call from Mama. She says they were about to set out earlier today when Father had a seizure. He was taken to hospital because they thought it was too serious to treat at home. She asks if you will go down there immediately.'

'Yes, of course I will,' Luke agreed at once. 'What about you? You can't abandon your guests, of course.'

'I wouldn't dream of it,' Marianne said. 'I couldn't do anything if I were there. Mama wants you. She has always relied on you and I would only be in the way. I'll come down in a few days when everyone else has gone.'

Luke looked at his sister. She didn't give a damn! She was a selfish bitch and he was tempted to tell her to her face, but he held back the angry words.

'I'll tell Father you will come as soon as you can,' he said. 'You know he thinks the world of you, Marianne.'

'Oh, he did when I was a girl,' Marianne replied carelessly. 'I think he admires Sarah for the way she stood by Troy. He may not say it but I've heard him talk about her to his friends.'

Sarah was worth two of her sister, Luke thought, though he doubted his father cared more for her than for his first daughter. Marianne had always been his favourite. He had been angry with her when she jilted Troy Pelham, but Luke was sure he had long forgiven her. He would want to see her, but it might be best if he were over the worst before Marianne arrived. She would probably burst into tears and distress him.

'I should leave,' Luke said. 'I won't bother to pack. You can send my things on to Trenwith.' He hesitated, then, 'Please apologise to Amanda. I shan't stop to explain.'

Marianne threw him a look of disgust. 'Really, Luke! You ought at least to tell her you are leaving. I am sure she was expecting you to give her an engagement ring tonight.'

'I don't recall asking her to marry me,' Luke said. 'I kissed her but that isn't a proposal in my book.'

'You can't jilt her!' Marianne looked shocked. 'Everyone is expecting an engagement – her father and ours have made no secret of their satisfaction.'

'I'm not sure it would suit me to wed Amanda.'

'Then you shouldn't have let everyone think you intended to,' Marianne told him. 'It is too bad of you, Luke. I wouldn't blame her if she sued you for breach of promise.'

'I haven't got time to argue with you now.'

Luke strode away, smarting from his sister's comments. She had no right to interfere in his life. He was sure he hadn't actually asked Amanda, though he might have said something that gave her the right to think he intended marriage. Indeed, it had been on his mind the night he'd taken her for a spin around the estate. He had thought then that he could do his duty towards his father and the estate, but that was before he had made love to Rose.

He couldn't give Rose up! He couldn't hurt her! She was everything he wanted. Amanda irritated him with her silly ways and inane conversation. She would accept the situation when he would apologise and tell her it was all a mistake. She would have to because he couldn't lose Rose.

* * *

Rose had decided to go shopping again. Luke had said he would be
back in three days but he had already been gone five and she
missed him terribly. The flat wasn't large but it seemed empty when
Luke was away. At first she had thought she wouldn't mind that
there was a part of his life she couldn't share, but she was feeling
shut out and she didn't much care for it. As she left a department
store in Oxford Street, lost in her thoughts, she didn't notice a
woman getting out of a car. She was walking away when someone
touched her arm and she looked round to see Lucy.

'Rose, you look wonderful,' Lucy said. 'I booked a ticket for that
show in the Haymarket, but your name isn't in the programme they
gave me.'

'It wouldn't be,' Rose said reluctantly. She didn't want to explain
because she feared she might say something she ought not to. 'I left
a few days ago. Things weren't quite how I'd expected them to be at
the theatre – so I walked out.'

'I'm so sorry.' Lucy looked at the bags Rose was carrying. 'I
always go shopping when I'm a bit down. It must be disappointing,
but I expect you will find something else soon.'

'Yes, I expect so,' Rose said. She knew Lucy was looking curiously at her clothes. They were more expensive than anything she'd
worn during the war; the kind of clothes Luke liked to see her
wearing – paid for by him. The knowledge of her secret relationship
lay like a weight on her mind. 'I had a little money left to me. I
thought I would spend some of it on myself.' Her cheeks heated as
she lied. What would Lucy say if she knew the truth? She felt guilty
and ashamed. She didn't want to lie to someone she thought of as a
friend.

'Oh, I don't blame you,' Lucy said and laughed. 'Rose, I have
nothing particular to do, because Andrew is busy all day. We could
go for lunch if you like.'

'I would love to if I could,' Rose said, 'but, I'm sorry, I have to be somewhere. Perhaps another day when you are in town?'

'I don't come very often,' Lucy said. 'I'm content at home – but, yes, perhaps another time. I mustn't delay you if you are busy, Rose.'

Lucy walked away into the department store, leaving Rose with the feeling that she had offended her friend. She ought to have accepted her invitation, but she'd felt awkward, on edge. It had been a surprise bumping into Lucy and she had been immediately uncomfortable. Deception did not come easily to her.

On the tram journey back to the flat, Rose couldn't get the look in Lucy's eyes out of her mind. Lucy had known she was lying. It wasn't likely that the relationship between Luke and Rose would remain a secret for ever. Once it became known to the family they would all hate her.

She longed for Luke to be waiting for her when she got back, but the flat was empty. Wandering around the rooms, staring out at the night, Rose realised that she was lonely. She missed being with the other girls at the theatre. Perhaps if she hadn't lost her job she wouldn't have noticed Luke's absence so much, but as it was she felt abandoned – and angry. Luke said he loved her, so why the hell didn't he have the courage to marry her and present his family with the truth?

* * *

'The doctor said it was touch and go for a while,' Luke said as he drove his mother home from the hospital. 'They think he will pull through this time, but if it happens again...'

'Your father has been unwell for longer than you realise,' Lady Trenwith said and frowned at him. 'He cannot shoulder the burden of the estate alone. I am aware that you have your art, Luke – but the estate is more important. It is your duty to spend more time at home, and I think it would please your father to see you married. Have you given Amanda Rawlings a ring yet? Your father thought you would use the ball as your chance to announce your engagement.'

'I don't actually recall asking Amanda to be my wife,' Luke said, a nerve flicking in his throat as he drove through the open gates of Trenwith. 'I'm not sure she is the one for me, Mama. I don't love her.'

'What has love to do with marriage?' Lady Trenwith demanded, giving him a hard stare. 'I married your father because my own father and his considered it a good match on both sides. My father settled thirty thousand pounds on me when I married, Luke. Your father allowed me the interest on that money and it is secured to you when I die. I have been prudent and added to the capital. I could let you have half of the money when you marry – providing you marry the right kind of girl.'

'I have sufficient funds for my needs at the moment,' Luke said. 'I'm not sure I can oblige you, Mama. A marriage of convenience may have been enough for you, but I don't think it will do for me.'

'I hope you haven't done anything foolish,' Lady Trenwith said as he brought the car to a standstill. 'I am aware that you have some capital of your own – left to you by my father, I might remind you. It would kill your father if you married beneath you.'

'What are you talking about?' Luke's face was pale as he turned to look at her. 'I don't understand you, Mother.'

'Do you not? I may live in the country, Luke, but I have friends in London. I received a letter telling me that you had been seen having dinner with a girl from a musical show. Normally, I would not have censured you, for men may have their little affairs – but that girl was Rose Barlow. You may think that I did not notice the way you lusted after her when she was a servant here, but I am not stupid, Luke. I cannot stop you having an affair with her – but if you distress your father by bringing that girl into the family I shall make you wish you had never been born.'

'Mother!' Luke was shocked by the vicious note in her voice. 'I can't believe you just said that.'

'Sarah may have accepted her as a friend, but I shall never accept her as my daughter-in-law. Marry her and I shall cut you out of my will. Your father will do the same. Trenwith may be entailed but you'll get nothing more – and none of us will speak to you again.'

'I don't much care about the money,' Luke said. 'I love Rose, Mother—'

'If your father learns of this I shall ruin her,' Lady Trenwith said. 'Either you marry a decent girl and keep that woman a secret or I'll make sure her name is dragged through all the scandal rags in the country. By the time I've finished with her she will never work again.'

'You can't do that!'

'I assure you that I have sufficient contacts to ruin both you and her,' Lady Trenwith told him. 'She would not be able to work, and you will lose your friends, Luke. You may think you could weather the storm, but my friends will not receive you nor will anyone of consequence. I do not believe you would care to be ostracised by society.'

'If it were just me I would tell you to do your damnedest,' Luke said. 'However, I care about what people think of Rose – and I care about Father. I don't want to be the cause of his death.'

'Then we understand each other.'

'You are a cold woman,' Luke said, staring at her in dislike. 'I thought you were hard on Sarah, but I didn't know the half of it. Have you ever loved anyone in your life?'

'I loved you,' she said. 'I may have indulged you too often, Luke. Please do not disappoint your father by forgetting your duty to us all. I shall say no more on the matter. Your affairs are your own but your marriage is for the family.'

Luke sat in the car, letting her open the door herself. He watched as she walked up to the house, her back ramrod straight. She need not have outlined his duty so plainly. He had always been aware of it, and even though he had longed to forget and follow his heart, he had always done what was required of him.

He felt sick inside as he realised he was going to do it again. He loved Rose, but he was going to marry a girl he felt nothing for because his father was ill and he could not let him down.

Luke hated himself in that moment; he hated his weakness and the way he had let himself be blackmailed all his life. His mother's threats were usually more subtly hinted at, and his father had simply made him aware of his duty. Nevertheless, their behaviour amounted to blackmail all the same. He was a damned fool to allow them to dictate his life, but what could he do? He felt trapped in a web of fine silk. He could break free of it, but he might bring everything and everyone down with him.

Sarah had been brave enough to follow her heart. Luke wished he dared emulate her example. He wanted to rush back to London and sweep Rose off to the register office, but he knew he wouldn't do it. He would delay proposing to Amanda for a little longer, but in the end he supposed he would have to marry her. What would Rose feel when she knew that he had promised to marry another woman? She would feel so terribly hurt – and betrayed. She would accuse him of breaking his word to her, and she would be right to hate him.

* * *

'It was good of you to come,' Sir James said from his bed. They had brought him home that morning but he was clearly still frail. 'Marianne hasn't arrived yet? I suppose she has too much to do with the children. She will come when she can.'

'Yes, Father, I am sure she will,' Luke said. The sight of his father lying in that large bed had affected him more than he'd imagined it might. Sir James looked shrunken, his eyes dark-shadowed by sickness. 'Sarah is here. She couldn't leave the children for a few days, but she is here now.'

Sir James nodded. 'I shall be pleased to see her. She was not always a dutiful child, but I am proud of her – as I am of you, Luke. You did your duty to your country. You won't let me down, will you?'

'Of course not, Father.' Luke reached for his hand, holding it awkwardly for a moment. 'Are you set on this marriage to Amanda?'

Sir James frowned. He removed his hand from Luke's grasp. 'She expects it and so does her father. I thought you would have the ring on her finger by now, Luke.'

'I didn't actually ask her, though I did kiss her.'

'Whatever you did or didn't do, you allowed her to expect it – and everyone has been told. Marianne shamed us by jilting Troy Pelham. I hope you will not behave as badly, Luke.'

'No, of course not, Father. I was just making sure the idea pleased you. I'll speak to her soon.'

'Do it now, Luke. I shall be well enough now that I am home. I would like to see you married before the year is out. I daresay Amanda will want some time to prepare her trousseau, which means the sooner you arrange your engagement party the better.'

'Yes.' Luke held the sigh inside. If he was going to ask Amanda, he might as well do it soon. He'd wanted to wait but his father might not see another year out. He owed it to him to marry well and take on the burden of the estate. He had hoped that perhaps there was another way, but the ties of duty had him tightly enmeshed. 'Yes, I'll go and see her before I return to London.'

'I know you have your show in London this month,' Sir James

said. 'But after that I think you should start to spend more time at home. I am relying on you, Luke. You will have to take over because I'm finished. It is time for me to hand over the trust to you.'

'Yes, Father.' Luke felt as if Sir James had hammered a stake through his heart. It would mean the end of his hopes and dreams. He couldn't expect Rose to sit around for weeks on end waiting for him to visit. He would have to tell her the truth.

* * *

'Back this evening. We'll go out.'

Rose looked at the telegram, which had come that morning. Luke had been away for almost two weeks, and when the boy had arrived with it she'd been terrified. A telegram had always meant bad news in the war. This time though, the news was good; Luke was coming back.

Rose had begun to fear that he had had an accident. She had been on the verge of telephoning Sarah for news when Janice had arrived at the flat with a letter.

'This came to the lodgings for you.' She looked around the studio curiously. 'Is your chap an artist?'

'Yes, he is,' Rose said. 'Thanks for bringing the letter, Janice. It's from a friend of mine, Sarah. I haven't given her my new address yet.' She knew that if she had given her address to her friend, Sarah would have guessed that Rose was living with Luke.

'I wanted to see if you were all right,' Janice said. 'It was rotten luck you getting the push like that.'

'Yes, I was angry at the time,' Rose said. 'I went to an audition the other day but I didn't get a recall.'

'You'll find something soon – or maybe your feller will marry you and you won't need to work.'

'I want to work,' Rose said. 'Luke would give me money but I want something to do when he isn't here. Anyway, tell me about you and Sally – how are you both getting on?'

'I'm leaving to get married,' Janice told her. 'Mike loves me and I'm giving up stage work.'

'That is wonderful!' Rose said and gave her a hug. 'I am so pleased for you, Janice.'

'I don't think I would ever have been a star,' Janice said. 'But you could, Rose. I hope you will find something soon.'

'Would you like to stay for a drink or a meal?'

'No, I have to meet Mike in an hour. I just wanted to bring the letter and tell you my news.'

Rose opened her letter after Janice had gone. She knew it was from Sarah and the first line told her that it was bad news. Sir James had been very ill. He was out of hospital now but still an invalid.

Father says it is time that he handed over to Luke completely. It is
a bit unfair on Luke, because I know he likes living in London a lot
of the time – and he has his show coming up. He really wants to
be an artist but Father expects him to give it up and live here. He
is insisting that Luke gets married. I think he will quite soon but I
am not sure it is what he wants...

Rose stared at the letter. Sarah had begun to tell her the news about her children and Troy, but Rose couldn't take it in. Luke was going to take over the estate. He would be living there most of the time and he was going to be married.

Rose felt sick as she replaced the letter in its envelope. Sarah didn't know she was living with Luke. She had just passed on the news, as she always did, not knowing that she would be hurting her friend.

Rose knew that the marriage being discussed was nothing to do with her. Luke was being pushed into the kind of arrangement that his family thought suitable.

How could he? A searing pain lanced through her and her legs turned to jelly. She sat down on the nearest chair. How could he make love to her – promise that he would always love her – and then marry another woman?

It wouldn't be fair to either of them. If he imagined that Rose would stay with him when he married... The thought made her feel ill. She would be his mistress, the woman he visited when he could spare a few hours. She would be expected to be here when he wanted her... and he would spend all the good times with his family: Christmas, holidays... All the special days of his life.

A wave of nausea overcame her. She went to the bathroom to be sick. She felt used, dirty – her heart breaking into pieces. How could Luke do this to her?

She had almost decided to pack and leave before he returned, but something made her stay. Perhaps Sarah had got it wrong. Luke's parents might wish him to marry but he would not oblige them. Surely he would refuse to be pushed into something he didn't want? If he loved her he would refuse; he must know that if he did not it would mean the end for them. But did he truly love her, or had she been a blind fool? She'd thrown away her chance as a singer because she refused to be treated like a whore by Harry Rhonda. And now Luke had lied to her and deceived her.

Rose didn't cry; she stored all the pain and hurt inside herself. And then the telegram had arrived.

* * *

'You look beautiful,' Luke said as Rose opened the door to him that evening. He came in carrying flowers and several packages. 'I'm sorry I was so much longer than I said, darling. Father was ill and I had things to do.'

Rose took the flowers through to the kitchen. She wondered if she would have sensed his apprehension if she hadn't read the letter from Sarah. Luke was nervous about something, and of course she knew what it was.

Luke came and put his arms about her, lifting her hair to kiss her neck. Rose moved away. She was hurting so much that she couldn't bear him to touch her.

'I know I should have written. We shall have to have a telephone put in so that I can ring you in future, but honestly, it was all so tense and upsetting.'

'Yes, of course it was,' Rose said. 'Your father was ill. You didn't have time to write or think of me. Why should you? I'm not important – not as important as Trenwith or your parents.'

'Rose...' Luke drew away as she turned to face him. 'You're angry. I'm sorry, but I'll make it up to you. Anything you want...'

'Like a wedding ring?' Rose lifted her head. 'You mean anything else but that, don't you? I'm not the one you're planning to give that to, am I?' Her eyes snapped with temper. 'When were you intending to tell me, Luke? At dinner – or after we'd been to bed?'

'Tell you what?' Luke had gone pale. 'Someone's been talking to you...'

'Sarah wrote to me. She told me that your father was ill and that you would be getting married soon. Were you hoping to keep it a secret? You must have known that I would find out sooner or later.'

Luke walked away from her. He threw himself down into an armchair, burying his face in his hands for a moment. Rose stood silently waiting. 'I was going to tell you later,' he said, looking up at last. 'Father wants me to have a child before he dies – and Mother... She knows about us somehow. She threatened all kinds of things if I married you...'

'Yes, of course. She would,' Rose said. 'You didn't have to listen to her, Luke. What could she do that is so terrible?'

'She said she would drag your name through the scandal rags. She said you would never work on the stage again.'

Rose gave a hollow laugh. She was probably never going to work in a show again anyway, but she didn't tell him that. All she had left now was her pride.

'She would do it too. Is that why you gave in?'

Luke shook his head. 'I don't care about the money or what society thinks of me, Rose. I don't even care about Trenwith – not the way Father does. But I do care about him. He could die at any time. I can't hurt him. If I told him I wanted to marry you – it would destroy him.'

'Yes, I see that,' Rose said bitterly. 'I'm not good enough to be the wife of the next master of Trenwith.'

Luke's face was tight with misery as he said, 'I've asked someone to marry me – but an engagement can be broken. If I delay the wedding... If Father dies... Besides, it doesn't have to affect us. We can still be together sometimes...'

'I think that is the most disgusting thing you've said so far.' Rose was furious. 'If you think I am going to be your mistress when you're married... That thought sickens me, Luke. I may have agreed to live with you, but that was because I loved you and I believed you loved me. I knew we couldn't marry yet. I was prepared to wait until your father was dead, even your mother – but I'm not a whore and I won't be treated like one.'

'Rose, I would never – you must know I would never make you feel like that.' Luke looked at her, a desperate appeal for understanding in his eyes. 'I love you – but I have to do this. It is my duty.'

'I hope you and your duty will be very happy together.' Rose's voice was cold. 'I almost walked out before you came back, but I thought I ought to give you a chance to explain. My things are packed. I shall leave in the morning. I think it is only fair that you go somewhere else for the night, don't you? In the morning I can arrange for a cab to take me...' She broke off; she had no idea where she was going.

'You can stay here,' Luke said. 'Stay for as long as you want. It's yours...' He got to his feet, taking her by the arms, his fingers pressing into the soft flesh. 'Please don't leave me, Rose. I can't bear to lose you.'

'I won't stay longer than tonight,' Rose said. 'Please let me go, Luke. You're hurting me. I can't stay – you know I can't.'

'I only know that I love you.' Luke pulled her hard against him, lowering his head to kiss her fiercely, his mouth bruising hers. He was breathing heavily, desperate to make her understand. 'She will never mean anything to me. It's you I love, Rose. We can do this...'

'No!' She thrust him away. 'I don't want to live like that, Luke. Let me go. You have to let me go.'

'Rose... no.' The words were torn from him. 'Please don't do this to me, Rose. You can't leave me. I need you...'

'This is impossible.' She walked resolutely into the bedroom. Her belongings were piled up ready for her to leave. Luke came after her, grabbing her wrist. He pulled her close to him and started to kiss her, but she pushed him away. She cried out: 'No! It's over, Luke. You're marrying someone else. It's over.'

He lowered his head and nodded slowly, a look of defeat in his eyes. He sat on the bed for a moment, head in hands, his shoulders shaking. He was crying. Rose put a hand on his arm.

'I'm sorry. You know I'm right, don't you? This has to end.'

'Yes.' His voice was muffled. He got to his feet and walked from the bedroom. She heard the door slam as he left.

Rose turned her face to the pillow and wept. She'd sent him away. He had let his family split them up and she couldn't bear it. He should have stood up to them; he should have put her first.

Angry and wretched by turns, Rose knew in her heart that their affair had always been doomed. They could never marry; the divide was too wide.

She got up, went to the bathroom and washed her face. She would leave now, tonight; take only what she could carry. She could come back for the rest in the morning. She wasn't sure where she was going, but there were hundreds of small hotels and lodging-houses in London. She would find somewhere.

Her heart was breaking. How could Luke have asked another woman to marry him when he said he loved her? Was he so weak that he would let his family push him into a marriage of convenience – or had he simply lied to her? Had Luke never loved her at all? No, she couldn't believe that. She was sure he had loved her. Perhaps he still did, but he hadn't been strong enough to resist the pressures his family had put upon him. Either way, the result was the same.

It was over.

4

'Rose!' Sally cried with delight as she opened the door. 'Come in. I'm so glad you called. Janice told me you'd split up with your chap. I've been wondering if you were all right.'

'Yes, I'm managing,' Rose said. 'I went to a theatrical lodging-house and they had a spare room – but I shan't be able to stay there long unless I find a job in the theatre. I've been looking in the papers but there isn't much. No one seems to be casting at the moment.'

'You've come to the right place,' Sally told her. 'I've just auditioned for a new show and I know they are still looking for singers. I'm sure I could get you a chance.'

'Would you really, Sally? You know what happened with Harry Rhonda?'

'That creep.' Sally shuddered. 'I can't stand him. All the girls dislike him, but he's good box office and he gets away with it.' She grinned at Rose. 'You look great. Is there a telephone where you're staying?'

'Yes. I'll give you the number.' Rose took a little notebook from her bag and scribbled it down. 'It is very good of you. I know I can find somewhere else to live – and I've been doing a few hours in a café, waiting tables, but I would like another chance to sing professionally.'

'We're having a bit of a party this evening.' Sally saw the doubt in her eyes and laughed. 'It won't be as bad as the other one. We've settled down since then and we only have friends round. We've all got our regular men and we behave ourselves these days, Rose. I could telephone you with the news, but if you come to the party you'll enjoy yourself. It can't have been much fun since you split up with Luke?'

'No, it hasn't,' Rose said. She had been feeling tired and miserable, but that was only because she'd cried a lot at the start. She couldn't afford to antagonise Sally. She was her only contact – the only person who might have some ideas about how Rose could get back on the stage. 'Yes, all right. I'll come – thank you.'

'I'll talk to a couple of people,' Sally promised. 'Wear something glamorous this evening. Have you got a good dress? I could lend you something if not.'

'I have an expensive evening gown that Luke bought me. It's green and cut rather low at the back. My mother would have a fit if she saw me wear it.'

'All our mothers would be shocked if they knew what we get up to,' Sally told her and laughed. 'It sounds just perfect. Be here at half past seven.'

Rose thanked her and left. She walked to the tram stop. As she was about to board the tram her head started to spin. She missed the step and might have fallen had a man not grabbed her arm and steadied her.

'Feeling a bit faint, love?'

'Yes, I was,' Rose said. 'Thanks. I'll be all right in a minute. It has happened a couple of times lately.'

'You want to see a doctor,' he said.

Rose nodded. She moved on to the tram, relieved to sit down. She had never felt quite like this before; there was nothing she could put her finger on, just odd sensations. She'd noticed a couple of small things lately – she'd experienced a little nausea, and there had been one or two occasions when the room had seemed to spin. She was more tired than usual too...

Oh, no. A wave of panic washed over her with the realisation that she might be carrying Luke's child. She had never even considered the possibility. She hadn't fallen for a baby when she was married to Rod, and until now it hadn't occurred to her that it could happen so quickly.

Life couldn't be that cruel! She had longed for Rod's baby after he'd been killed, and wished she could have conceived a child on their honeymoon. It hadn't happened then, but she was very much afraid that it might have happened with Luke.

If they had still been together she would have been so happy. She knew that Luke would have taken care of her if she'd allowed him to – but she'd sent him away. Her pride would prevent her from asking for help, so she would have to manage alone. She knew that it would be a few weeks before her pregnancy became obvious. Perhaps she would be lucky and get a spot in the show Sally had told her about. She would have to be more careful about what she spent, because she had already used some of the money her mother had given her after her father died. There was always Jack's money, but she didn't want to use that, just in case...

Rose sighed. It wasn't likely that her brother would come back after all this time. Everyone else had accepted that he was dead, but somehow there was a spark of hope inside her that just would not die.

* * *

Jack left the garage and cycled back to the café. He was feeling pleased with the world because he had managed to repair a car that everyone else had thought was finished. It had been rusting in a shed for some years, but he'd cleaned the bodywork and tinkered with the engine until he had a vehicle that anyone would admire, even though it was much slower on the road than the newer cars. A customer had come in to look at it while he was working on the engine and he'd put in an offer to the garage owner.

'You are marvellous,' his boss told him. 'I do not wish to lose you, Georges. I know you dream of your own business one day but I have no sons. If you will give me your promise to stay I shall make you my partner.'

Jack had agreed to talk it over with Louise and give his answer the next day. André was a good employer and he got on well with the man. However, his dream was to have his own garage and he had been saving towards that ideal for a while. He didn't want to leave his employer, but he was afraid he might not be kept on if he refused André's generous offer.

Jack thought longingly of the money he had saved in England before the war. If he had that he could set himself up in business immediately, though he wouldn't try to compete with André. He had seen premises in another district of the city, which would suit him very well.

He was thoughtful as he walked through the back door of the café, and then stopped as he saw a man sitting at one of the tables. He was drinking a glass of red wine and talking to Louise. As the man turned his head and Jack saw his face, he felt a spasm of something like fear in his stomach.

'Henri,' he said, his mouth suddenly dry, because this man was the only other person in Paris besides Louise who knew that Jack's papers were false. 'What are you doing in Paris?'

'I am here on business,' Henri said, and something in his eyes warned Jack to be wary. 'Louise tells me she is very busy in the café and I hear you've found yourself a job at a local garage. You always were a good mechanic, Georges.'

'It's what I've always wanted,' Jack told him. 'Is there something I can do for you?'

'Nothing that won't keep for a while,' Henri said. 'I just wanted to make sure all was well with you. You understand what I mean?'

'Yes, I believe I do,' Jack said. Outwardly calm, he felt a surge of anger. Henri had blackmailed him into joining the freedom fighters during the war, though in the end Jack had stayed for Louise's sake, and also because he liked what he was doing. However, it had been Henri who had provided the false papers that allowed Jack to stay and work in France. He had earned those papers many times over, but a prickling sensation at the nape of his neck was warning Jack that he was about to be asked for a further payment. He smiled at Louise. 'You get back to the customers, love. I'll join Henri for a drink.'

He fetched a fresh bottle of wine and sat down, pouring the rich ruby liquid for them both, his manner easy, friendly, as he took his first sip. His eyes held a glitter of warning as he looked across the table at Henri.

'So, what do you want?' he asked. 'I know it wasn't just a spur of the moment thing, Henri. Tell me and we'll talk about it.'

'I always admired you for your honesty,' Henri said, and he toyed with his wineglass. 'We have discovered the identity of a traitor. He caused the deaths of many Frenchmen during the war. We want revenge.'

'It has happened often enough since the war ended,' Jack said. 'You don't need my help for that, my friend. The papers have reported revenge attacks for months. The police turn a blind eye most of the time. Germans have been pelted in the streets, their businesses set on fire. Traitors are treated as they deserve – beaten, tarred and feathered...'

'This one has to die,' Henri said. 'But we need it to look like an accident. He drives a car...'

'No!' Jack shook his head. 'I won't murder for you, Henri. How do I know he deserves to die?'

'I can bring you the proof,' Henri said, his eyes narrow and hard. 'I give you my word this will be the last time I ask a favour.'

'Bring me proof,' Jack said. A little pulse was flicking at his temple. 'I'm not saying I'll do it, but I might tell you how...'

* * *

Rose felt a flutter of nerves in her stomach as she approached the front door of Sally's flat. Remembering how long it was since she'd seen her monthly flow, she was almost certain that she was carrying Luke's baby. If anyone guessed the truth she wouldn't stand a chance of getting back on the stage. Theatre managers didn't like girls leaving in the middle of a successful run to have a baby. She hesitated outside the door but then, just as she was deciding not to go in, the door opened and Sally pulled her into the hall.

'I saw you come,' she said. 'I was afraid you might change your mind – and there is someone here who wants to see you.'

'Someone to see me?' Rose noticed that Sally was looking excited and her heart pounded madly. Was it Luke? Had he discovered where she would be that evening?

'Do you remember Jason Brent?' Sally asked as she closed the door behind them. 'He remembers you very well and he wants you to audition for him.'

'Really?' Rose wasn't sure whether to be elated or nervous. She had never forgotten Jason Brent or his bold eyes – 'bedroom eyes' was the expression the other girls used for eyes like his. 'Is he the one putting on your show?'

'Yes, he is. I didn't tell you because I wasn't sure he would be interested, but he is. He wanted to know why you'd left the other show, and... well, I'll let him tell you himself. Come into the parlour and meet everyone.'

Rose felt nervous as she took off her coat. The dress was new. She had intended to wear it for Luke the next time they went out together, but all that was over. She had to put the past behind her and try to forget, at least for this evening. She was very conscious of how low the back of her gown was cut. It was fashionable and a lot of the women who frequented the expensive restaurants that Luke had taken her to were wearing similar gowns. However, for a girl from a family who considered it decadent to undress in front of another person, the style was almost shameless.

She was aware of several heads turning to look at her, and her cheeks were a little pink as one or two of the men raised their wine-glasses to her. Someone was playing background music and a couple were dancing. However, it was a much quieter affair than the last party she had been to at Sally's flat.

'I'll get you a drink,' Sally said and left her.

Rose saw Jason Brent immediately. He stood out from all the other men present, his clothes quietly expensive and his manner that of a wealthy man who didn't need to try too hard. He walked unhurriedly towards her, a smile on his lips.

'Rose Barlow,' he said. 'I wondered where you had gone when you dropped out of the show. I asked but they said they didn't know. I'm sorry for the way you were treated. If it were my show I would have thrown Harry Rhonda out. He will never work in any of my productions.'

'Unfortunately, they didn't see it that way. He is big box office.'

'So will you be by the time I've finished with you.'

Rose gasped. She raised her gaze, seeing the amusement in his eyes. He had intended to pull the rug from under her feet and he had succeeded. For a moment she couldn't think of anything to say.

'No questions? You surprise me, Rose.'

'I'm getting my breath back,' she said and smiled. She had thought him arrogant, dangerous, but maybe he wasn't so bad. 'What makes you think I could be a star, Mr Brent?'

'Ah, that question,' he laughed softly in his throat. 'I don't *think* anything, Rose. I know star quality when I see it – that is my talent, just as singing is yours. You have a good voice and it will be better when we have trained you. Yes, I know you have had lessons, but you need more – and you need to learn how to be a star. You look the part, but you have to believe in yourself.'

'I know I want to sing. I love being on stage, but I'm not sure I'm good enough to be the star of your show, Mr Brent.'

'Call me Jason. I know you aren't good enough yet, but you will be if you listen to me. You have raw talent. It needs to be cultivated... nurtured. I'm the man to do it. We'll start tomorrow – unless there is a reason you can't be a part of the show I'm planning for the West End?'

'The West End...' Rose stared at him in wonder. He wasn't talking about a small theatre and chorus work. He was talking about her name up in lights, pictures in the papers and fame. 'No – there's no reason why I shouldn't work for you, if you want me. You may change your mind once you hear me sing again.'

'There is no chance of that,' Jason told her. 'I sat out front and listened to you every night you were at the Haymarket. I asked them to release you from your contract but they wouldn't oblige me. They were damned fools to let you go. But that is their bad luck and my good fortune. You are going to make my show a success, Rose Barlow.'

Rose studied his expression. He seemed to be sincere, but what would he ask in return? Most people wanted something in return when they did you a favour – very few people gave something for nothing.

'I should enjoy the chance to try,' she said and licked her lips. 'But...'

'No strings attached,' he promised. 'You don't have to sleep with me to get to the top, Rose. Maybe one day – if it suits us both – but at the moment I have a relationship.' He smiled as Sally brought a drink for Rose. 'Sally is a lovely girl and we get on well...'

'Sally...' Rose caught her breath and then laughed. 'In that case I am delighted to be auditioning for you tomorrow.' She took the glass of champagne from Sally and sipped at it. 'Thank you so much, Jason.'

'You may not thank me tomorrow,' he said, and his eyes gleamed. 'Fame doesn't come easily, Rose. It has to be worked for – and they tell me I am a hard taskmaster.'

'I've never minded hard work. I was in the VADs during the war.'

'Then you know what hard work is,' Jason said. 'You girls worked your hearts out for us, and I should know. I had six months in hospital towards the end of 1917.'

His eyes held a challenge. Rose wasn't sure what it meant. If he hadn't told her he was in a relationship with Sally she would have thought he was interested in her. But why would he want Rose when he had a beautiful girl like Sally?

She felt a little uncomfortable as Sally started to chatter on about her solo spot in Jason's show. She obviously had no idea that he was thinking of giving Rose star billing. She couldn't help wondering if Sally would be as friendly towards her when she knew.

Her own secret was lodged heavily at the back of her mind; she wasn't sure how long she would be able to keep the pregnancy to herself or what Jason would say when he discovered the truth. He might not be too pleased if he had invested a lot of time and money into moulding her as his star.

*   *   *

Luke entered the house via a back door. He sensed at once that the expected visitors had arrived. Amanda and her father had been invited to spend a week or two at Trenwith, and Lady Trenwith had brought in extra staff to make sure that everything was perfect.

'We do not want Amanda or her father having second thoughts,' she'd told Luke earlier that morning when he questioned some of her arrangements. 'Amanda expects us to give a ball for her and we shall show them that we know how to do things properly. Some of the staff are not as well trained as I would like, but I daresay we can manage for a few days.'

'I think you were lucky to get those who did come back,' Luke told her. 'I did not think Jarvis or his wife would stay as long as they have – and Emily Redfern is related to the Barlow family...'

'Emily's manner is a little pert,' his mother replied frostily. 'Had she not come with good references I should not have taken her. Whether I shall keep her here is another matter.'

'Do not cut off your nose to spite your face, Mama,' Luke said, a note of bitterness in his voice. 'You got your own way. Be grateful that Emily is here. I doubt if she will stay long. She is too bright to work as a servant. She will either marry or leave to work in a shop – and I for one would not blame her.'

The look in his mother's eyes told him that he had not been

forgiven, even though he had asked Amanda to marry him. He doubted that she would forget he had dared to flout her wishes by having an affair with Rose.

Was that all it had been? Merely an affair? Luke felt regret slice through him like a knife through butter. Sometimes when he looked at Amanda he loathed her. He knew it wasn't her fault that he had been weak enough to submit to his parents' demands, but he wished that she had refused him. Amanda had been delighted with her ring, a large and expensive emerald and diamond that had been produced from among the family heirlooms by his father. He'd wanted to give Rose diamonds and lavish her with gifts, but she had sent him away.

He was ashamed how he'd acted with her that last night. He'd wanted her so badly, but Rose had got through to him – and he'd known she was talking sense. It was wrong and cruel to think of carrying on an affair after he had asked Amanda to be his wife. She didn't deserve to be deceived and Rose certainly didn't deserve to be hidden away as if he were ashamed of her.

He wondered what Rose was doing now. He knew she wasn't in the show at the Haymarket, because Barney had been to see it and was disappointed. Luke hadn't been back to his flat so he wasn't sure whether Rose was still staying there or not. He had written to apologise to her and to tell her that he had opened an account for her. He could at least make sure that she had enough money to live on... especially if she should be carrying his child.

Would she tell him if she discovered that their brief affair had resulted in trouble for her? Luke doubted it. Rose had her pride. He thought that he would never cease to regret his own weakness, but it was too late to go back. Rose would never forgive him. He couldn't expect it of her and he couldn't let everyone else down. Amanda was making endless plans for the wedding; plans he found irritating. Sometimes he felt that he could not bear to listen to another description of her trousseau, but he controlled his irritation because it was his own fault. He should never have kissed her, never have given her cause to believe they were engaged.

Sighing, he straightened his shoulders and went through to the back parlour where his mother and her guests had gathered to talk and take tea. Luke wondered how long after his marriage he could suggest that Amanda lived in the house her father was giving them in London, while he pleaded pressure of work at Trenwith.

He supposed he would have to make certain there was an heir on the way first. It was a damned coil! He knew his attitude was all wrong. Amanda deserved so much more than he could ever give her. He must at least make an effort to please her and to make her stay at Trenwith as pleasant as possible.

'Ah, there you are, darling,' he said and smiled as he went over to kiss her cheek. 'I hope you had a good journey down?'

'Thank you, yes,' Amanda said. 'Daddy was fretting because of the delay, but I told him I simply could not leave before my new ball gown was delivered. They were an hour late sending it, which isn't at all acceptable. I may have to change my dressmaker. Daddy will not put up with shoddy service from anyone.'

'I do so agree,' Lady Trenwith said, giving her a nod of approval. 'I am not sure how you manage for servants, Mr Rawlings – but I find that standards have slipped since the war. We still have some of the servants that stayed with us, thank goodness, but I dread to think what will happen when they are forced to retire through age or ill health.'

'Mother...' Luke glanced at the girl who had just brought in the tea tray. Emily might not quite match Rose's standards, but the Barlow family had come from a long line of men and women trained to serve. Emily was a cousin of Rose's and had been too young to know what things were like here before the war. She did her best and there was absolutely no reason why she should stay if she wasn't happy.

Lady Trenwith glared at him from across the room. She had always ignored servants other than to give orders. She expected silent obedience – and for the most part that was what she got. Even from him, Luke thought resentfully.

His father had not come down for tea, though if he was feeling well enough he might put in an appearance at dinner. Sometimes he dined with the family, but more often he had a tray in his room. Luke knew that his mother still worried about his father, but for himself he believed that Sir James simply preferred his own company.

'I've given the best part of my life to Trenwith,' he told Luke when they had their daily talks. 'I've preserved it for you, Luke. Now it is up to you to make what you will of it. After I've gone you can make changes – but I should be grateful if you will keep things as they are for the present.'

'Of course, Father. I wouldn't dream of going against your wishes.'

It wasn't quite true, of course. Luke had already made changes to the way the land was farmed. Trenwith land had always been arable, mainly wheat, barley and oats rotated with a root crop every other year to clear it of pests and sweeten the soil. Luke had decided to diversify into some soft fruit and salad vegetables; he had also increased the dairy side, bringing in a small herd of Jersey cows. As yet he had only put a small part of the land into market garden produce, but if things went well he might increase it over the years. He had discussed his plans with Terry Jarvis. Terry's father and mother were among those who had never left Trenwith. After serving in the army and receiving a wound that caused him to walk with a heavy limp, Terry had come back to Trenwith looking for a job.

'I'm not sure what I can do, sir,' he'd told Luke. 'My leg won't stand up to hard manual labour and I'm not sure I'd be any good in the house.'

'You used to like helping in the kitchen gardens before the war,' Luke said. 'How would you like to oversee it as a commercial project? You will be in charge of the men and of the distribution. Does that appeal?'

'I was with the army logistics for part of the time during the war,' Terry told him. 'But I daresay you knew that, sir. I may have contacts in the food department.'

'Yes, I rather thought you were the man for the job. Can you drive? I thought you might want a small van or truck – something to help you get about?'

'That's very good of you, sir. The army taught me to drive. I'll make this pay for you, sir.'

'The old days are done, Terry. You may call me Luke or Trenwith, it's your choice – but, please, not sir.'

'If you wish it, Mr Luke,' the young sergeant said and grinned. 'Captain Trenwith it ought to be by rights.'

'Thank goodness the war is over! You army boys had it hard. I don't think I could have stood it in the trenches.'

'You'd have done it if you had to,' Terry said. 'Folks back home didn't know what it was all about and, bless 'em, it don't seem right to tell 'em. We understand, Mr Luke. I told my father, when he asked me why I'd come back, I've had enough of foreign parts; this is home and I'm grateful for a job.'

'I wish more felt as you do, Terry.'

'The girls had a taste of freedom. That Emily was talking of leaving and going for shop work, but I told her it ain't all it's cracked up to be. I doubt she'll stay long, though she's a smashing girl.'

'Yes, I think we are lucky to have her. You should ask her to marry you, Terry. We might hang on to her then for a bit longer.'

'She wouldn't look at me, sir.'

'Well, you never know. The kind of work you will be doing has a bit of status, besides offering decent money and one of the better cottages. I've set some work in hand and there will be a cottage for you in a month or so if you want your own place.'

'I shan't say no, Mr Luke. Living at home was all right before the war, but I shout a bit in the night sometimes...' Terry kicked at a stone with the toe of his boot. 'You know how it is.'

'Yes, I do. I can get away from my parents at Trenwith, but it isn't so easy in a cottage. They tell me it will pass in time.'

'Aye, they say so.' Terry shrugged. 'I daresay they don't know what it was like, listening to men what got shot in no-man's-land – listening to 'em scream all night and not being able to do anything.'

'Or seeing a friend crash in flames,' Luke agreed, a nerve flicking at his right temple. 'I'll leave you to get started. You can recruit the men you need and tell me what you require in the way of equipment and storage.'

'I think we might have some soft fruit bushes as part of the project,' Terry said, lifting his cap to brush back his thick dark hair. 'Gooseberries and raspberries; blackcurrants too. Most of the year they don't need much looking after, and if you get the right varieties they crop heavy.'

'I'll leave it to you then,' Luke said, feeling an inward satisfaction. He had made a good choice in Jarvis.

Luke considered they had weathered the war and its aftermath pretty well at Trenwith. It was a pity his mother wasn't easier to please, more satisfied with the way things were now. She wouldn't approve of most of his plans for Trenwith, but he was determined to go ahead with them. It would be a slow process, but he was going to drag this place into the modern world despite his mother's opposition.

* * *

'You should have heard her,' Emily said when she returned to the kitchen. 'I don't know if she thinks I'm deaf or daft, but the way she talks about us is enough to make me see red.'

'The old bitch thinks we're slaves,' Maisie Black said, looking surly. 'I've worked in this kitchen since I was a lass younger than you – and what thanks have I had for it? If I were your age I should be off to the town, girl. I'm too old to make the change, and my Bill is set in his ways, but I wouldn't put up with her tongue if I were you.'

'You will not talk like that in my kitchen,' Mrs Jarvis said. 'If you'd had any ambition, Maisie Black, you could have found work elsewhere years ago. You look at Rose Barlow. She enrolled in the VADs when the war started and now she's singing in a show in London.'

'How did she get that job then?' Emily asked. 'I remember Rose going in the VADs but I didn't know she was singing. She doesn't come near now her ma's gone away. I haven't heard from her for ages.'

'I should have thought she would write to you, send you a few bob now she's rich, seein' as you're cousins,' Maisie said and pulled a face. 'Still, I suppose she's above herself now.'

'Being in a show doesn't make you rich,' Emily said, defending her cousin. 'I like Rose. I should like to hear her sing on stage.'

'Well, you could if you went off to London,' Maisie said. 'I don't know what you want to stay here for.'

'Because she's got more sense than you,' Mrs Jarvis said. 'My Terry came back here and Mr Luke has been real good to him, giving him that job and a cottage of his own. Terry says it has running water and an inside lavvy – and there's going to be a real bath when it's finished.'

'Bloody hell,' Maisie said. 'The old bitch will raise hell when she hears about that – I can just hear her – giving them what should know their place ideas above their stations! You see if I'm not right.'

'A bathroom?' Emily looked at Mrs Jarvis. 'That sounds a bit of all right. Your Terry is lucky.'

'He's got something to offer now,' Mrs Jarvis said. 'He may have a limp but he's found himself a good job here. He wouldn't have got that in the town now, would he?'

'No, I don't suppose he would,' Emily said, looking thoughtful. 'I've heard some of the slums are going to be cleared in places like London and Liverpool, but a proper bathroom – that's special.' She washed her dusters in the stone sink. 'Mr Luke is all right anyway – it's only her ladyship...'

'Well, she can't bring herself to accept that the old ways have gone,' Mrs Jarvis said. 'She'll cling on for as long as she can, but things are changing whether she likes it or not.'

'I shan't leave just yet,' Emily said. 'I like Mr Luke, but I'm not sure I shall stay when he's married. That fiancée of his is a stuck-up miss and she leaves everything on the floor for me to pick up.'

'Well, you please yourself,' Mrs Jarvis told her. 'But in my opinion you could do a lot worse.'

* * *

Rose finished singing her last song of the morning. They had been rehearsing hard for the past two weeks, and she'd realised how much she had to learn. She had soon discovered that Jason wasn't joking when he said he was hard to please. He had been present at every rehearsal and constantly critical of everything she did, every note she sang, every move she made. Rose had been pushed almost to the limit, holding on to her temper with great difficulty.

However, this morning he had been absent and she had been

surprised to discover that she missed him. He was critical but also lavish in his praise when she got it right.

'That is fine, Rose. You can go now. We'll have the chorus girls on next. I want to go through their dance routine.' Jason's assistant dismissed her with a smile. 'You were good, Rose. You shouldn't look so worried. Take the rest of the day off and enjoy yourself. One more week of rehearsal and we shall be opening on stage.'

'Are you sure Jason would approve?' Rose asked. 'Yesterday he said I had a long way to go still.'

'You're doing just fine,' Mike Branning said. 'Trust me, Rose. Jason is a bear where you're concerned. It beats me why you put up with him.'

'I'm grateful he gave me this chance.'

'You could get work anywhere.'

'You've taught me a lot, Mike – you and Jason.'

'You just needed a few raw edges smoothing,' he said and grinned at her. 'Don't be too grateful, Rose. Jason wouldn't have bothered if he didn't think he'd struck gold. Go on, scarper. You've worked hard and you deserve a bit of fun.'

Rose thanked him and left the stage. She talked to one or two of the other girls for a few minutes and then changed into her street clothes. As she was leaving her dressing-room she saw Sally and called to her.

'Did Mike say you could have the rest of the day off too? Shall we go for a coffee and a sandwich?'

'I've got something on,' Sally said and pulled a wry face. 'Maybe another time.'

Rose nodded. Sally had been a bit distant of late. She had wondered if her friend was upset because Jason had been spending so much time with her on stage, but Sally didn't seem jealous, just preoccupied.

Rose decided to wander round the shops. She had no intention of buying anything, because even though she was earning three times what she'd ever earned before, she was trying to be careful. She'd noticed a slight thickening about her waist, and she was apprehensive of what would happen once she began to show her condition. Would Jason be angry and throw her out? He would have every right to be angry; she ought to have been honest with him at the start. She hadn't been absolutely certain then that she was carrying Luke's child, but she was now.

She was thinking it was time to catch a tram back to her lodgings when she caught sight of the one person she did not wish to see. Luke had just come out of an expensive jeweller's shop. He had a pretty girl with him. She was younger than Rose, fair and obviously the daughter of a rich man, her clothes expensive and tasteful. Rose watched as she reached up to kiss Luke's cheek, dimpling at him and laughing confidently.

Rose turned away without waiting to see Luke's reaction. It hurt too much to see him with the woman he intended to marry, and she felt angry and resentful. He had made those empty promises to her when he'd known all the time he was going to marry this girl.

Tears blinded her eyes as she walked hurriedly away, and in her urgency she almost collided with a man. She apologised, bringing her head up sharply, then drew in her breath as she saw that it was Jason Brent.

'I'm sorry,' she said, and she tried to smile but failed miserably. 'I didn't see you. I should have looked where I was going.'

'No harm done,' he said. 'Something has upset you. Come on, I'm taking you to tea at the Savoy and you can tell me all about it.'

'It doesn't matter. I'll get over it.'

'Rose, you are going to be a star. When something moves you to tears I want to know about it.' Jason summoned a passing cab and ushered her inside despite her protests. 'I'm the one you talk to in times of crisis, right?'

Rose laughed despite herself. Jason was so sure of himself and his right to take over her life. She didn't notice that Luke had seen them. She didn't see the smile leave his face or the way his eyes darkened with pain.

* * *

'He told you he loved you and promised it wouldn't be a brief affair and then you found out he was getting married a few weeks later?' Jason's eyes glinted with anger. 'He sounds a complete bastard, Rose. I don't think you lost much. Once you open in the show you will have all the men in love with you – you'll be able to pick and choose.'

Rose hesitated, and then took a deep breath. 'There's something else I have to tell you, Jason. I wouldn't blame you if you threw me out... but I'm having a baby.'

'His, I suppose?'

'Yes,' Rose admitted. 'He isn't that bad, Jason. He would help me with money if I asked, but I shan't because I can manage alone.'

'You're not going to tell him he has a child even when the baby is born?'

'He is getting married,' Rose said. 'It would only complicate things for him. He wanted me to go on being his mistress. He was going to give me the flat but I walked out that night.'

'You should have taken all he offered,' Jason said, and then he smiled. 'I'm glad you didn't – and I'm glad you've told me the truth, Rose.'

'Are you angry? I know I've wasted your time.'

'I might have been if you hadn't told me,' Jason said. 'It means we shall have to design your clothes to disguise the bump for as long as possible – and you will have to leave the show for a while when it becomes too obvious or the work is too hard for you. But that doesn't mean I'm throwing you out. There may be some scandal, though we might hush it up if you go away to have the child – or you could marry me and make it respectable.'

'Marry you?' Rose stared at him. 'Don't be daft, Jason! You don't want to marry me! Besides, it wouldn't be fair to Sally.'

'What has Sally to do with this?'

'You said – that night when you asked me to be in the show – you told me you were with Sally.'

'I let you believe it because you thought I was coming on to you,' Jason said and grinned. 'Sally has someone but it isn't me – she has been seeing a man secretly for a while now and she keeps his identity to herself, but I happen to know who he is. He is married and titled, and besotted with her. He is never going to marry her, of course, but he wants her to move into a house he owns so that he can visit her more easily. Sally is holding out for the deeds and a settlement. If she gets what she wants she will probably leave the show.'

'No wonder she has been a bit preoccupied recently,' Rose said. 'I thought perhaps she was upset because you had spent so much time with me.'

'Sally is a friend. I've never had a fling with her – or any of the other girls.' He hesitated, then, 'I'm going to tell you something that I don't tell many people, Rose. My sexual tastes are for something rather different. I could go to prison for my preferences if they became public knowledge. I am trusting you with this knowledge so that you will understand. If you married me it would just be for public show.'

'Your tastes...' Rose stared at him because it had simply never occurred to her that Jason might prefer men to women. 'I must be a complete fool but I've never seen... noticed... anything.'

'You thought I was after your body the first time we met. It amused me, Rose, because I was interested in your voice from the start. I'm not saying I don't find you attractive, because I do – and there was once a woman I occasionally slept with, but it didn't work for either of us and I finally admitted what I really wanted. It took me a long time to accept it myself, and I can't let it be known publicly because I should be ruined.'

'It is unfair that you should have to lie about something like that,' Rose said. 'Oscar Wilde stood out against the law but it destroyed him. You know I would never tell anyone the truth, Jason.' She supposed that a lot of people would find what he had just told her disgusting; homosexuals were regarded with abhorrence by many, and the practice was illegal. However, she had learned to like and respect Jason, and knowing the truth didn't change how she felt about him as a friend. 'It must have been hard for you, always having to lie and hide what you truly feel.'

'It isn't easy. Think about my proposal,' Jason told her with a smile. 'It wouldn't be ideal, but I would give you a divorce if you met someone else you could love. You may be brave enough to have the child and carry on without marriage, but the offer is there if it appeals to you.'

'I am grateful – honoured – that you should want to help me in this way,' Rose said. 'I'm not sure what I want to do at the moment. I need to think it over for a couple of days.'

'Of course, but remember that you would be doing me a favour as well,' Jason said. 'A lot of men in my situation marry to deflect scandal. I couldn't pretend that it would be a proper marriage, but you never know.'

'I'm still in love with Luke,' Rose told him. 'I think I always shall be – but I have to forget him. Let me think about it, Jason.'

'I don't want to pressure you into anything,' he said. 'I'll be your friend or your husband, Rose. It is entirely up to you.'

'You are my friend. You've made me feel much better. I can't wait for opening night.'

'You are going to be a big success,' Jason told her. 'I have a feeling about you, Rose, and I'm seldom wrong. I think you will go a long way in this business. It is a little unfortunate about the baby, because the news is bound to get out and the moral brigade will be after you – but I daresay we can brush through it if we try. The public can be fickle in their reaction to that sort of thing. Some people seem to be able to do whatever they like and get away with it, whereas others – well, if an audience takes against you, you are finished.'

5

It hadn't taken Rose long to find another man! Luke felt the bitter jealousy spiral inside him. He ought to have known she wouldn't grieve for him long. He had thought he wanted her to be happy, but seeing her with a man who was obviously rich and able to give her the kind of things Luke had wanted to give her made him angry.

Luke's anger was short-lived. He knew that he had only himself to blame; he had let her down. He'd given in to his conscience and done what his family required of him. Even after the quarrel with Rose, he had clung on to the idea that perhaps they could get back together. In his heart he had known that Rose would not consent to be his mistress when he married, but he'd delayed fixing the date, hoping that something might happen and he would not have to marry Amanda.

What a damned fool he had been! It was over. He'd had his chance with Rose. Now he had to put the past behind him and get on with life. There was no point in putting off the wedding. His father and Amanda's father had been pressing for a date. He would tell Amanda that she could choose the day whenever she liked.

'Would you mind awfully if we had a Christmas wedding?'

Amanda asked when he told her she could pick the day as soon as she liked. 'I've always loved Christmas – and my godmother, Lady Jane Marshall, has asked me if I would like to accompany her on a cruise. We shall be away for almost three months, which means that it would be too much of a rush to get ready for the wedding before Christmas.'

Luke would have been relieved had she suggested the delay a few days earlier; now he was merely frustrated. It would have been good to get it over and done with so that he could settle things in his mind, but of course he couldn't say that to Amanda.

'Yes, of course, darling, if that is what you want.'

'You won't miss me too dreadfully?'

'I shall miss you, of course – but if your godmother wants to take you on this cruise...'

'I sort of promised her before you gave me the ring,' Amanda told him, looking doubtful. 'If you said I couldn't go, I would stay with you, Luke – but she would be so disappointed.'

'You are fond of her, aren't you?'

'She was so good to me after Mama died. I should hate to let her down – but I don't want you to be cross, Luke.'

'I shan't be cross. What makes you think I might?'

'You look so cross sometimes,' Amanda said, and her bottom lip quivered. 'I know I'm young and silly and you must know lots of clever women. I'm not sure why you asked me to marry you, Luke.'

'I asked you because I care for you, of course.'

'I thought it might just be because Daddy and your father are friends,' she said uncertainly. 'I was excited about getting engaged, and you've given me so many lovely things – you and Daddy – but I wouldn't want you to marry me just because I am suitable. You do love me, don't you?'

'Yes, of course I do.' Luke leaned down to kiss her softly on the lips. He realised that his behaviour might have hurt her and he felt a stab of remorse. It was the first time Amanda had spoken to him like this and he felt closer to her because of it. 'I've had a lot to do with the estate, darling – and Father being ill doesn't help. I want to do things he wouldn't like and yet I do not want to distress him; but I can't help seeing the things that need doing.'

'Daddy thinks you are showing wonderful restraint,' Amanda told him. 'He believes your ideas are sensible for the most part, though he says there is no need to open a shop, or the gardens, because his wedding present will ensure the future is good for us.'

'Your father is generous,' Luke said, 'but Trenwith has to be a business if it is to survive in the modern world, Amanda. Either that or I shall have to earn a fortune some other way.'

'Have you been painting recently?'

'I don't get much time, I'm afraid.'

'You shouldn't give it up if it makes you happy,' Amanda said seriously. She put out a tentative hand to touch his. 'Sometimes you look so terribly unhappy, Luke. Is it my fault?'

'Certainly not!' Luke's conscience smote him. 'You are beautiful, young and innocent, Amanda – I'm an old grump and I shouldn't take my bad temper out on you. Please forgive me if I've made you unhappy.'

'You haven't,' Amanda said and smiled. 'I shall enjoy being your wife, but I want you to be happy too.'

'I shall be,' Luke promised her. He would have to make more of an effort. He had gone into this with his eyes open and it was time he started to behave like a prospective bridegroom. 'Shall we go to the theatre this evening, darling? Or would you prefer to go dancing?'

'Oh, dancing please.' Amanda gave him a look of appeal. 'And you really don't mind me going with my godmother – or that the wedding will be delayed until Christmas?'

'Of course I don't. It is a bride's prerogative to choose. When do you leave on this world cruise?'

'In three weeks – so we have plenty of time to be together before then,' Amanda said. 'Thank you for taking me to the jeweller's this morning – you will spoil me if you keep giving me things.'

'I like to give you pretty things,' Luke told her, though he knew the gifts were a sop to his conscience. He couldn't give her love so he was giving her jewellery. In future he would have to make sure his black moods were banished when he was in Amanda's company.

She wasn't Rose, but she would be his wife and he did not want to hurt her.

* * *

Rose came off stage to rapturous applause. Mike was in the wings and pushed her back on again to take another bow. The audience stood up and called for an encore. Rose hesitated but the orchestra started up again so she sang her final song once more and then took her bow. Still the audience refused to let her leave the stage and she had to take two more encores before they brought the curtain down.

'You were wonderful,' Jason said when he came to her dressing-room a little later. 'I knew you would be a success, Rose, but I didn't expect quite that reaction on your first night.'

'It's because of you and Mike. You've taught me so much. I was a good singer before, but this evening it felt so different. I've never felt that way on stage before.'

'They loved you. When an audience loves you, it lifts you – carries you to the stars.'

'Yes, that is just how I felt,' Rose said and laughed. 'You know so much about the theatre, Jason – and you are a wonderful pianist. Haven't you ever wanted to perform yourself?'

'I'm not good enough. I wanted to be a concert pianist once but I realised I was never going to make it – which is why I take an interest in those who I can see have real talent. I suppose I'm taking my bow through you, Rose. You are my star. I feel that I had a part in making your success.'

'You did – a large part,' Rose agreed. 'I think you play well enough to perform on stage.'

'I'm a perfectionist. Second best will not do.' Jason glanced round the dressing-room, which was filling up with baskets of flowers. He picked up one of the cards. 'Who is this from? It says "Good luck, from Barney". I don't think he's one of the regular crowd, is he?' Jason raised his eyebrows.

'Barney's wife is the sister of a friend of mine,' Rose said. 'I'm surprised he even knew I was appearing this evening.'

'I've been promoting you and the show in all the papers. I knew I had a star. I just didn't know how big you would be... You will be on Broadway before you know it.'

Rose laughed and shook her head. 'I can't think that far ahead. You've forgotten that I may have to give up in a few months from now.'

'I haven't forgotten that you will need to take a rest, but you'll come back, Rose. You were born to be a singer.' He looked at her questioningly. 'You haven't changed your mind about my offer?'

She reached out to touch his hand. 'I think it is best that we remain friends, Jason. I'm so grateful for the offer, but I don't think it would work. I shall try to keep my secret for as long as I can – and if it comes out I shall just have to put up with the consequences.'

'If you are popular enough the people will forgive you,' Jason said. 'But my offer stands if you change your mind.'

'You are a good friend.' Rose stood up and he arranged her cloak around her shoulders. 'I think—'

There was a knock at the door and one of the dressers put her head round it. 'A Mr Barney Hale is here to see you, Rose. Shall I send him up or will you see him at the door?'

'Barney is here?' Rose hesitated. 'If I let him come up, will you stay, Jason?'

'Yes, of course. I am taking you out, Rose; we have to celebrate. People will want to see you – and photographers will be there to take pictures of us for the papers tomorrow. If you leave with this man, he will have his picture taken too.'

'That would not suit his wife,' Rose said. She turned to the dresser. 'Please ask Mr Hale to come up for a few minutes, Jean.'

'I told you all the men would fall in love with you,' Jason said as the dresser went away. 'He won't be the only one, believe me.'

'Barney is just a friend. He isn't interested in anything else, but his wife has a temper and she would be angry if he was pictured in the newspapers with a singer.'

'Might do her the world of good,' Jason said, a wicked gleam in his eyes. 'Shall I make him jealous for you, Rose?'

'Don't be silly! I told you, Barney is married.'

'That doesn't stop them lusting after you.' Jason grinned.

Rose was about to reply when someone knocked at the door and, after waiting politely for her response, Barney came in. He looked at her uncertainly.

'I hope you didn't mind my asking to see you?'

'Of course not,' Rose replied with a warm smile. 'This is Mr Jason Brent – it is his show, Barney. I hope you enjoyed the performance?'

'I wouldn't have missed it for the world. I came to see you at the Haymarket once but the next time I went you weren't there.'

'I had to leave,' Rose said. 'I have a much better job here – thanks to Jason.'

'We are going out to celebrate.' Jason hesitated, then, 'You're welcome to come with us – but I have to warn you, the photogra-

phers will be taking pictures outside the theatre and at the nightclub later.'

'Oh, no, thanks all the same,' Barney said. 'I just came to
congratulate Rose. You were very good. I always knew you had a
lovely voice – heard you in church. Sarah will be delighted to hear
of your success. She was talking of coming up to see you one day.
She is always so busy with the convalescent home and her family,
but I'm sure she and Troy will find time for a visit one of these days.'

'That would be lovely. I'll send some tickets if she knows when
she would like to come.'

'She would be thrilled.'

'And thank you for the lovely flowers, Barney. It was so good of
you to come.'

'I'll go then,' Barney said. 'I don't want to hold you up.'

'You're not,' Rose replied warmly. 'I shall always be pleased to
see you, Barney. We are friends.'

'You have a lot of flowers,' Barney said and glanced at Jason. 'I
may see you another day. I come to London quite often. Marianne
prefers it to the country, especially in the Season.'

'Yes, I expect so.' Rose smiled. 'It was lovely to see you. Marianne isn't with you this evening?'

'She went to a party with some friends,' Barney said. 'I'll probably pop in later and take her home.'

Jason looked at Rose after he'd gone. 'Sounds like the ideal
marriage,' he said wryly. 'What is Marianne like?'

'Beautiful... Spoiled.'

'Makes sense,' Jason said with a wicked grin. 'Are you ready to
face the cameras?'

'Yes, of course.' Rose stood up and took his arm. 'They will think
we are lovers, you know. I'm sure most of the cast think it already.'

'I don't mind – if you don't?' Rose shook her head. 'Shall we go?'

* * *

Luke opened the morning paper by his plate. Amanda had gone to stay with her godmother prior to leaving on the cruise. He had returned to Trenwith, feeling no better than he had when he'd accompanied her to London for a shopping trip. His frustration at the delay to the wedding had gone. He hoped that he had made Amanda believe that he loved her before she left for her godmother's. He prayed it was so because the success of their marriage would depend on his ability to make his wife happy.

Luke had abandoned all hope of finding happiness for himself. He hadn't touched a painting in weeks, because there seemed no point. His show had done well, though it hadn't been a huge success. The agent who had arranged it believed that the war was too recent for people to want to see such graphic depictions of its horrors.

'People want to forget,' he'd said. 'Try landscapes or water – something with movement and life. You're talented but you need to lighten up. Go away for six months, paint, and then come back to me.'

Luke had listened but made no attempt to follow the man's advice. He had put his heart and soul into the pictures he'd painted in France. At least he had been alive then, even though he'd witnessed such horrors that still gave him nightmares. These days he felt as if he were simply going through the motions, existing rather than living. Most mornings he got up, ate his breakfast alone and then went to the estate office to discuss business with the various members of his staff. The bailiffs had found some traps in the woods at the far edge of the estate. Luke knew he had to put a stop to it, though he was reluctant to prosecute. The villagers had needed extra meat during the war and his father had turned a blind

eye to poaching, but the traps were crude and caused pain to the
animals caught by the cruel wire. Besides, life was slowly getting
back to normal and there was no longer so great a need for it.

Every day there was a new or different problem to keep his mind
active. For Luke, the more he worked the better he felt. Just as
during the war he had channelled his excess energy into painting,
now he worked long hours trying to put the estate into order. It
didn't satisfy his creative urges, but it helped him to sleep at night.

Sighing as he thought of the day ahead, Luke opened his paper
and saw pictures of the latest singer to hit the headlines. Miss Rose
Barlow was the new darling of the West End. People were flocking
to buy tickets for her show and she had been offered a recording
contract. It was rumoured that *Vogue* was going to feature her on its
front page.

Luke stared at the picture of Rose leaving a nightclub with Jason
Brent – the man he'd seen her with in London. So that was his
name! Brent was the money behind the show – behind several of
the successful shows in London. He read the article that appeared
underneath the photograph.

'I believe Rose is going to be the biggest star for a decade this
side of the Atlantic,' Jason Brent told reporters last night. 'I knew
the first time I heard her sing that she had star quality. I am
expecting to hear from the Broadway producers very soon.'

Luke turned to the inside pages and stared at Rose's pictures.
The photographers had gone to town and there were six in all:
pictures of Rose laughing, smiling up at her companion, clinging to
his arm. He was probably her lover. Unknown artistes didn't get the
chance to be a star for nothing.

Luke's jealousy was grinding away at him as he folded the paper and pushed his plate away. His appetite had left him the moment he saw her picture. He got to his feet and left the room. Rose was happy and that was all that mattered. He had to be glad for her, because there was nothing else he could do but accept things the way they were.

* * *

'What's the matter, Sally?' Rose had found her friend sobbing in her dressing-room. Sally had wiped her hand across her eyes, smearing kohl garishly over her cheeks. 'Are you feeling ill?'

'I'm having a baby,' Sally said. 'It's William Trent's. He is Lord Trent really, but he never uses his title when he's with anyone from the theatre. He says I've got to get rid of it, because he doesn't want a child around when he comes to see me.'

'Oh, Sally – that is awful! I'm so sorry, love. What are you going to do?'

'I don't know,' Sally wailed, looking so miserable that Rose's heart wrenched for her. 'The house is in his name – he wouldn't give me the deeds. If I say I want to have the baby he might throw me out – and then what do I do?'

'Are you in love with him?'

'I thought I was, but...' Sally shook her head. 'Not after the way he was last night. I thought he really cared, Rose. He said he loved me. He said that one day we would be together. He can't divorce his wife, though he says she can't live for many more years due to her illness... But last night he was so horrible. He doesn't want a child with me. He is insisting that I have an abortion.'

'That is horrible,' Rose said and shuddered. 'Look, Sally, I haven't told anyone else, but I'm also having a baby...'

'You're having Jason's child?'

'No, it's Luke's. I found out after I left him.'

'Does he know?'

'I haven't told him.'

'Would he ask you to get rid of it?'

'No – not if he knew I wanted to keep it. Luke loved me. I still believe it even though he let me down. His family would never accept me so he had to marry a suitable girl, but he would have looked after me if I had let him.'

'Does Jason know?'

'Yes.'

'He doesn't mind?'

'Jason just wants me to be a star. It means I shall have to leave the show for a while, but he says I can come back. We shall try to keep it a secret if we can but, if not, I'll have to take the consequences. It all depends on what the papers decide to say. They might want to destroy me...' Rose shrugged. 'I never expected all this fuss, Sally. I didn't think I would be a star. I just wanted a chance to be on stage. I shall make the most of it and when it's over I'll move on.'

'You're so brave,' Sally said. 'I wish I had your courage.'

'If you want the baby, tell William. If he throws you out you can move in with me until you find somewhere else.'

'Rose, you're such a good friend,' Sally said. She accepted Rose's handkerchief and wiped her eyes, then looked at it ruefully. 'It's all black now. I'll wash it and give it back later. I thought everything was all going to be so wonderful when I met William, but I'm just a girl he visits when he has the time. I don't know what to do, Rose.'

'Isn't there anyone you could go to – someone who cares?'

'My mother wouldn't have me in the house. She threw me out when she caught my stepfather trying to put his hand up my skirt. I wanted to be a singer but I'm never going to be more than a chorus girl. Oh, I know Jason gave me a solo spot but that was just because he needed someone at the time. If I left he would soon find someone else to take my place. I'm not like you...'

'I didn't expect success either. It might happen to you too, Sally.' Sally shook her head. 'William isn't the only fish in the sea. You could find someone else.'

'Not with a baby to look after.' Sally started to cream her face, wiping off the stage make-up. 'I suppose there's my answer; I shall have to have the abortion. I may not stay with William. After this, I'll be looking for someone else – but I won't find someone if I have a baby in my arms. Besides, I think if I defied William he might harm me.'

'He wouldn't dare. Tell Jason. He would sort him out.'

'I told you, I'm not you, Rose. Jason would tell me it was sensible to get rid of the child.' Sally's head came up. 'I've made up my mind. I had already done so last night really, but this morning it all came over me and I couldn't help having a few tears. William is fixing it up for me. I shall have the abortion done soon – the sooner the better. It is too dangerous if you leave it too late.'

'Oh, Sally, I am so sorry.' Rose stared at her. She knew how her friend was feeling, but she wasn't sure Sally had made the right decision.

Rose felt sad that Sally had been forced into an abortion against her will, and she was concerned for her welfare. She knew it was possible to get a termination if you went to one of the back-street women who knew various ways of bringing on a miscarriage. Sometimes the methods they used were brutal and could result in the death of both the unborn child and the mother. It was difficult to find a doctor who would perform an abortion, because only a few would attempt it: those who had been struck off the medical register for some misdemeanour. And most of them were little better than the untrained women who offered the same service.

Rose knew that she would never have done what Sally was

going to do. She would have liked to dissuade her friend, but Sally had made up her mind. She went around with a face like thunder for two days and then turned up for rehearsals looking washed out.

'It's over,' she told Rose when they had a moment alone. 'I feel like death. He was supposed to be a doctor but he was a butcher. He didn't care what happened to me. He wanted his money before he started and afterwards he just told me to go home and stay in bed until I stopped bleeding.'

'You should go to the hospital,' Rose said. 'Tell them you had a miscarriage and let them take a look at you.'

'I will if I don't feel better soon,' Sally replied. 'It wasn't just what he did or the way he treated me. I feel hollow inside, Rose. I killed my baby...' She smothered a sob. 'I know it was hardly there, but it was mine and now it has gone...'

'Oh, Sally...' Rose put her arms about her, feeling her shake with suppressed sobs. 'I am so sorry, love. I wish there were something I could do to help.'

'You offered to take me in, and like a fool I refused,' Sally said. 'I'm leaving the house William set up for me. I'm going to find somewhere else to stay.'

'Come back with me,' Rose offered at once. 'I shan't take no for an answer, Sally. You need looking after and we're friends. You got me this job and I'm grateful.'

'Jason would have found you even if you hadn't come to the party that night,' Sally told her. 'He wanted you, and when he wants something he usually gets it.'

'Whether he would or not doesn't matter. I'm taking you home with me when we leave. You shouldn't have come to rehearsals today, Sally. You're not fit to be on stage. I'll tell Jason you have a stomach upset. You can go to bed and rest.'

'Yes, I think I shall,' Sally agreed. 'I did feel shaky, but I didn't want to stay where I was. I'll take a few days off to get over it.'

'Don't bother about your things for now,' Rose said. 'I moved into a nice little flat with a garden after I started to work for Jason. You can stay at my place. Give me your key and I'll fetch them for you after rehearsals. My spare key is under a brick at the back door. Why don't you go now and let yourself in? My room is the first bedroom along the hall. The second will be yours for as long as you want to stay.'

'You are so generous,' Sally said. 'I don't know how to thank you, Rose.'

'You don't have to. I shall enjoy having you to stay. Get off now, love, and I'll explain to the others.'

Jason insisted on seeing Rose to her door that evening. Sometimes he simply called her a cab but at other times he made a point of coming with her. Rose unlocked the door and he followed her inside.

'You've had something on your mind all day. You might as well tell me, Rose.'

'I'm a bit worried about Sally,' Rose said. 'Help yourself to a drink if you want one, Jason. I'm just going to check on her.'

'She's had an abortion, hasn't she? Don't bother to deny it, Rose. I'm not a fool; I've seen the signs before. Go and take a look at her. It is just as well that you made her come here. If she starts to bleed you'll need a doctor quickly. I'll write down the telephone number of one you can trust—' Jason broke off as they both heard a feeble cry and then a crash.

Rose shot him a look of alarm and rushed through the hall to the guest room. Sally was lying on the floor, wearing one of Rose's nightgowns. It was stained heavily with blood, as were the sheets on the bed.

'Rose... Help me...' she whispered.

'Sally!' Rose rushed to her. 'Let me get you back to bed.'

'I'll do it.' Jason had entered the room behind her. 'If you try, you may bring on a miscarriage yourself.' He bent down, scooped Sally up and laid her gently on the bed. 'You silly girl, you should have come to me. I know someone who would have looked after you instead of half killing you. I'm going to telephone him now. You need help quickly.'

Jason left the room and Rose sat down by Sally's side, reaching out to capture her restless hand. 'Thank goodness you came here and that Jason was with me, love. You should have asked him for help. Jason knows everyone.'

Sally gripped her hand so tightly, it hurt. 'Perhaps it is my punishment. I killed my baby. Perhaps I should die...'

'Don't say that, Sally. It wasn't your idea to get rid of the baby. If anything happens I shall know who to blame – but it won't. You're going to get better and you'll be back in the show before you know it.'

'If Jason will have me back after this.' Sally lay back against the pillows, her face pale. 'I feel awful.'

'I know you do,' Rose replied and squeezed her hand gently. 'The doctor is on his way. He will be here soon, love.'

Sally's eyes were closed. Her eyelids fluttered but she didn't speak.

Jason came to the door and looked in. 'Edgar will probably take her to a private clinic. As you know, it is against the law to practise abortion, but he has to tidy up after so many damned charlatans that he gets angry. He says abortion should be made legal in certain cases, but he doesn't approve of girls going to these back-street butchers.'

'William fixed it up for me,' Sally said weakly. 'He made me go...' She sighed and closed her eyes.

Jason took her wrist, feeling for a pulse. 'She is getting weaker. I just hope Edgar will get here in time. He was at a dinner party but I told him it was urgent.'

Edgar arrived in a shorter time than Rose would have thought possible. He took a brief look at his patient and nodded to Jason, and between them they carried her down to the waiting ambulance. Rose went to the door, watching as they drove away. She had offered to go with her friend, but the doctor had turned her down.

'You can't do anything to help,' he told her bluntly, 'and to be honest you will be in the way. Come and see her tomorrow. We should have her on the mend by then. It was lucky she wasn't alone.'

'Yes, very lucky,' Jason said. 'Keep her at the clinic for as long as necessary. Your bill will come to me.'

'You know I help these cases for nothing.' The doctor glared at him as if he thought it was Jason's fault that Sally was in trouble.

'Then I'll make a donation,' Jason said. 'I want Sally back – and the less scandal the better.'

'I shan't go to the police, but they may come to me.' Edgar looked grim. He was a thin, dark man with serious eyes. 'I'll do what I can to protect her – as always.'

'It wasn't her fault,' Rose told him as he closed the ambulance door on Sally, leaving her in the care of a nurse. 'Her lover forced her to have the abortion. He arranged it. He is the one who should be punished.'

'I couldn't agree more,' Edgar said, and he shot a curious glance at her, as if noticing her for the first time. 'There are too many that just walk away from a situation and make a mess for others to clear up.'

'He won't get off altogether, I promise,' Jason said, looking grim. 'By the time I've finished with him he will wish he had thought a little more before he pushed Sally into this business.'

Rose glanced at him and saw the way his mouth hardened. She had a feeling that Sally's lover would be made to pay more than he anticipated for what he had done.

* * *

The following day Sally was sitting up in bed against a pile of
pillows when Rose took some flowers, fruit and magazines to her.
Her eyes had deep shadows under them, but she had regained a
little of her normal colour.

'Are you feeling better?'

'I still feel as weak as a kitten,' Sally told her, 'but I've stopped
hurting. They've given me medicine that makes me feel sick, but the
bleeding has stopped and most of the pain has gone.'

'You are in the right place. It's a pity you didn't come here to
have the abortion.'

'They would probably have talked me out of it. I've already had
a lecture about what I've done – and I was feeling guilty enough as
it was.' Sally plucked at the bed covers. 'I wish I had taken notice of
you, Rose. I was afraid of William, but if I'd moved out he might
have left me alone. I could have had the baby and managed
somehow.'

'I wish you had. You scared me last night.'

'I scared myself,' Sally said with a wry look. 'I thought I was
dying. I was haemorrhaging and I could have bled to death if no
one had found me.'

'Yes, I know.' Rose shuddered. 'It was so lucky that Jason knew
whom to contact. Otherwise I should have had to get you to a
hospital and you could have been in trouble if they had guessed
what you'd done.'

'I was a fool. I trusted William to see me through this, but he
hasn't come near me since I went to that horrible place.' Sally's face
clouded. 'I hate him! I really hate him!'

'I don't think he will come near the theatre once Jason has had
his say. He will stay clear if he has any sense.'

'If I know Jason, he'll do more than give him a lecture,' Sally said and her eyes glittered. 'The rotten bastard deserves all he gets after what he said and did.'

'What do you mean? What will Jason do to him?'

Sally's eyes slid away. 'You know...'

'No, I don't,' Rose replied with a frown. 'Are you saying that Jason will thump him?'

'He might not do it himself. Jason has a lot of friends and some of them are not exactly law-abiding.'

'You mean he would have William beaten up?'

'You didn't hear it from me, but it wouldn't be the first time. I don't know much but I've heard people say that he can be ruthless. When Jason wants something, he gets it – and when he decides to punish, he doesn't run scared of the law.'

Rose felt a cold shiver down her spine. She had seen Jason's anger the previous evening, but she hadn't thought he would go that far. He was powerful and rich, but there must be other ways to punish the man who had hurt Sally.

Rose was disturbed by the idea of Jason being in touch with the kind of men who would beat others up at his bidding. It sounded as if he were some kind of high-powered criminal. She realised that she hardly knew him at all. He had given her a chance and it was owing to him that she was pulling in the crowds and being offered all kinds of exciting projects. There was a possibility that she might make a record, and she had been invited to pose for the front cover of a prestigious magazine – but she didn't like the idea that it was all at the behest of a man who, from what Sally had just told her, might be a gangster.

* * *

Luke sat in the darkened theatre and listened as Rose performed her last solo of the evening. As she finished, the audience got to its feet as one and clapped her, hoping for an encore. She obliged and sang one more popular ballad before the curtain came down for the last time. He judged by all the chatter and laughter that Rose was popular, because the atmosphere was one of good humour.

'They say she is Jason Brent's mistress,' one girl said to her friend as they stood behind Luke in the queue to get out after the final curtain came down. 'I wouldn't mind changing places with her.'

'Nor me,' the second girl giggled. 'She's got everything any girl could want.' She sighed and pulled a face at her companion. 'Money, clothes, jewels. Do you think they were real diamonds she was wearing on stage?'

'I'm not sure if she would wear real ones on stage,' the first girl went on, 'but I should think he has given her some. They say he's crazy about her.'

'She can certainly sing...'

Luke had considered going round to the stage door to ask if Rose would see him, but why should she? As the girls behind him had said, she had all she could possibly want. Why would she want to hear from a man who had let her down?

Besides, nothing had changed. He was as committed as ever. He had come up to town to speak to the gallery owner about some of his paintings. Unexpectedly, a collector had walked in and asked to buy several of them. Luke was meeting Sam Bronstein for lunch the next day. He had decided to come up to London that afternoon and stay over somewhere. He'd found the flat empty, all Rose's things gone. The rooms had a neglected air, as if no one had been there for weeks.

Since she wasn't using the flat, Luke had decided that he might as well stay there. On his return from the theatre, he spent an hour wandering about his studio because the gallery owner was asking for more of his work. There were a few pictures that he had thought he would hang on to, but he had decided they might as well go – and there was one really good portrait of Rose. He had painted quite a few from memory, but this one had been done just after she moved into the flat and it was of Rose in an evening dress with a very low-cut back. She had posed turned away from him, looking back over her shoulder. It was a very sensual portrait – a compelling study of a young woman gazing at her lover.

On impulse, Luke put it with the others he intended to show Sam the next day. It would be ridiculous to keep it for sentimental reasons. He would put a high price on it, because he didn't want it to go to just anyone. It showed that he was capable of painting subjects other than war scenes. He knew though that he ought to get rid of all his sketches and paintings of Rose. They would only remind him of what he could never have.

Luke frowned as he went into the bedroom. Amanda had been away a month and he hadn't missed her at all; he was still missing Rose like hell. The sheets on the bed had not been slept in, but the scent of her seemed to cling to everything she had touched. All evening he had felt that at any moment she might walk in, smiling, and everything would be as it had been during those glorious few weeks they'd had together. It had been such a short while – and it was all he had to last him a lifetime.

Once again he cursed himself for being a fool. He should never have got involved with Amanda. Rose would have stayed with him if she hadn't discovered he was going to marry someone else. In time his father might have accepted their relationship – and it probably wouldn't have mattered for long, in any case, because Sir James was failing.

Luke had discovered that he didn't care much what his mother thought. He would never forgive her the threats she had made to ruin Rose's career. It was her bullying that had finally made him give in and ask Amanda to marry him.

He had to stop this. Dwelling on the past would do no one any good. He had to move on and look to the future. Selling his picture of Rose was a start, and perhaps, one of these days, he might sell the others.

6

Rose was surprised when the dresser brought her a huge basket of yellow roses and told her that Mr Barney Hale was asking to see her. The card congratulated her on her success and was signed simply 'Barney'.

'Yes, please ask Mr Hale to come in,' Rose said. She went behind a Chinese painted screen, took off her stage gown and replaced it with an evening dress she had recently purchased. It was green silk with embroidery at the hem and across one shoulder. Hearing the door open, she called out, 'I shan't be a moment.' She came out from behind the screen, still fiddling with the catch at her nape.

'Can I help? I'm quite good at hooks.'

Rose hesitated and then, smiling, turned her back and lifted her hair. 'Thank you.' She faced him. 'You are good at...' The words died on her lips. Barney was looking at her and there was no mistaking the hunger in his eyes. 'Barney?'

He seemed to become aware that he was staring and a deep colour crept up his neck. 'Sorry, Rose. I didn't mean to embarrass you – or myself.'

'You haven't,' she replied. 'The flowers are gorgeous. Thank you so much, but you really shouldn't, Barney. You've sent me at least six baskets since I opened here.'

'I wanted to show you how wonderful I think you are,' Barney said, his eyes going over her. 'I've always admired the way you just got on with life, Rose – but now... you are marvellous!'

'I have been very lucky. Jason gave me the chance and he and Mike taught me so much. I could always sing but I didn't know how to present myself. Now I do.' She looked away from Barney's burning gaze, shocked to discover his attraction to her. She had thought of him as a friend, nothing more. 'How are Marianne and the children?'

'All well,' Barney assured her. 'Marianne has her friends. Don't think ill of me, Rose. We have separate rooms and Marianne keeps the connecting door locked. She doesn't want me near her. I should have known it would turn out this way. Marianne married me on the rebound. If it weren't for the fear of scandal she would divorce me.'

'I'm so sorry, Barney. I guessed that things weren't as good as they might be between you at the christening, but I didn't think they were that bad.'

'I think Marianne is too cold to really want any man in her bed,' Barney said. 'She isn't even a loving mother. When I look at the way Sarah and Troy are together – and Lucy and Andrew...' He broke off and made a face. 'I shouldn't be telling you all this, should I?' Rose shook her head and he smiled ruefully. 'I've always been able to talk to you. I know you would never look at me but I can't help feeling the way I do about you.'

'I like you a lot,' Rose told him. She hesitated, then continued. 'I must ask you to keep this a secret for the time being, Barney – I am having a child. I want to stay in the show for as long as possible, but when I can't carry on I shall go away somewhere and have the baby.

Perhaps abroad where I'm not known.' Barney was silent. Was that disappointment in his eyes? 'Have I shocked you terribly?'

'No, of course not. I always knew I didn't stand much of a chance – but I want you to know that I'm here for you if you need me, Rose. I couldn't divorce Marianne, of course, but I would be happy to take care of you, and perhaps one day...'

'You are such a good friend. I've never forgotten how kind you were the day my father was taken ill. At the moment I can manage. I have friends, and Jason has promised to arrange everything, but if...' She hesitated. 'If something went wrong I might ask for your help.'

'Is Jason Brent the father?'

'No, he isn't. There was someone else – someone I loved. I believed we would be together for always, but it didn't work out.'

Barney nodded. 'Does he know about the baby?'

'No, I haven't told him and I'm not going to, for the moment anyway. He would give me money, but he can't marry me, if that is what you were wondering.'

'I would marry you if I could,' Barney said, surprising her. 'You might not believe me, but I mean it, Rose. You're worth ten of Marianne!'

'No, you mustn't say that.' Rose shook her head. 'You love her, Barney. You know you do – it's just that she has hurt you by shutting you out of her bed and her life. Why don't you talk to her? Tell her how you feel? If she really doesn't want to be your wife – and you've had enough of it – you shouldn't stay married simply to avoid a scandal. I know that when my baby is born it will be only a matter of time before someone finds out. I may be torn to pieces in the press. They've built me up and they can bring me down just like that – but I am not going to give up my baby. I'll take all the adulation and the money for as long as I can get it, but when it is over I'll go away somewhere and do something else.'

Barney looked at her with undisguised adoration. 'You have such courage, Rose. I think it is why I admire you so much.'

'I'm just doing what I have to do.' Rose reached out to touch his hand. 'Why don't you take me out to supper somewhere? We can still be friends, if nothing more – can't we?'

'Yes, of course we can,' Barney said. 'I'm not going to pretend that I don't want more, Rose. Just remember that I'm around if you need me.'

'I shan't forget,' she said, picking up her stole. 'I'm hungry – let's go somewhere discreet where they serve excellent food.'

* * *

Rose found Sally cooking them both breakfast the next morning. 'You've been so good to me,' she said, 'I want to do something for you.'

'You don't have to. If you're feeling well enough to do some of the chores it is up to you, but don't make yourself ill, please. I've enjoyed having you here. It has been no trouble looking after you, love.'

'I'm feeling much better than when I left the clinic,' Sally said. 'As well as I shall, anyway. Edgar told me that it is unlikely I shall have another child. I was so badly damaged inside by what that butcher did to me that I need to heal before I can go with anyone. It may take months. I could be permanently damaged.'

'Oh, Sally, love.' Rose looked at her in dismay. 'I am so sorry.'

'It makes me so angry when I think of what William said to me.' Sally's eyes glittered. 'I really hate him, Rose. I wish he was dead – I wish he felt bad, the way I do, the way I always shall...'

'Sally...' Rose looked at her sadly. 'I know you must be feeling miserable, but please don't let it make you bitter, love.'

'I can't help it,' Sally said. 'I know I told you I'd made up my mind to have the abortion, but I wasn't sure, even then. Sometimes I think I should like to kill him for what he has done to me! He hasn't asked after me or sent me anything. It's as if I no longer exist.'

Rose nodded. She had seen William Trent with another young woman the previous evening. He had been dining at the restaurant Barney had taken her to and she knew he'd seen her, but he had totally ignored her. He hadn't even asked how Sally was, and he must have known that she was staying with Rose. However, she couldn't tell her friend that piece of news.

'Maybe he has been busy,' she suggested. 'Anyway, he isn't worth breaking your heart over, Sally. Forget him. Concentrate on getting well and coming back to the show.'

'Jason said I could when I was ready,' Sally said, looking thoughtful. 'You didn't tell him what I said – about him having William roughed up? I spoke out of turn and I doubt if he will. I asked him not to bother.'

'No, I haven't said anything. Jason has kept that side of his affairs secret from me. I think he knows that I wouldn't appreciate anything of a criminal nature.'

'I didn't say he was a criminal.'

'No, of course you didn't,' Rose said. 'But the kind of men who beat others up for a living are gangsters – in my opinion, anyway. The East End is full of criminal gangs. I saw the kind of things they do to each other when they came to the hospital, and I don't want anything to do with that sort of behaviour.'

'I don't really know much. I should keep my mouth shut – but I think Jason owns some nightclubs; the kind of places where he needs to employ men who are handy with their fists.'

'Is that where his money comes from?' Rose frowned, because she knew that behind the gangs of thugs there was often a wealthy, outwardly respectable man in the shadows.

'I don't know. Please don't say anything. Jason would be furious with me for telling you – but I think William was involved in something a bit underhand with Jason.'

'You're telling me they are partners?'

'I think they were, though they may have split over a disagreement. William never told me any of this, but I heard him having an argument with Jason once. They both thought I'd gone shopping, but I came back and they didn't hear me...'

'What were they saying?'

'William accused Jason of cheating him and Jason told him he was a fool and he'd best keep his mouth shut or he would shut it for him.'

'That sounds like a threat.'

'I am sure he meant it as one. I know it frightened William. He was very quiet that evening and when I asked him what was wrong he said that he could be in a lot of trouble. He wouldn't say any more, but I'd heard them arguing so I knew it must be to do with Jason.'

Rose nodded. The more Sally told her about Jason's shady business dealings, the less she liked it. She had thought the shows were the source of his wealth, had admired him for being able to spot talent – but now she had begun to wonder if much of his money came from less worthy ventures. He had asked her to marry him once to cover his sexual practices – what more did Jason have to hide?

* * *

'It is lovely to see you,' Sarah said when Luke walked into the sitting-room. She had been nursing her daughter but she placed the child back in the cot and stood up to kiss her brother's cheek. 'It's odd, because I was thinking about you earlier. I was going to write and ask if you would like to be Mary Anne's godfather. We were thinking of having the christening next month – it won't clash with anything you and Amanda have on, will it? Do you expect her back soon?'

'I think they plan to be away at least another month,' Luke said and frowned. 'I got a letter yesterday as a matter of fact. It was very brief. Just to tell me that Amanda was enjoying the trip and was pleased she had accompanied her godmother.'

'That sounds a bit cold.' Sarah looked at him closely. 'I don't understand why she went off like that, Luke. I should have thought she would want to spend the summer getting to know you better.'

'Oh, I think she had more or less promised before I popped the question,' Luke said. 'She didn't want to let her godmother down.'

'You *are* happy about this marriage?' Sarah asked, her eyes dwelling on him for a long moment. 'You haven't given up on your painting, have you? I know Father expects you to look after the estate, but you need some time for yourself too.'

'I've sold quite a few of my pictures, far more than I expected,' Luke told her, looking pleased. 'There wasn't much interest when we had the show, but Sam put them up in the gallery and someone walked in and bought most of them in one go. He was an American, I think. Sam wanted some more stuff. I took him a portrait I did of someone and he wants more of that kind of thing. He thinks I should do exotic landscapes and portraits, but I'm not sure. I would need a model.'

'What about the girl you painted – the portrait he likes?'

'Oh...' Luke bent over his niece and smiled. 'She is a beautiful baby, Sarah. I doubt Rose would want to pose for me these days. She is too busy being a success on the stage.'

'She is doing well,' Sarah agreed, her face lighting up. 'Rose has a telephone now. I rang her and asked if she could come down for the christening, but she doesn't think she can get away.'

'I suppose she is in demand.' Luke struggled to keep his voice casual. 'I've seen several photographs of her being escorted by various men.'

'I've only seen her with one,' Sarah said. She looked at him; there had been something odd about the tone of Luke's voice. 'Barney told me he had visited her. He says she doesn't often go out with anyone other than her manager, Jason Brent. He gave Rose her chance, of course. Rose said he has taught her a lot. She went out to supper with Barney one evening. He has always liked Rose. He took her to the station the day her father was taken suddenly ill.'

'Yes, I remember,' Luke said and felt a pang of jealousy. If he hadn't rushed Rose into an affair he too might still have been her friend. 'Did he say how she was?'

'He said she was looking very well. I should like to see the show, but Troy has been busy and there's always something happening with the children. I hope I get to see it before it closes. I'm not sure how long it will run for.'

'As long as people keep buying the tickets, I imagine.' Luke hesitated. 'So Rose isn't coming to the christening then?'

'She doesn't think she will be able to manage it,' Sarah said. 'She sounded a little odd when she rang me back. She asked about you, Luke – just how you were and when the wedding would be. I told her I thought at Christmas. You haven't changed it?'

'No, but it was Amanda's choice. We are going to start planning it in detail when she gets back.'

Sarah looked thoughtful. 'I still think it strange that she simply went off and left everything hanging. Young girls in love usually can't wait to plan their wedding.'

'Amanda has all that to look forward to when she gets back,' Luke said and frowned. 'Besides, we shan't live in each other's pockets, Sarah. I daresay Amanda will want to spend time with her friends, the way Marianne does.'

'Poor Barney,' Sarah said. 'He looks so miserable all the time.

Marianne should be ashamed of herself. He doesn't deserve to be treated so shabbily.' She hesitated, then continued. 'I shouldn't say this – I wouldn't to anyone else – but I think she might be having an affair.'

'Surely not, Sarah! Think of the scandal if it were discovered. Barney might divorce her – and that would kill Father.'

'He may not be around for much longer.' Sarah looked sad. 'We've had our differences, but I hate to see him so frail.'

'I feel as if I'm walking on eggshells,' Luke admitted. 'He gets so upset if I do something he feels isn't right for the estate. I'm doing my best, Sarah. It isn't possible to carry on just as we were before the war. A lot of the men who were content to work on the land just aren't around any longer. We lost almost a whole generation of young men and their younger brothers don't want to be labourers. I've employed some foreign workers for the market garden stuff, which is doing well – better than anything else. Father hit the roof when someone told him. One of the workers is a German and he asked me if I had gone mad. I tried to explain that Hans came here before the war. He was detained during the conflict but he thinks of this country as home.'

'You know how some people hate the Germans. A shop owned by a German was set on fire locally during the war. Mr Bergman had lived here since he was five and he condemned the Kaiser from the beginning, but it didn't save him from the spite of ignorant people who hate all Germans.'

'I imagine jealousy played a part,' Luke said. 'Mother thinks things should be as they were when the Barlow family all worked for us, but it isn't like that any more.'

'Perhaps if Jack Barlow hadn't been killed he might have returned and then his mother might have stayed – though I don't think Rose would ever have gone back to service.'

'No, I don't think she would – and a good thing too,' Luke said.

Sarah stared at him because his emotion was becoming evident. 'Anyway, Mother has to move on like the rest of us.'

'Yes, of course,' Sarah replied. 'I like Rose. She was a good friend to me during the war.'

'I liked her too.' A little nerve flicked at Luke's temple. 'But she has her own life now.'

'Yes.' Sarah hesitated. 'There was a time when I thought you might feel something more than liking, Luke.'

'You can imagine what Mother would have made of that,' Luke said and, try as he might, he was not able to keep the bitterness out of his voice.

'I would have supported you, Luke.'

He looked at his sister and saw quiet understanding in her eyes. 'I know,' he murmured thickly. 'But I couldn't do it to Father.'

He turned away from her, crossed the room and walked through the open French doors into the garden. He took a cigarette from his silver case and lit it. As he replaced the case, which was very like one he'd given to Jack Barlow during the war, he was thoughtful. He had kept the knowledge of Jack's secret life from his sister, but was he wrong to do so? Jack had wanted him to tell Rose, but for various reasons he had held back. Perhaps he ought to make an effort to see her one last time and tell her what he knew.

He wondered where Jack was living. He'd had one letter towards the end of the war telling him that Jack and Louise were going to Paris to open a small café, but nothing more since. Perhaps he should go to Paris and try to find Jack; just to make sure it was still all right for his sister to know he was a deserter.

* * *

'You would not like your neighbours to know that you are really a deserter from the British army, would you?' Henri's eyes met Jack's across the kitchen table. 'And you could be deported – I wonder what would happen then?'

'Damn you, Henri! I've had enough of your blackmail.' Jack's temper snapped. 'I joined the freedom fighters and earned my papers. That was supposed to be the end of it. I've told you once, I will not murder for you. I've told you how to file into the brake wires to cause an accident, but I won't do more. The rest is up to you.'

'He is a Frenchman who betrayed his friends and neighbours,' Henri said. 'I promise you that this is the last time I shall ask – and it will be easy for you, because he brings his automobile to you. It would be an easy matter for you to do the deed.'

'And have everyone point the finger at me?' Jack shook his head. 'I won't do it, Henri. Do your damnedest – tell everyone that my name is Jack, not Georges, and get it over.'

'Then leave the garage unlocked overnight so that we can do it ourselves,' Henri said. 'You owe us this, Georges.'

'I owe you nothing.' Jack stood up. 'I must ask you to stay away, Henri. I've given you my answer. You have no proof that the man is who you say he is – and if you can prove it you should let the law take its course.'

'The fools say the proof is inconclusive, but we have witnesses. We know what he did.'

'Then he deserves to be caught and punished,' Jack agreed. 'But murder is wrong.'

'You murdered a German officer. I saw you drive the body away.'

'That was war.' Jack's frown forbade further discussion of an incident that he preferred to forget. 'I shall not help you murder this Frenchman, Henri. I paid for my papers time and time again.'

'Yes, you did.' Henri finished his wine. 'If you won't help us, you won't, and that's an end to it.'

'Are you going to betray me?'

Henri smiled enigmatically. 'You have proved yourself a good Frenchman, Georges. I shall not betray you, but I hoped I might persuade you. I shall have to do this alone.'

Jack stared after him as he left. Could he trust Henri? Was he really just going to walk away, or would he be back when it suited him? If the Frenchman truly had done all Henri claimed, he probably deserved to come to a sticky end, but Jack couldn't murder in cold blood. If he had been asked to do anything else – a robbery or some sabotage – he would probably have agreed to help, providing no one got killed, but not murder.

He'd killed often enough during the war but that was different. The only time he had killed a man out of sheer rage was when the German officer tried to rape Louise at the farm. The memory still haunted him.

'Has he gone?' Louise entered the room. 'You didn't agree to help him, did you?' She shuddered. 'I don't trust him, Jack. He is trouble.'

'Yes, I know,' Jack agreed. 'No, I sent him away. I hope he knows I mean it this time. He threatened to expose me, but he won't do anything, Louise. I think he knows most people round here would just accept that I helped as best I could. It's only back home that they would see me as a traitor – and I'm never going back.'

'I wish he hadn't turned up,' Louise said. 'I shan't feel safe while I know he is still lurking about.'

'I promise you all that is over.' Jack reached out and drew her close. He looked down into her eyes as he kissed her. 'I love you, my darling. I had to do something once I made up my mind not to go back to my unit – and Henri was OK. He kept his word and got me the papers.'

'You won't leave me?'

'I shan't leave you,' Jack promised. 'All I want is to open my own garage one day and live here with you.'

'Another good year and we might be able to afford for you to work for yourself. I wish you could have what you want, Jack, instead of working for someone else.'

'I'm doing all right for the moment,' Jack told her. 'I'm building a reputation and one day I'll move to my own place.'

'Will Henri give up and go away?'

'He is after a traitor. You know Henri never gives up. I doubt if he'll leave until the man is dead.'

Louise shivered. 'I have a bad feeling about this,' she said. 'You are sure you didn't promise to help him do whatever he intends?'

'I'm quite sure. I fear he is going to kill the traitor and I don't want anything to do with murder.'

* * *

'Have you heard the news?' Renee, one of the chorus girls, approached Rose as she walked off stage at the end of her first solo spot that evening. Rose shook her head. 'They are saying that William Trent has been found dead. Shot three times...' Renee shuddered. 'Sally will thank God she wasn't with him. He was killed at the house they used to share. His new mistress found his body and became hysterical.'

'How do you know?' Rose felt an icy prickle down her spine.

'It's in the papers. One of the girls saw the headlines and bought one. Everyone has been reading it. The police took his new woman away for questioning. Like I said, it was a good thing Sally wasn't still living with him.'

'This is the last thing she needs at the moment,' Rose said. 'She is feeling bad enough about what happened.' She shook her head. Everyone had guessed about the abortion, but it wasn't spoken about. The girls wouldn't have betrayed Sally themselves, because more than one of them had been through a similar experience. 'I know she doesn't love him any longer, but I'm glad she wasn't the one to find him. Has anyone heard anything more about what happened? Do they have any idea who killed him?'

'There's a lot of talk,' Renee said, 'but no one knows anything yet, other than what the papers say, and that isn't very much.'

'No, I suppose not.' Rose sighed. 'I can't leave the theatre until I've finished for the evening, but I hope Sally hasn't heard yet. I'd like to try and break it to her gently if I can.'

'How long will it be before the police want to question her?' Renee wondered. 'I bet someone will tell them that he was with her until a few weeks ago.'

'I don't suppose it will take them long to find out.'

* * *

'Sally – are you there?' Rose called when she got in. She'd taken a cab to get home as quickly as possible. However, she was fairly certain that no one was at home and a brief look through the flat confirmed it. She found evidence that Sally, who was a very good needlewoman, had started to cut out a dress pattern. It was to be a maternity gown for Rose, but it would be heavily disguised as a stage costume and help to hide the fact that Rose was now nearly five months pregnant.

Rose went back to the kitchen. She poured herself a glass of milk from the small ice cabinet that Jason had bought for her. It kept milk and food wonderfully cool; much better than her mother's pantry at home. She wound up the phonograph and sat down to sip her drink and listen to the music. It sounded a bit tinny, not as lovely as the music at the theatre, but it helped her to think.

Where was Sally – and where had Jason been for a couple of days? She shivered as she thought about Sally's ex-lover being shot. Who had killed him? Various suspicions went through her mind, but they were all too horrible to dwell on. Sally had talked wildly about wishing him dead, but she wouldn't get involved in murder – would she?

Rose dismissed the idea immediately. William Trent had been a rotter, but Sally wouldn't be so foolish as to kill him! Would Jason Brent have had him killed? Again, Rose felt cold at the thought. Jason had been wonderful to her, but there were times when he had let his ruthless side show. She felt that he might be capable of murder. At the very least he was probably capable of ordering the murder of someone he felt had wronged him – or someone he cared about. No, she mustn't think like that. If she truly believed that Jason was involved in any way in William's murder, she wouldn't be able to bear to be near him. She would have to leave the show.

Rose was brought out of her reverie as the front door opened and then Sally came in. One look at her frightened face told Rose that her friend had heard the news. She got to her feet, her back aching. It was the first time since early pregnancy that she had felt any ill effects from the baby, and she realised that there would be more aches and pains from now on.

'Sally? Have you seen the newspapers?'

Sally stared at her. Her hands were trembling as she clasped them in front of her. 'I don't need to see the paper,' she whispered. 'I went there, Rose. I wanted to fetch something I'd left there – and I saw him lying on the floor.'

'Did you touch him?' Sally shook her head. 'You didn't get blood on yourself?'

'No. I was going to touch him, but then the door opened and she came in. I heard her coming and hid in the kitchen. When she started screaming I ran out the back way. I still had a key to the kitchen door. I was going to take a few things – bits of silver – but I was too scared.' She raised her head defiantly. 'He owes me.'

'Yes, he does, but you shouldn't have to steal,' Rose said. 'He should have given you money to make up for the time you had to take off work. I would have asked him for you if you'd told me how you feel. It's too late for that now though.'

'Yes.' Sally sat down abruptly. 'I feel sick. It was horrible seeing him like that, Rose. I hated him but when I saw his eyes staring up at me...' She got up and ran through to the bathroom. Rose heard her being sick and then the sound of water running. After a few minutes she came back, her face pale. 'What should I do if the police come here? Should I tell them I was there, or should I lie?'

'Did anyone see you going in or leaving?'

'I don't think so. I went through the alley at the back, same as I often did when I lived there. I had been brooding over what happened, Rose – thinking, why should he get away with it? I went to get what I could, or to have a row with him if he was there, but I didn't kill him. In any case, I don't like guns.'

'How did you know he had been shot?'

'He was lying in a pool of blood, but there was a gun nearby on the ground – a little pistol with a pearl handle...' Sally broke off, her eyes widening. 'I've seen a pistol like that before.'

'Where?' Rose's gaze narrowed. 'Go on, tell me.'

'Jason has one. He brought it to one of the shows – not this one – some time ago. He said we could use it as a prop in one of the sketches the actors were doing, and he made a big show of making sure it wasn't loaded. He said it would kill at close range but probably not from a distance because it was old-fashioned.'

'He wouldn't have left it there if he had killed William Trent.'

'No, of course he wouldn't,' Sally admitted. 'He is too clever for that – besides, I've got an idea it was stolen. Jason didn't get it back at the end of that show.'

'We don't know if it was his or if it was simply like one he once had,' Rose said carefully. 'In any case, I can't believe he would kill someone like that.'

'It isn't his style,' Sally agreed. 'If he'd wanted William Trent dead, he would have got someone to do it for him. So who does that leave as suspects? His mistress and me – or is there someone else?'

'You said he was involved in shady dealings with Jason. Perhaps he had something going on with others who might have fallen out with him.'

'What am I going to do if the police come looking for me?'

'Just say that you were here all day and all last night,' Rose said. 'As long as no one saw you they can't prove anything – and they might not believe you are innocent if you say you were there. After all, if it is Jason's gun and it was stolen, anyone could have taken it...'

'Including me.' Sally looked scared. Her hands shook. 'They might think it was me, Rose. I swear to you, it wasn't! You have to believe me. Please say you believe me.'

'I believe you. It just depends when he was killed. If it was today, I can't say you were with me – but if it was last night, then that is just what I shall say.'

'You don't think it was Jason?'

'No. I hope it wasn't,' Rose said grimly. 'If I thought he was involved I should leave the show straight away. I'm not sure how long I can stay on and still keep my secret, but I would like a little longer if I can manage it.'

* * *

Jason arrived the next morning as they were having breakfast. Neither of them had slept much and they had been drinking tea for much of the night. They had been anticipating a knock at the door, but as yet it hadn't come. Now they looked at each other as Jason went to the sideboard and poured himself brandy from the decanter.

'You've heard about Trent, of course,' he said. 'I got back late last night. I had been away on business and I didn't know anything until the police came knocking at my door at eleven o'clock. I've been at the station all night, answering questions. They would have known I was away if they had checked my story, but they found a gun – and it was mine.'

'The one that was stolen from the show last year?'

'Yes.' Jason looked at Rose with narrowed eyes. 'Sally told you then – and before you ask, I didn't have anything to do with Trent's death. I admit it was my intention to punish him for what he did to Sally, but he owed me money. I was going to have a lawyer take him to court. Since he probably couldn't pay, he would have been in serious trouble.'

'I thought he was rich,' Rose said. 'He always acted as if he had money.'

'Trent liked to live beyond his means,' Jason explained. 'While I funded him he kept going pretty well, but we had an argument some weeks ago about the money he owed me. I told him then that I intended to get it one way or the other and I refused to let him have another advance on some property he had mortgaged to me. It was all done legally and will revert to me once things are sorted. The police knew he was in debt to me and that is why they thought I might have sent the heavies in to get it. As I told them, I wouldn't have wanted him dead because I now have to wait until his estate is settled to get what belongs to me.'

Rose studied him for a moment. She had a distinct feeling he was lying. Why was he telling them all this in so much detail? It wasn't anything to do with either Sally or Rose.

'Did the police believe you?'

'They had no choice. I've been in Manchester and I have the hotel bill to prove it, also the testimony of several people who saw me at a shareholders' meeting I attended.'

It was a watertight alibi. Jason certainly couldn't have killed William Trent himself. However, a man with his wealth and connections could have arranged for the murder to be done while he was conveniently out of town.

'Sally was afraid they might think it was her,' Rose said. 'Do you know when it happened?'

'They think sometime during the previous night,' Jason said. 'His mistress had been staying at her sister's, because she thought he would be away for another day or so. He had told her he was going somewhere on business, but he must have returned earlier than planned and been killed on his return. The police are inclined to think it may have been a robbery that went wrong. Fortunately, I reported my pistol had gone missing at the time and when they looked they had the theft on record.'

'That was fortunate,' Rose said. 'Otherwise you might have remained under suspicion even though you were not in London.'

'Yes.' Jason gave her a penetrating look. 'But you were worried about the timing. Where was Sally that night?'

'Here with me from ten thirty onwards,' Rose said. 'I came straight back as soon as the performance was over. I locked up and the doors were as I left them when we got up in the morning.'

'Looks as if we're both in the clear.' Jason nodded and looked pleased. 'A man like Trent probably had a lot of enemies. I know he had an interest in some seedy nightclubs. If you mix with the kind of people who frequent those places anything can happen.'

'You're not involved with anything like that?'

'I had an interest some years ago but I sold out,' Jason said. 'I don't need anything that isn't legal. I've nothing to hide in my business.'

Once again, Rose suspected he was lying but she could not be sure. She got up and went into the kitchen, taking a tray of cups and plates with her. Jason followed her in, watching her as she put them into the sink and poured hot water from the kettle over them.

'Is something wrong, Rose?'

'I've been getting quite a bit of backache,' she said. 'I may not be able to keep going as long as I had hoped, Jason. I think you should start looking for a replacement for me.'

'A temporary replacement?'

'Yes – at least, shall we see what happens? If the newspapers get wind of the fact that I've had a child you may not want, or be able, to take me back.'

'What will you do if that happens?'

'I'm going to see my mother when I leave the show. She will think I am a damned fool for getting myself into trouble but she will help me until the baby is born. Afterwards, I'll find someone to live in and help with the child while I'm at work. Even if I can't come back to London I might get work in a seaside show.'

'I doubt it,' Jason said. 'If the papers get their knife into you, you'll be finished, Rose. You might be able to go abroad and work in Paris, or even America. You would probably get away with it there.'

'Then I may have to do that if it comes to it. I would like to go on singing if I could.' She raised her gaze to look at him. 'I want to thank you for all you've done for me, Jason. I've had a wonderful experience in the show, and if it all ends tomorrow I shall never forget it – or you.'

'That sounds suspiciously like goodbye to me.'

'Why don't you give Sally a chance?' Rose wiped her hands on a towel. 'She has a good voice and she won't be getting into trouble again. I think I shall give it one more week and then leave – if that is all right for you? Can you find someone in that time?'

'I can find someone to fill in, but it will not be the same. You were my star, Rose. Why didn't you marry me? You would not have had to bother about any scandal then. You could have taken some time off and come back.'

'Well, perhaps I shall be able to come back now,' Rose said, and she smiled a little wearily. 'I have money in the bank and I've had a wonderful time, Jason. I never expected any of it to happen. I can't complain if the wheel turns full circle.'

'You can't go back to being a VAD.'

'No, I can't do that,' Rose agreed. 'But I might set up a little business making dresses. I'm fairly competent with a sewing machine and I'm good at designing clothes, especially for pregnant women. Wealthy ladies have theirs made to order but the ordinary woman in the street can't afford to go to a couturier. I could start a new fashion. I might make lots of money with clothes that most women can afford.'

'You never give up, do you, Rose?' Jason said with a look of reluctant admiration. 'I believe you would make a success of it too – but I hope you won't give up your singing without a fight.'

'It depends on what the press think of me,' Rose said. 'If they let me, I shall carry on. I might even come back to London in a few months' time when it has all died down. If not...' She shrugged.

'You will know where to find me,' Jason reminded her. 'You only have to ask, Rose.'

'Thank you. I shall remember that, if I think the time is right.'

Jason nodded. 'I have somewhere to go now but, before I do, I have a gift for you. I saw it in a gallery before I went to Manchester and bought it. I was going to hang it at the theatre but I'll send it to you instead as a farewell present.'

'A painting?'

'She looks like you.' Jason's expression was thoughtful. 'It might even be you. I'm not sure. Have you had your portrait painted?'

'Yes. Someone told me that they had done a portrait from memory,' Rose said, her heart catching. Had Luke sold the painting of her? Why would he do that – why sell something so intimate and personal to them both? 'I should like to have it if it is of me.'

'I think it is, though I've never seen that expression on your face,' Jason said. 'It made me wish I were straight. I would have liked to see you look at me that way. I think I have been a little in love with you, Rose – even though I told you I was of another persuasion.'

'Perhaps in another life?' Rose smiled wryly. 'You've been a good friend, Jason, but I'm not in love with you.'

'I know. I've always known that,' he said, and he moved away as Sally entered the kitchen. 'Are you feeling well enough to start rehearsals on Monday, Sally? I shall be offering you two solo spots if you're up to it.'

Sally's face lit up. 'You're the best, Jason. Thank you so much!'

Rose turned away to stack clean cups on the dresser. Sally seemed to have forgotten her suspicions of Jason in the excitement of getting an extra solo spot in the show. Rose didn't find it so easy to suppress her fears. Jason had an alibi and, because he had reported his pistol stolen at the time, he was probably in the clear. However, she had an uneasy feeling that he knew a lot more about William Trent's murder than would ever come to light. She wondered if the gun had gone missing for the very purpose it had been used, but she squashed the thought. Jason had been a good friend and she had never liked William Trent, though of course she hadn't known him well.

She went into the bedroom as Jason took his leave and began looking through her clothes. Some of her gowns could be reused because they had hardly been worn. Others had been altered to accommodate her advancing pregnancy until she had been forced to make special ones to hide her condition. There were about six that she did not think she wanted to take with her. She decided that she would give them to Sally. Sally could have them altered to fit her or sell them if she wished, because they had been expensive gifts from Jason.

She took an armful of dresses through to Sally's bedroom and put them on the bed, then turned to look for something to hang them on. A piece of white cloth was sticking out of the wardrobe. Rose opened the door and saw that it was an apron – and it had dark splashes on it that looked like blood.

Sally came in as Rose was staring at the apron. 'I ought to have dumped it before I came home,' she said, and the guilt was plain on her face. 'I went there to steal, Rose. I took the apron from a cupboard upstairs and I was putting silver and jewellery into it when someone came in. I hid and then I heard a shot and someone ran out. When I went into the parlour I saw William's body lying there in a pool of blood. I was terrified and I put the apron on over my gown as I knelt down to look at the pistol by his side. I remembered the pistol Jason had lost and wondered if it was his. I suppose I should have called for help but when I heard someone – his woman – coming I panicked. I ran away and it wasn't until I got home that I realised I'd put my coat on over the apron.'

'I thought it might have been Jason. I am sure he is hiding something – but I'm not sure what. If you heard the shot, it means he lied about the time of William's death – but you lied to me too. Will you give me your word that it wasn't you?'

'I swear I didn't kill him. I shouldn't have gone near him but I wanted to make sure he was dead.'

'And if he'd still been alive?'

'I would have called a doctor. You must believe me, Rose. Please don't tell the police I was there.'

'Supposing Jason is blamed for the murder?'

'I don't know if he killed William, but he's had other people beaten or killed – and he is involved in seedy nightclubs even if he denied it. Maybe he thought he was telling the truth about the time of the murder; it might be that it was supposed to happen the previous night...' Sally threw her a look of appeal. 'I only know that I heard a shot and found William lying there.'

'Perhaps that was what Jason was hiding. Yes, you could be right. I'm sure he was guilty about something.' She felt sick inside, because she didn't know what to believe. Either Jason or Sally had to be lying.

'Are you still going to leave the show?'

'Yes. I couldn't have stayed much longer. I shall leave at the end of next week and visit my mother. I may not stay there for long, but I want to see her.'

'Do you hate me for lying to you?'

'Would you have told me the truth if I hadn't found this?' Rose asked. Sally shook her head. 'I don't hate you, but I wish you had told me the first time. I think you should get rid of this apron. If the police found it here they would arrest you immediately. They wouldn't believe your story.' Rose wasn't sure she did either. Sally was still hiding something – but what?

'I'll burn it in the range,' Sally said. 'Shall I see you again after you leave the show?'

'I don't know if I shall come back to London.' Rose was thoughtful. 'It depends whether the papers tear me to shreds once they find out about the child.'

'I shall miss you, Rose. You've been good to me and I liked staying here.'

'My rent is paid until the end of the month. You can stay until then – after that it is up to you.'

'Thank you,' Sally said, and her face lit up. 'You have to believe me, Rose. I really didn't kill him – even though I said I would, and I'm not sorry he's dead.'

Rose nodded. She went back to her own room to finish sorting through her clothes. She wasn't sure whether she believed Sally or not. Sally had hinted that Jason was mixed up in criminal activities but Rose had only her word for it, though she had sensed for a while that something was not right as far as he was concerned.

Suddenly, Rose was glad she had decided to leave the show. Being a popular singer had been good while it lasted, but for the next few months all she wanted was to be quiet and have her baby in peace.

7

Jack noticed the fire as he cycled to work in the morning. A dark cloud of smoke was hanging overhead, and the smell of burning was strong. At first he couldn't believe that it was the garage, but as he got closer he saw that there was a fire engine and a small crowd of onlookers clustered near the forecourt. He joined his employer, who was standing to one side looking anxious.

'What happened?' Jack asked. 'How did the fire start?'

'They think there was an explosion inside.' André looked distraught. 'We stored paint for bodywork renovations but nothing more. Thankfully, the petrol was stored in the shed out at the back or it would have been worse.'

'But what could have caused an explosion? We had nothing unstable in there.'

'They think it may have been done deliberately – sabotage.' André shook his head. 'Why would anyone do this to me?' He spread his hands, his shoulders hunching. 'I am ruined. I cannot pay for the repair to the building – and the cars inside were expensive. One belonged to Monsieur Eustace.'

'Yes, I was due to work on that today.' Jack's stomach lurched as he saw the gendarmes carry out a body on a stretcher. It was covered with a blanket so that they could not see the corpse, which must have been badly burned, perhaps blown apart by the explosion. However, a beret had been placed on top of the blanket. It was black, and distinguished from thousands of others only by a small badge sewn on the front. Jack knew the badge and the owner of the beret immediately. It had belonged to Henri. He must have blown himself up trying to attach explosives to the car of the man he believed had been a traitor to the French people during the war. Jack made the sign of the cross over his breast and André hurriedly did the same.

'Poor devil,' Jack whispered in English. 'He did not deserve that.'

'What did you say?' André looked at him questioningly. Jack shook his head and his employer shrugged his shoulders. 'You must look for new work. I have no money to pay you – and I do not know when I shall open again.'

'Were you insured?' Jack asked, and he gave a sympathetic look as André shook his head. So many people did not bother to take out insurance and were ruined when disaster struck. 'I am sorry. If there is anything I can do to help...'

'I have a little money put by. I may sell what remains of this place – let someone else have the trouble of rebuilding.'

'How much do you want?' Jack's heart thudded with sudden excitement. 'I wouldn't mind doing the work myself. I could rebuild it at my own pace and get this place going again gradually. It looks as if they've managed to save most of the brickwork. It will need a new roof and of course everything inside will be destroyed.'

'I will think about it and let you know,' André said. 'Go home, Georges. You might as well help that pretty wife of yours in the café as waste your time here.'

Louise stared at Jack in disbelief as he told her the news. 'Henri is dead?' she said. 'Are you sure?'

'Pretty sure,' Jack replied. 'The badge on his beret was distinctive. I haven't seen another one in Paris – except the one he gave me, which I've never worn.'

'I'm glad,' Louise said. 'I know you shouldn't speak ill of the dead – but he would never have left us alone, Jack. He wouldn't have stopped there even if he'd managed to kill the man he was after. It would just have gone on and on until you gave in.'

'I should never have given in.' Jack looked grim. 'I can't understand what happened. Henri was an expert in explosive devices. He used them over and over again during the war.'

'God was on his side during the war,' Louise said and crossed herself. 'I thank God that it wasn't you, Jack.'

'I told him that if he cut the brake leads I would get the blame, so he used explosives. I suppose he meant the device to go off when his victim was driving, but it killed him instead. Perhaps the explosive material had been stored for years and had become unstable.' Jack reached for Louise, pulling her to him and kissing the top of her head. 'We are in the clear now, Louise. No one else knows my true identity.'

'No one but Madame Bonnier – and your English friend.'

'I shall never see Luke again,' Jack told her. 'And your friend will never betray us – so you can stop worrying.'

'Yes.' Louise gave him a brilliant smile. 'I love you so much. I just didn't want to lose you, Jack.'

'You won't lose me,' he promised. 'The garage has been badly damaged by fire. It will need a lot of work to put it right – but if I'm lucky it could be ours.'

'Really?' Louise looked at him in delight. She knew that Jack would never truly settle until he owned the business he craved. 'I had a letter from my lawyer this morning, Jack. He says that at last he has had an offer for the house Maman left me. It should be enough for you to get started with the garage.'

'Are you sure you want to give me that money?' Jack gazed at her intently, but his pleasure and relief were obvious. 'I'll pay you back every penny, I promise.'

'You are my husband, Jack.' Louise smiled up at him. 'I have my café and you will have your garage – what more could we want?'

'Nothing.' Jack kissed her. 'We have been lucky, Louise.'

They both knew that the one other thing they both wanted was a child. Since their marriage, Louise had twice miscarried in the early weeks of pregnancy. Her first husband had brutally kicked her in the stomach, causing her to lose their baby. The doctor had told her that because of some old scarring caused by this injury, it was unlikely that she would carry a child to full term.

'I am sorry for Henri,' Jack said, as Louise did not answer. 'But he brought this on himself and I can't pretend I'm not relieved that it's over. He threatened to betray me and, although he did not carry out the threat, that might not have been the end of it.' He held her close. 'You are right. We should never have felt truly safe while he lived.'

* * *

Luke frowned over Amanda's latest, very brief letter, written on headed notepaper from a Paris hotel. The cruise was over but she and her godmother had decided to return to Paris for a few weeks. She hoped Luke would forgive her but she was having too much fun to come back to England just yet.

What was he supposed to make of that? He put the letter away in his desk. Far more pressing was the matter of what he was going to do with the estate cottages. Several of them were empty and likely to remain that way. The estate was employing far fewer men on the land than it once had; traction engines had replaced most of the heavy horses, and the new machines that were being invented to take over traditional jobs were saving on manpower.

Luke had even turned a couple of men away recently. His mother had been right to a certain extent; some of the men had come back, seeking their old jobs. They had tried working in the factories, but the work wasn't as plentiful as it had been during the war. Many men were on the streets. Sometimes their plight was due to an injury that meant they couldn't do manual work; sometimes it was because the war had left scars that could only be healed by drinking too much; but others were out of work simply because the jobs were not there.

The girls in the house came and went. Luke was becoming used to seeing new faces appearing at regular intervals. He knew his mother was difficult to work for, and the girls soon tired of her rules and went off in search of greener pastures. The men, however, stayed. The market garden was doing well and Luke was satisfied that the estate was just about paying its way – which still left the problem of the empty cottages.

He could simply pull them down, or he could spend money on doing them up and let them to families from the village. If he had his way though he would turn them into a restaurant and a gift shop.

'Mr Luke, sir?' He lifted his head as a voice spoke to him from the door. It was the new man his father had employed to replace Barlow. Jenkins was in his forties and one of the old school. 'Sir James has taken a turn for the worse this morning. He says he is all right but I don't like his colour. I have taken the liberty of ringing for the doctor. Sir James is asking for you, sir.'

'My father is ill?' Luke got to his feet. 'I'll come at once. How long has he been like this?'

'He seemed uncomfortable when I took up his morning tray, sir, and when I went to fetch it he complained of a pain in his chest. I was worried so I rang the doctor straight away and then came to you.'

'You did exactly right,' Luke assured him. He took the stairs in a hurry and almost ran the length of the landing to his father's room. Pausing outside, he gathered his breath, then knocked and went in. Sir James was lying back against a pile of pillows, his face white and his hands working on the bed as if in distress. He was clenching his fingers, his legs moving restlessly beneath the covers.

'Father,' Luke said, approaching him as calmly as he could, 'where is the pain?'

'In my chest...' Sir James gasped, opening his eyes to look at his son. 'I think it is my heart. This is the end for me...'

'No, Father. Jenkins has sent for the doctor. He will soon put you right.'

Sir James shook his head, looking weary. 'I don't think so, not this time, Luke.' He smiled as Luke took his hand and held it. 'You've been a good son to me, though I was unfair to you, insisting you came back here when your life was in London. I'm sorry about Amanda. I was wrong to push you into that – if she knew her duty she would be here and married to you rather than...' He gasped and his clasp on Luke tightened as the pain struck. His body arched and his lips drew back in a grimace.

'Don't try to talk, Father. It was my duty to look after the estate.'

'You've done well. You will do better when I'm not here to hold you back – but don't let it take over your life as I did, Luke. I was a slave to tradition. I married a woman I didn't love. She didn't love me either, but she wanted a husband and I asked. I'm sorry if you're unhappy.'

'I'm not miserable, Father.'

'But you're not happy either. You should do more painting, Luke. I never told you, but I thought some of that stuff you did during the war was good.'

'Thank you.' His father's hand eased its grip and then slipped away. 'But I think...' Luke stopped speaking as air was expelled from Sir James's throat. He watched the colour fade from his father's face. 'Father...' Tears slid down Luke's cheeks. He sat with his head bowed, feeling grief wash over him. 'Why didn't you ever speak like this to me before?' He got up and closed his father's staring eyes. Why couldn't you talk to me, Father? The question was in his mind, but unspoken. Luke knew the answer already.

It had been too hard for his father to voice his feelings. Even now he hadn't told Luke he loved him, but the sentiment, though unspoken, had been implicit.

'Oh, Father...' Luke felt a deep sense of loss.

'So he has gone? I'm too late?'

Luke turned his head to see his mother standing in the doorway. She approached the bed and stood looking down at her husband's white face, but made no attempt to touch him. It was impossible to know whether she was distressed; her face remained impassive, without emotion.

'I suppose it does not matter. We had nothing further to say to each other.'

'Mother.' Luke was angry but controlled himself. 'He was your husband. You must have felt something for him.'

'I respected your father. He knew how to be a gentleman – which you do not, Luke. I suppose you will do exactly as you please now he has gone.' Her eyes were cold and unfeeling.

'The estate needs to grow, Mother. If it stagnates it will die; slowly, perhaps, but in the end it will die.'

'We all die in the end,' Lady Trenwith said, and she walked from the room.

Luke sat where he was long after she had gone. He kissed his father's cheek, sitting in silence until Jenkins brought the doctor in.

They spoke in low tones about what must be done and then Luke left.

He went back downstairs to his study. The problem of the empty cottages could be left for the time being. He had a funeral to arrange, people to tell. It must and would be done properly. Sir James might not have been generally loved but he was well respected in the neighbourhood. The church would be filled and people would come back for refreshments. His mother would no doubt see to that part of it, but Luke would write the letters himself.

* * *

'So you've come to me now that you're in trouble.' Mrs Barlow looked at her daughter and frowned. She was clearly disappointed and upset. 'Rose, what made you do it? I thought you had more sense.'

'I'm sorry, Ma,' Rose said. 'I'm not exactly in trouble. I've got money and I can go somewhere else if you would rather not have me here.'

'Don't talk so daft!' Mrs Barlow snorted. 'You are my daughter, Rose. I'm glad you came to me, though I'm sorry you've got yourself in trouble – for trouble it is, money or no. You're having a child that will have no father and that's never good news.'

'I wish it had been different, but I'm not sorry about the baby. I wanted Rod's baby, but it didn't happen. Now I have a chance and I'm keeping the child, so if your cousin doesn't want me here...'

'Myrtle may have something to say about you living here in the circumstances. You can't blame her if she says it will be too much trouble having a young baby in the hotel, Rose. If she does, you can find a little cottage somewhere nearby so that I can look after you when the baby is born.' Mrs Barlow frowned. 'You were doing so well, Rose. Your name in the papers like that, and all that talk of a recording contract and a show on Broadway. You could have been really famous one day.'

'It was a lot of paper talk, Ma,' Rose said. 'I might have got the contract for a record in time but I'm not sure I would have wanted to go to America if they'd asked me, which as far as I know, they didn't. Anyway, I doubt if they will ask once they know I've had a baby.'

'Who is the father?' Mrs Barlow's gaze narrowed. 'The man you were with in the papers – Brent, was that his name?'

'Jason is the man who produced and paid for the show,' Rose said. 'No, he wasn't my lover, just a good friend. He says I can go back afterwards, but it depends on what the papers have to say when they find out.'

'Oh, Rose, never say we're going to have them queuing outside our door? I've no idea what Myrtle will think to that.'

'Good business if they come in and buy a meal,' Myrtle said and entered the room. 'I'm sorry, Rose. I couldn't help overhearing what you were saying – and your mother being daft. I shall be pleased to have a young one in the house, girl. It don't matter to me that you haven't got a husband. It's not as if you were a virgin. You were married before and it stands to reason with you being up there and everyone after you that something might happen.'

'Don't encourage her, Myrtle. She may have been married but it isn't her husband's child.' Mrs Barlow glanced at her daughter. 'I suppose he won't marry you?'

'He can't, Ma.'

'Oh, Rose – not a married man!'

'He wasn't married then but he may be by now.' Rose turned away from her mother's accusing eyes. 'I loved him, Ma. I still love him.'

'Well, you know your own business best,' Myrtle said, but Mrs Barlow was silent and thoughtful. 'Whatever happens, we'll see you through it, Rose lass. All you have to do is keep well and take care of yourself.'

'I can work for a while,' Rose said. 'Just light things – like accounts and a bit of dusting...'

'Can you do accounts?' Myrtle looked at her sharply.

'I taught myself when I was in the VADs,' Rose told her. 'Sister Harris wanted someone to check the stores and she trusted me more than most of the others. She suspected some things were going missing and I proved that she was right.'

'What happened?' Myrtle was fascinated.

'One of the nurses left in a hurry. I wasn't told anything, but Sister Harris thanked me and I was given a special services medal when I left. Not all the girls got one, though we all worked hard.'

'It just shows she thought a lot of you.' Myrtle hesitated, then said, 'I've got a bit behind with me accounts recently. If you could check them for me regular that would be lovely, Rose. You needn't bother about the dusting, but you might stand in on the reception sometimes – just answering the phone and making bookings.' She looked at Mrs Barlow. 'You want to be proud of your Rose. I reckon she's a grand lass.'

'I've never said different,' Mrs Barlow retorted. 'Her father was proud of her nursing in the war, but I still wish she hadn't landed herself in this bother. We've always kept ourselves decent as a family and you can say what you like, but this isn't proper.'

Rose sighed. Her mother was perfectly right to be upset that she was having a child out of wedlock. She couldn't blame her; she knew she had been foolish. Rose should have known that men like Luke Trenwith never married girls like her. She shouldn't have let herself get carried away by his talk of love and a relationship that mattered. It still hurt that he had lied to her, because he must have known that he was planning to wed that girl.

* * *

'I should have thought Amanda could be here today for the funeral,' Lady Trenwith said and glared at her son. She was dressed in black from head to foot. Luke couldn't help thinking she resembled a scrawny crow, then immediately felt ashamed of his uncharitable sentiments. 'If she had any respect for you she would have come home immediately. She had your telegram.'

'Amanda is enjoying herself. I did not ask her to come, Mother. She hardly knew Father. Why should she cut short her holiday?'

'She has been away far longer than she intended. If she doesn't come back soon it will be too late to arrange a wedding at Christmas.'

'Well, that is her choice. Perhaps she has decided she would prefer the wedding in the spring.'

'Are you sure she hasn't decided to call it off?'

'I do not know, Mother – and to be honest I'm not that concerned. I asked Amanda to marry me because it was what Father wanted. He hoped to see my first child born but it is too late for that and so it hardly matters.'

Lady Trenwith gave him a withering look. 'I suppose you will be off to London with your friends now that your father has gone, leaving everything to me.'

'I might sell the estate,' Luke said, and he felt an unworthy satisfaction as her face went white. It was wrong of him to taunt her because he had no intention of selling, but he was sick of her ceaseless nagging. 'We shall have to see what happens, Mother. The dower house is yours, naturally, for as long as you want it.'

'You can't sell.' Lady Trenwith had recovered herself. 'Trenwith is entailed.'

'But there are no more male heirs at present,' Luke said. 'Besides, I think you will find that I can do pretty much as I like,

Mother. If you will excuse me I must go down and speak to Sarah. She and Troy arrived a short time ago. Come down when you are ready.'

'Luke!'

He turned and smiled. 'Yes, Mother? Do you not think we should get Father buried before we start arguing about the future of Trenwith?'

He walked out before she could answer. He had almost lost his temper with her; her behaviour these past few days had pushed him to the limits. He knew that it was probably caused by fear of the changes he would make now that his father had gone.

Luke had not made any firm decisions. His efforts in these past months had pulled their finances back on track, and the managers he had employed would keep things running when he was away. He had a few ideas about things that he would like to do in the immediate future. One of them was a trip to Paris, where he might be able to kill two birds with one stone.

Sarah was alone, staring out of the window at the park. She turned as he approached and smiled a little sadly. 'Troy will be down in a few minutes. He had a telephone call from his father and was delayed.'

'We're not due in church for another half an hour.'

'It's odd how much you miss someone when they are gone, isn't it?' Sarah pulled a wry face. 'I didn't always see eye to eye with Father, but I've discovered that I loved him.'

'He cared for you as much as he was able,' Luke said. 'I can't tell you he loved you because I don't know. He said some things to me just before he died – things that made me feel he cared, but he never used the word love. Except to say that he did not love Mother and she never loved him.'

'It was a marriage of convenience. She was a better wife to him than she was a mother to us.'

'Yes, that is the odd thing,' Luke said, looking thoughtful. 'You would think she would love her children, but I don't think she does – do you?'

'I know she disapproves of me,' Sarah said. 'I used to think you were her favourite, but somehow...' She broke off and shook her head.

'Mother thinks I let her down because I had an affair with someone she disapproves of,' Luke said. 'We had a big row about it and she hasn't forgiven me. I'm not sure she ever will.'

'She doesn't – forgive. We sort of made up our differences, but she never forgave me for being pregnant when I married Troy. I love you, Luke. You know I would stand by you, whatever you did.'

'What does that mean?'

'I think you should ask Amanda to release you from your engagement,' Sarah told him. 'If she loved you she wouldn't have stayed away all these months. You don't love her – do you?'

'No, I don't love her,' Luke said. 'I didn't want to ask her; I got myself backed into a corner. She must be the one to break it off.'

'Don't ruin your life, Luke. You don't want to end up like Mother and Father. You were pushed into it; Amanda was never the one for you.'

Luke ran restless fingers through his hair 'No, I wouldn't want that – but I can't jilt Amanda. I think I shall go over to Paris when this is done, Sarah. I would like to do a bit of business there – and I'll talk to Amanda, see what she has to say...' He broke off as the door opened and Troy came in. He was closely followed by Marianne and Barney, and the chance for private conversation was at an end when Lady Trenwith arrived.

'We're all here,' Luke said. 'The cars are waiting; we might as well go.'

* * *

Jack came down from the ladder. He had been inspecting the work on the new roof, which had an asbestos lining and was far more modern and in line with the fire regulations of the day. It was almost finished and he would be able to start replacing the benches and electrical wiring inside soon. He had worked hard and the garage was taking shape sooner than he could have imagined. The pit had survived the fire but all the machinery had twisted or melted with the heat. He would have to buy everything new, but he'd expected that, and modern machinery was a great improvement on the old. He wanted to invest in a quality sprayer because he was going to be doing bodywork improvements – rebuilding some of the lovely old automobiles that had been rusting in sheds during the war. He would repair newer cars, of course, but it was the restoration of older models that he liked best.

His head filled with plans for the future, Jack locked up and took his bicycle from the wall, beginning to pedal along the tree-lined avenue towards the café. He saw a car drawn up outside but did not recognise it. Louise's customers sometimes came by car; her reputation for good food was growing, and people came from the other side of the city to dine. It was too early for dinner though and the casual customers who dropped in for a glass of wine or a cup of coffee usually walked.

It appeared that they had a visitor. Jack walked round to the back of the house and parked his bicycle. He opened the door and entered the kitchen, stopping to wash his hands at the sink before going through the hall to the café. He heard Louise's voice and then a man's laughter, and his heart stopped for a moment. Surely it couldn't be! What was Luke Trenwith doing here?

Jack entered the café. It was empty apart from Louise and their visitor. The man turned his head as Jack stood just inside the door from the hall, and their eyes met.

'Captain Trenwith.' Jack took a few steps forward, his hand outstretched. 'This is a surprise. How did you find us?'

'I asked around for a Monsieur Georges Marly and was directed here,' Luke replied and smiled. 'You are both looking very well. I was told that this was one of the best places to come for a meal.'

'What can I do for you? Or do you have some news for me?'

'I do have news,' Luke said. 'Sir James has recently died and I had business here so I thought I would call on you if I could find you. I suppose you've heard about Rose?'

'What about Rose? The last I heard she was married.'

'Didn't I tell you her husband was killed in the war?' Luke frowned. 'I'm sorry, I thought I had when I wrote about your father – but perhaps I didn't. Anyway, she has been singing in a West End production and doing rather well, I think. Sarah says she left the show some weeks ago, but I don't know why.' He hesitated, then, 'I have never told her what happened, Jack. I know you said I could tell Rose, but your father died and somehow I never found the right time to tell her. I wondered if you still wanted her to know?'

'We are pretty settled here. If you think Rose is happy, then don't tell her – but I'll leave it to you. If you think she would like to know I'm still alive...' He shrugged his shoulders.

'Right, I'll use my discretion then. I should like to dine here one evening before I leave Paris.'

'Come this evening,' Jack said instantly. 'It's on the house.'

'Thank you, that is awfully good of you, but I'm not sure about this evening. I shall come before I leave, I promise you.' His eyes went from Jack to Louise. 'I've wondered sometimes... It must have been hard, knowing you can't go back... But you're happy?'

'Very happy.' Jack put his arm about Louise's shoulders. 'We have each other. It is all we want.'

'I wondered if love would be enough.' Luke gave an odd, twisted smile. 'I am very glad to see that in your case it is.'

'Yes, but we have been lucky. If I hadn't been sent on special duties by a sergeant who hated me I might never have met Louise – and she might be dead.'

'Jack saved me from a German officer,' Louise said. 'I'm not sure if we told you when you were at the farm. Jack stayed at the farm because I was afraid of being alone, but he wasn't a coward. He was awarded a medal for serving with the freedom fighters.'

'Yes, I saw his name in a list somewhere. Besides, Jack saved my life when my plane went down and I shall always be grateful.' He got to his feet. 'I have to see someone but I shall come back. I should like to visit from time to time when I am in Paris – if that is agreeable?'

'Yes, why not?' Jack said, and they shook hands again. 'It's nice to see you, sir.'

'It's Luke or Trenwith to you. My employees don't pull their caps to me these days, Jack. I don't expect it from them or you.'

'Right you are, Captain. Come to dinner with us one night – and visit whenever you are in Paris. We shall be pleased to see you.'

Louise looked at Jack as Luke went out. 'He is much nicer than I realised when he stayed with us at the farm. I was afraid of him then and thought he would persuade you to go back through the German lines with him, but he is a gentleman.'

'Yes, he is,' Jack confirmed. 'His parents expected a servant to know their place. You weren't supposed to look them in the eye, and the men had to touch their caps and the girls had to curtsy when they spoke to Lady Trenwith. Mr Luke was never like that, and he meant what he said – but calling him by his name doesn't come easy.' He frowned and looked thoughtful. 'I always thought he liked Rose more than he ought. It is a wonder he didn't tell her about me.'

'Why don't you write to her?' Louise asked. 'She wouldn't betray you, would she?'

'Rose? She's a great girl, brave as a lion,' Jack said. 'We used to fight all the time when we were kids, but she cared for me and I cared for her. I don't know how to write a letter like that, Louise. I hoped Mr Luke might know how to explain it better than I ever could.'

'Just tell her that you love her,' Louise suggested. 'She will understand that – and when she comes here I'll explain.'

'I'll think about it,' Jack said, and he turned away to pour a glass of wine. 'I wonder what brought Mr Luke to Paris. I don't think it was us.'

'He said he had some business, but I think it may have been personal.'

Louise's intuition was often spot on, Jack reflected. 'Yes, you may be right. There was a strange look in his eyes as he said it.' He handed Louise a glass of wine. 'It isn't our business. Still, I'm glad he called. I always liked Mr Luke.'

* * *

Luke was thoughtful as he drove away. He had been pleasantly surprised by the café, which had a warm, prosperous feel. Before Jack arrived home, Louise had told him about the fire at the garage and the rebuilding Jack had undertaken. It looked as if they were settled here for life, which was just as well because Jack could still be in trouble if he returned to England. The war was over and it was unlikely that he would be shot as a deserter, but he could still be arrested, tried and sentenced to several years in prison. No, Jack would stay where he was and grow old as a Frenchman with his lovely wife.

Luke wondered if he might have been tempted to do the same if he'd found someone like Louise. There had been a girl in the French village where he was stationed, but Lillian had never meant anything to him. He'd done what he could for her and her child, which wasn't his – but he'd never been back to see if she had received money from the child's father's family after he was killed. He considered making a detour to visit Lillian and then decided against it. He didn't want to get involved. That period of his life was over and done with as far as he was concerned.

Luke returned to his hotel and went up to change for the evening. He had deliberately chosen to stay at a different hotel from Amanda. He was going to walk in on her just before dinner and hope to surprise her. Amanda had got used to the idea of freedom, but Luke thought it was time that she made her decision one way or the other. Either she wanted to be married or she didn't.

He went down to the lobby and asked the doorman to get him a taxi. After giving the name of the hotel to his driver, he sat back, opened his cigarette case and extracted a slim white tube. He tapped the ends and then lit it, drawing a long breath of tobacco smoke.

He felt quite calm. He wasn't sure why.

* * *

'Have you seen the evening papers?' Myrtle asked as she came into their private sitting-room.

Rose was knitting something in pink. She had convinced herself the baby was a girl and Myrtle agreed with her, but Mrs Barlow said she ought to make some of the coats in white, just in case.

'Has something important happened?' Rose put her knitting to one side. 'You look serious. There isn't going to be another war, is there?'

'I'm not sure the last one is over yet,' Myrtle said. 'They keep arguing over everything and I'm not convinced we're any better off than the Germans, even though they say we won.' She thrust the paper at Rose. 'I thought you ought to see this.'

Rose sighed, putting a hand to her back. The months had flown and she was getting near her time. Sometimes she thought the waiting would never be over, but she must have only a few days to go now. She took the newspaper and scanned the headlines, then turned cold as she realised why Myrtle had brought it to her.

'The police have arrested Jason Brent on suspicion of murder and running illegal brothels and gambling clubs.' She looked up at Myrtle. 'This is awful.'

'Just look a bit further down the page. They've brought your name into it, Rose. Someone must have discovered where you're staying – and that you are having a baby.'

Rose looked further down the page. The report seemed to suggest that she was, or had been, Jason's mistress.

There is a rumour that a certain songstress has retired to the sea to have her nestling. Maybe she should have stayed in town and kept her lover on the straight and narrow. When asked if he was the father of Rose Barlow's child, the impresario denied it – but who believes a man the police have arrested on suspicion of murder and running a brothel?

'They've got a damned cheek if you ask me,' Myrtle said. 'It is none of their business who your child's father is, Rose.'

'No, it isn't,' Rose agreed. 'It says the police have taken Jason in for questioning. They haven't charged him yet.' She scanned the rest of the page and then gasped. 'Oh, no! Not Sally! He couldn't... He wouldn't have murdered Sally... He just wouldn't...'

'Is that the girl they found dead of an overdose of opium?' Myrtle asked. 'I read something yesterday but they didn't name her then.'

Rose read further and nodded. 'Yes, it looks like it. Oh, poor

Sally. But I can't understand it. Sally didn't take drugs. At least, she didn't when I knew her.'

Rose frowned as she handed the paper back to Myrtle. She hadn't heard a word from Sally since she left the show, even though she'd written as she'd promised. Sally hadn't taken the trouble to reply, but perhaps she hadn't known what to say. Rose knew she had been feeling guilty about the day William Trent was murdered. Rose had never been sure whether Sally was guilty of a crime or if she was just an unfortunate girl who had got mixed up in something nasty.

Now Sally was dead of an overdose of drugs. It was hard to believe that such a vibrant, lovely girl had killed herself deliberately. Obviously, the police were suspicious or they wouldn't have arrested Jason. They had arrested him once before but were forced to let him go for lack of evidence. It might be the same this time.

Rose stood up, preparing to go upstairs. She gave a little gasp as the pain struck hard in her back, her eyes widening as she looked at Myrtle.

'I think it is the baby. I wasn't expecting anything to happen just yet.'

'I thought it might be soon.' Myrtle smiled at her reassuringly. 'Is that the first time you've felt the pain, love?'

'Yes. I was fine sitting there, but when I stood up it came suddenly.'

'I should say there is a way to go yet,' Myrtle said. 'There's plenty of time to get you to the hospital – though in my day we had babies at home.'

'It will be less work for you and Mum,' Rose said, and she gasped as she felt another sharp pain. 'Oh God, that was a bad one. I'm not sure there is enough time, Myrtle. I think this baby is in a hurry to be born...'

Rose suddenly felt near to tears. She wanted Luke to be here with her now. For months she had managed not to think about him, but now that the birth of their child was imminent, she longed for him to hold her hand.

* * *

Luke saw Amanda as soon as he entered the hotel lounge. She looked extremely beautiful in a dress that shouted Paris at him, and her hair had been styled in a new way. She had grown up an awful lot in the past few months and Luke felt a stirring of interest in the new Amanda. She was more of a woman and less of a child than she had been. He smiled and started to cross the room towards her when he saw her wave. She wasn't waving at him though; she hadn't yet seen him. He watched as a young man walked towards her. He was dark-haired, handsome and looked wealthy. He reached her side and Amanda moved towards him impulsively. He put his arms about her and kissed her. It wasn't the casual kiss of friends, but the more intimate embrace of lovers.

Amanda was in love with him! Luke saw her face, the way her eyes sparkled, the joy in her movements. He continued to watch for some minutes, debating whether to walk away or confront them. He wasn't angry, just a little shocked that she had found someone else and hadn't told him. As he stood, undecided, Amanda glanced towards him and her face went pale. She looked frightened. She obviously thought Luke was going to make a fuss and cause trouble. He inclined his head to her, turned and walked away, out of the hotel into the busy boulevard.

There were cabs passing that he could have hailed, but he ignored them. It was a beautiful night for a walk and he had nothing particular to do. He considered returning to Jack and Louise but decided that he wasn't in the mood for company. He needed to think about the future.

Amanda knew he had seen her. If she had been torn between becoming his wife and the wife of the young man she was with that evening, she would know that she must make up her mind. Luke didn't need to do anything. He was amazed that he felt so calm. Once upon a time Amanda's behaviour would have made him angry, but now he merely felt a little sad. It had all gone so wrong and he had only himself to blame. If he had stood up for what he really wanted he would still be with Rose.

At that moment he felt such a tearing pain in his stomach that he gave a moan and almost staggered. He had to stop for a second and draw a deep breath. It was odd but he'd had a few unexplained pains in his back and stomach for the past few hours. He had taken no notice, but that last one had nearly floored him. At first he thought it must have been something he'd eaten, and then he remembered he hadn't eaten since breakfast. Perhaps that was it; he should find a café and order something light. However, the pain eased off and he was able to breathe again.

Luke strolled down to the river, watching the Batons Rouges going up and down the Seine; their decks were strung with lights that twinkled in the dusk. Paris was a romantic city, particularly at night when the bustle of the day eased and the pace became slower, more leisurely. He could hear singing from one of the many cafés and he was aware of laughter, of people strolling together, arm-in-arm, on their way to a theatre or a restaurant.

He saw a café with outside tables and sat down, ordering coffee and soup with bread. A couple got up from the next table and left behind a newspaper. When the waiter returned he picked it up, glanced at it and then handed it to Luke.

'It is English,' he said. 'I don't read so good the English – perhaps you would like?'

'Thank you. I haven't bought one today.' Luke folded the paper and laid it beside his plate. He might read it later in his room.

8

'You've got a beautiful baby girl,' Myrtle cooed. 'You were right, love. She is a little darling, a real charmer – and her hair is going to be a reddish gold. It is a lot lighter than yours.'

'Yes, it is but it has a reddish tint,' Rose pointed out and gazed fondly at the baby in her arms. 'She is so gorgeous, and her eyes are blue.'

'They might change later,' Mrs Barlow said. 'She will suit all those pink coats and dresses you've been making, Rose. What are you going to call her?'

'I think... Elspeth. Or do you think that is too posh?'

'It's a lovely name,' Myrtle said and laughed. 'I wish my mother had thought of it when she had me.'

Rose smiled. 'Elspeth it will be then. I shall have her christened Elspeth Sarah Myrtle.'

'What about the last name?' Mrs Barlow asked. 'Are you going to put her father's name on the birth certificate? She'll want to know it when she grows up.'

'I shall put Barlow,' Rose said. 'She isn't Rod's daughter so I can't use Carne and I've been using my own name for a while now.'

'What about her father?' Mrs Barlow went on. 'Are you going to tell him now she's born? I didn't press it until she came, because I knew you didn't want him thinking you need help – but don't you think he should be told he has a child – whoever he is?'

'Leave Rose be,' Myrtle said. 'She's just given birth and here you are, bullying her.'

'I'm not bullying her, Rose knows that,' Mrs Barlow retorted. 'You don't have to ask for anything, Rose. Your baby will have everything she needs between the three of us – but he might want to know.'

'I doubt it,' Rose said, but she wouldn't meet her mother's eyes because she knew that Luke would want to be told that he had a child. 'I shall think about it, Ma. Please do not look at me like that – as if I'm being silly. I do know what I'm doing.'

'Do you?' Mrs Barlow gave a disbelieving sniff. 'I can't force you, but if I were you I should tell him.'

The look in her eyes was so suspicious that Rose was almost certain she had guessed the name of Elspeth's father – but how could she? Rose had kept her feelings for Luke very much to herself. It wasn't possible that her mother could know that for a very short time she had been his mistress.

* * *

'Miss Rawlings says will you go up, sir,' the receptionist said. 'Take the lift to the second floor. It is the Green Dragon suite.'

Luke thanked her and made his way to the lift. He had sent a message to Amanda that morning asking to speak to her alone. She'd sent a message by return asking him to call. He was in two minds what to say to her. If she asked him to release her he would of course oblige, but supposing she turned on the tears and begged him to forgive her?

He took the lift, listening to it whirr its way between floors. Did he really want to go through with this marriage? He had never loved Amanda. Surely he had every right to break off the engagement now? He got out of the lift and crossed the plush carpet that seemed to be everywhere in this exclusive hotel to the door of Amanda's suite. She must have been waiting, for the door opened at once in response to his knock, and there she stood, looking nervous.

'Luke, I can explain.'

'Can you, Amanda?' he asked and smiled. 'I am sure you can – but I would prefer the truth if you do not mind too much. I think we should be honest with each other, my dear.'

Amanda turned and walked into the room. Luke followed silently. When she turned towards him her expression was defiant. 'You don't really care about me, Luke. Please do not pretend that you love me, because I know it's not true. When you asked me to marry you I didn't understand. I thought that was all there was and so I said yes – but I know differently now. I am in love with Alan and he adores me.'

'That was obvious last evening,' Luke said. 'No one can help falling in love, but when were you going to tell me – after you had exchanged his ring for mine?' Luke glanced at her finger and saw that she was wearing a huge clear white diamond. It must have cost five times the price of his ring.

'Alan asked me last night and I said yes,' Amanda said, remaining defiant. 'I wasn't sure until last night that he would ask me and I...'

'Was afraid that I would barge in and spoil it all?' Luke smiled wryly as she flushed. 'It was in your eyes last night, Amanda. I preferred to walk away from a confrontation. Tell me, does your father know about this?'

'Not yet.' Amanda bit her lip. 'He may be cross. Daddy didn't approve of me coming on this trip and he wants me to marry you and become Lady Trenwith.'

'I take it that Alan doesn't have a title?'

'He is an American, very rich and well educated – but they don't care about titles over there. He says they are outdated and belong to the dark ages.'

'Good for him,' Luke said. 'I'm not at all keen on titles myself. I tell everyone not to use mine but unfortunately they seem to delight in it. I never could see why.'

Amanda looked at him uncertainly. 'Do you hate me?'

'Certainly not. Why should I? I am pleased that you have decided to tell me the truth at last – and I wish you happiness.'

'You really don't mind?' Amanda seemed vaguely disappointed, as if she would have liked him to declare himself broken-hearted. 'You never were in love with me, were you?'

'No, Amanda, I was not,' Luke agreed honestly. 'I kissed you in the moonlight because you were pretty – but I can't think what I said to make you think we were engaged.'

'You didn't say anything. I told Daddy you had kissed me and he told your father you had talked about marriage. Sir James said you were a bit slow about things like that and I should act innocent and look at you adoringly and he would do the rest.'

'Well, it certainly worked,' Luke said. 'I hope your father doesn't scold you too much for breaking it off.'

'I'm going to run off with Alan to Gretna Green and get married over the anvil,' Amanda said. 'I told him I thought it was romantic and he said we should do it – so we shall.'

'Was that what you were hoping for from me – romance?' Luke laughed softly. 'I must have been a sad disappointment to you, Amanda. I am sorry I let you down.'

'You didn't, because if you had been more romantic I shouldn't have come on this trip and then I wouldn't have met Alan. I ought to give you your ring back, but I took it off ages ago and I can't find it. I think I must have lost it in one of the hotels we stayed at on our tour.'

Luke looked at her and then chuckled, much amused by her flippant dismissal of the ring he'd given her. 'I think that is the best place for it, Amanda – lost somewhere in a hotel. I shall say goodbye now. I'm returning to England this evening. I shall put a notice in *The Times* to say that we have terminated our engagement by mutual agreement and remain friends – will that do?'

'Yes. It is very generous of you, Luke.'

'I don't want to label you a jilt,' he said. 'I should never have asked you. This ridiculous business was my fault, Amanda – as it usually is.'

'No, it wasn't your fault. Daddy and your father pushed us both into it. I'm sorry I wasn't brave enough to say no at the start.'

'So am I,' Luke said, and he shook his head as she lifted her brows. 'It doesn't matter. Goodbye, Amanda. I don't think we need to prolong this. I am sure you have better things to do.'

As he walked back to the lift, Luke felt as if a weight had been lifted from his shoulders. His mother would create hell when he got home and told her the wedding was off, but he didn't give a damn. She could do her worst. He should have told her to go to hell the last time she interfered, but he had opted for the least damaging option – only it hadn't turned out that way. He had been living under a cloud ever since he'd parted from Rose.

Luke acknowledged that he had treated Rose badly. He had persuaded her to trust him and then he'd let her down. He resolved that, if she would allow him to, he would try to make it up to her.

He was smiling as he walked into the hotel, his thoughts busy with plans for the future. It was a moment or two before the girl's voice got through to him.

'Sir Luke?'

'Yes.' He glanced at the receptionist. 'I am sorry, I was miles away. Did you call me?'

'Yes, sir. An urgent telegram came for you while you were out.'

'Thank you.' Luke frowned as he opened it. 'Damn! Forgive me,' he said as the girl looked startled. 'It is bad news, I'm afraid. I shall have to leave at once on an earlier train, if I can get one.'

'I am sorry, sir. I'll have your bill made up.'

'Thank you. It is my sister. She and her husband have been involved in a car accident...' Luke hurried to his room, shaken. Marianne had been badly injured – the doctors were uncertain if she would live. Barney must be in a terrible state. The least he could do was to be there. His own plans would have to be put on hold once again – but not for ever. Luke nursed the secret knowledge that he was free. For the present he must be there for his family while they needed him, but when this latest crisis was over he would go in search of Rose.

* * *

'Can I leave Elspeth with you for a few days?' Rose asked her mother one morning. 'I'm going to London and I would rather not take her with me. She takes her bottle well, and my milk has more or less dried up anyway.'

'Of course we'll have her,' Myrtle said. 'Are you going for a job?'

'I want to see Jason,' Rose told her. 'The police have let him go. There was insufficient evidence that he gave Sally those drugs, but they are still investigating him for other offences.'

'Are you sure you should go?' her mother demanded. 'There hasn't been much about you in the papers so far – just a few hints and some pictures – but if you are seen with him it may all start up again.'

'Jason has something of mine – a painting someone did of me.

He said I could have it and I would like to bring it here. And I do need to ask him about Sally.'

'You won't settle until you get it out of your head,' Myrtle said. 'If you decide to go back to work you'll need a nurse for Elspeth. We shall miss you both, but if it is what you want you should do it, love.'

'I'm not sure. I need to talk to Jason about a few things, but I don't know if I want to work for him again.'

'Well, there are other theatres and other producers,' Myrtle said. 'You've got a lovely voice, Rose. You shouldn't just give the singing up.'

'I thought there would be more comment about me in the papers than there was,' Rose admitted. 'Perhaps I'm not as famous as I thought.' She laughed a little ruefully. 'They hardly missed me.'

'Don't you believe it,' her mother said. 'In my experience there is always the calm before the storm. I think you would do better to leave well alone, but if you must go you must.'

Rose nodded. She knew that in a way her mother was right, and yet she wouldn't rest until she had settled a few things in her mind. Sally had been through a lot and she'd been frightened and guilty over something. Rose had never been entirely sure that her friend had not killed her ex-lover. Had Sally turned to drink and drugs because she couldn't face what she had done?

* * *

'She will never forgive me,' Barney groaned. He hadn't slept since the accident and his face was white, his eyes dark-shadowed. 'When she sees the scar on her face, she will hate me.'

'It wasn't your fault you hit that lamppost.'

'I was driving too fast and I'd been drinking,' Barney confessed guiltily. 'We had been quarrelling for days. She said that if I didn't like things the way they were I should leave her – and, God forgive me, I said I was tired of her behaving like a miserable bitch and I wanted a divorce. She went for my face with her nails and I swerved...' Barney dashed away the tears that trickled down his cheeks. 'Why couldn't I be the one to be scarred? I don't care about my appearance. I've never been much to look at – but Marianne was perfect. She didn't have a blemish.'

'I still say it is as much her fault as yours,' Luke said. 'One person doesn't make a quarrel, Barney. It takes two in my experience.'

'Did you quarrel with Amanda?' Barney asked. 'Sarah told me the engagement was over. She too said I shouldn't feel so guilty – but when I look at Marianne's face I can't help it. I see what I've done to her and it makes me want to spew my guts.'

'You still love her – don't you?'

'Do I?' Barney looked even guiltier. 'I worshipped her for years, Luke – but she had an affair. She won't admit to it but I know it's true. I thought I'd stopped loving her. I meant it when I told her I wanted a divorce, but now...' He shook his head. 'I can't do it. I'm not that much of a rotter. I'll have to try and make it up to her somehow.'

'The physicians here in this hospital aren't experts in facial surgery, but I know there are doctors in America who could probably do something for Marianne. Why don't you persuade her to go there?'

'At the moment she screams and throws things every time I enter the room,' Barney said. 'To be honest, I don't want to visit her, Luke. I think it is really over now. I shan't divorce her, but we get on each other's nerves too much to stay together.' He hesitated, then said, 'I suppose you wouldn't take her to America?'

'I'm not sure I can. I do have commitments here, Barney. Talk to Marianne; see if you can get her to see sense. She is lucky to be alive. For the first few hours it was touch and go – a scar isn't that important, surely?'

'You know Marianne. She cares about things like that too much. Please talk to her. Tell her that they can do things to make her beautiful again.'

'Good heavens, it isn't that bad,' Luke said. 'If it were anyone but Marianne I would ask what all the fuss was about – but she was very beautiful and looks are important to her.'

'I wish I were dead,' Barney said dramatically. 'Please get her to listen, Luke. I suppose I can put up with her temper a bit longer. If she has the operation I could at least let her divorce me with an easy mind.'

'Mother is outraged enough that Amanda and I broke up.' Luke hadn't told his mother that Amanda had jilted him for another man, though she had probably guessed because Amanda's engagement to her American had been published in *The Times* a few days after his own announcement. Amanda's father had presumably vetoed the idea of a marriage over the anvil. 'She will go mad if you and Marianne divorce.'

'Your mother scares me to death,' Barney told him. 'I honestly don't know how you stand living with her.'

'Sometimes I wonder myself,' Luke admitted. 'Look, I'll talk to Marianne and tell her that I'm going to make inquiries in Harley Street. They will know the best place to have whatever she needs done. I can't promise I'll take her to America, but I'll fix it all up for you.'

'Thank you. I'm such a coward. It's no wonder Rose Barlow never looked at me twice.'

'What do you mean?' Luke asked sharply. 'Have you seen Rose? I know she left the show but I'm trying to trace her.'

'You're trying...' Barney went still, then he nodded. 'I knew there was someone. I thought you were sweet on her but she never told anyone. Is it your child?'

'What are you saying?' Luke stared, his heart beginning to hammer. 'Is Rose having a baby?'

'She had it some weeks ago from what I've heard. She left the show and went off to the seaside to have the child. I'm not sure exactly where, but I bumped into Jason Brent the other day and he told me she was doing well and had a daughter.'

Luke's stomach clenched. It was the first time he'd heard anything about Rose having a child. He'd seen an article about Jason Brent in a newspaper someone had given him in Paris, but he hadn't bothered to read more than a few lines.

'I thought he was arrested for murder and running illegal gambling clubs?'

'He got off again. The man always has cast-iron alibis. If you ask me he is a rogue, but so far the police haven't managed to pin enough on him to bring him to court.'

'Damn!' Luke glared at him. 'Where did you meet him? I should like to have a word with Jason Brent myself.'

'Please speak to Marianne before you go chasing after Rose,' Barney said. 'She won't listen to me. When we brought her home from the hospital she was too ill to do more than lie in her bed, but now she is feeling better she is like a raging tigress.'

'You shouldn't be afraid of her! Stand up to her like a man, Barney. Marianne will never respect you unless you do.'

* * *

'Come back to the theatre, Rose. I know there may be some bad press, but I am sure we can weather it together. If you married me they would soon get bored and go away.'

'I gave you my answer long ago,' Rose said. 'You were good to me, Jason, but I don't want to marry you.' She looked him straight in the eyes. 'You know why I've come to see you.'

'I was hoping it was for a job.'

'I am thinking about it. Elspeth is a little young just yet for me to leave her with a nurse all day. I've been wondering about Sally. I need to know what went wrong. Why did she start taking drugs? I know she drank too much sometimes – but drugs?'

'She got in with the wrong sort.' Jason frowned. 'I tried to tell her, Rose but – she seemed haunted. I think she had a terrible secret, but I'm damned if I know what it was.'

'I think she may have shot William Trent,' Rose confided. 'She had an apron spattered with blood. At first, she said the stains came from kneeling by his body when she found him. She'd gone to the house to fetch some things that belonged to her and heard someone come in and then a shot. She swore she didn't kill him. I believed her then, but now I'm not sure if she was lying.'

'She was certainly driven. I had to speak to her several times because she turned up unfit for work.' Jason frowned. 'The day her body was found... I'd told her the previous day that she would be sacked if she didn't pull herself together.'

Rose wrinkled her brow in thought. 'You believe she may have taken her own life because she thought you were going to sack her – would you have done it?'

'I might,' Jason confessed. 'Don't look at me as if I'm a monster, Rose. I have a show to put on. I can't employ girls I can't trust – and, let's face it, there are plenty of better singers than Sally.'

'That's not very nice!'

'You think I shouldn't speak ill of the dead?' Jason looked at her hard, his blue eyes glinting. 'Well, I'm sorry if it offends you, Rose – but Sally was always headed for a bad end. She couldn't keep on the straight and narrow. She went off men after the abortion, but she took to drink and drugs instead. You are more sensible. You went ahead and had your child...'

'And I'm going to keep her,' Rose said. 'My mother's cousin

would take care of her if I paid for help – but I want Elspeth with me. If I came back I would bring her with me.'

'I would accept that, naturally. There would be some scandal but if you can take it I certainly can. There's hardly a day that passes without some new accusation or innuendo in the papers concerning my life.'

'Is there any truth in what the papers said when the police arrested you?' Rose demanded, her eyes on his face. 'Tell me the truth, Jason. I know when you hide something – you *have* been hiding something from me, haven't you?'

Jason hesitated and then nodded. 'I was involved in some of those clubs a few years ago, but I sold out – some of them to Trent. He thought he was buying a gold-mine and when he found out there wasn't as much money in them as he thought, he accused me of cheating him.'

'Is that why you quarrelled?'

'Yes.'

'And you don't have an interest in a brothel or an illegal gambling club?'

'No, I don't. I have a half share in a nightclub, but we don't have a back room for gambling. The police tried to prove otherwise but couldn't. I'm clean, Rose. I might have a shady past, but I'm legit now.'

'So what were you hiding from me just before I left the show? Don't lie, please. I know there was something.'

'I had an offer for you from a Broadway producer,' Jason said. 'It was a lot of money, Rose, and a wonderful opportunity for you. I didn't tell you because I didn't want you to go. I knew about the baby and I hoped that after the child was born you would come back to me. I know that wasn't fair, because you could make a fortune if things went well over there.' His smile challenged her. 'Will you think about working for me again? I'll give you top billing, the same as before. If the takings are good I'll give you more money.'

'And will you tell me next time you get an offer for me to sing somewhere else?'

'Yes.' He grinned and crossed his chest, tongue in cheek. 'On my mother's life – and she was a saint, Rose. Not a bit like her rogue of a son. Give me another chance, will you?'

'I'll need a flat and a nurse – and sometimes I shall bring Elspeth to rehearsals.'

'You make your own terms this time. I haven't found anyone to replace you, Rose.'

'All right...' She smiled at him. 'I'll go home and fetch Elspeth and bring her back with me.'

'We'll start rehearsals straight away.' His eyes roamed over her. 'You haven't got fat – maybe a bit bigger round the bust, but that is natural. Are you still feeding her?'

'No, she takes the bottle. My milk wasn't enough for her so the midwife suggested the bottle. I couldn't work otherwise.'

'I'm going to announce your return to the papers. Let them have a field day before you get here – but be prepared for a lot of rubbish. I'll do my best to stop them annoying you, but I'm afraid it is going to be open season once you start work.'

'Yes, I know. We'll see how it goes, but I'm not going to run away and hide, Jason. If the shows are busy they can do their damnedest!'

* * *

'I'm sorry, Sir Luke, but Rose isn't here,' Mrs Barlow said. She gave him a look that was little short of scathing. 'She was staying with us but she left two days ago.'

'I have been searching for her for some weeks. My sister told me she might be here,' Luke confessed. 'I would be very grateful if you could tell me where she has gone please.'

'I could but I am not sure that I should.' Mrs Barlow's tone was brusque. 'I think you've done her enough harm – don't you?'

Luke was shocked by the look she gave him. 'Are you saying that her child is mine?'

'Your own conscience should tell you that, sir. You had a love affair with her and left her – didn't you? She didn't tell me, but I know my Rose. She isn't one for going with just anyone. Someone hurt her badly and I think it was you.'

'I shan't deny it,' Luke told her. 'I have treated Rose abominably, but I would like to speak to her. If the child is mine, I should...' His voice trailed away as he saw the anger in her eyes. 'I couldn't marry Rose at the time, Mrs Barlow. My father would have been upset and he was ill.' He hesitated. 'I'm afraid I entered into an engagement to please him.'

'Then leave Rose alone,' her mother advised. 'If you can't offer her marriage, stay away from her. It is the decent thing to do, sir. She won't let you give her money for Elspeth so there's no sense in upsetting her all over again.'

'I am no longer engaged,' Luke assured her. 'I would very much like to speak to Rose – discover how she feels. I am not sure whether she would have me now even if I asked her.'

'Well, you won't get her address from me,' Mrs Barlow told him firmly. 'I warned her against you years ago. I saw the way you looked at her, sir. It wouldn't have done then and it won't do now, even if you were wishful to marry her. Why don't you just leave her be?'

'I'm sorry you feel this way, because I can't do that. I'm afraid I can't promise you that I am going to marry Rose, because naturally that is up to her – but I am going to ask her whether you help me or not. I didn't mean to hurt Rose, Mrs Barlow. You may not believe it, but I suffered as much as she did. Thank you for seeing me today. Goodbye.'

Luke walked away, humiliated. Mrs Barlow had made him feel about two feet high; worse than his mother had ever managed with her air of reproach. He hadn't yet told Lady Trenwith of his intentions. He knew that she would cut him out of her life if he married Rose, but he no longer cared what she thought. If Rose had given birth to his child he wanted to know about it and, if she would let him, he wanted to marry her. He had been a damned fool to let duty and concern for his father separate him from the woman he loved.

If Rose was no longer living with her mother at the hotel she might have gone back to work in London. He would concentrate his search on the theatres and eventually he would find her. Perhaps Rose would send his sister her new address in time, but if not he would find her somehow.

* * *

'You sing even better than before,' Jason said as Rose came to the end of her last song at rehearsal. 'We'll start you off with those two songs on Monday and then build it up as we go along.' He smiled at her. 'How do you like your flat?'

'I'm glad it has a garden,' Rose replied. 'It isn't warm enough to put Elspeth's pram out for the moment, but it will be lovely when the summer comes.'

'And how is the nurse?'

'Jean is a lovely girl. I was lucky to find her. She loves Elspeth and she is very good with her – but don't think I can leave her with Jean all the time. I want my child to know her mummy.'

'You are a good mother,' Jason said and looked rueful. 'I almost wish I'd never told you the truth about my preferences. We could have been together and I would have been Elspeth's father.'

'Would you like children?' Rose caught an oddly wistful expression on his face.

'Sometimes I think I might, especially when I see you with your daughter,' Jason admitted. 'Would you have married me if I'd told you I was in love with you?'

'No. I might not have come to work for you,' Rose told him. 'I needed a job badly, but I was feeling bruised. I was glad you told me the truth – and I've enjoyed your friendship, Jason.'

He nodded. 'I didn't think it would work if I lied to you, and I trusted you. Most people have no idea of my private life, Rose. The police have been trying to get me for everything else under the sun, but they haven't caught on to the one thing I couldn't wriggle out of...'

'That is because you are always seen with beautiful girls, Jason.'

'I take care to keep my private life out of the papers, but one day they will catch on and then...' He shrugged. 'I expect they will throw me in prison and lose the key.'

'It seems unfair that you can be imprisoned because of the way you love,' Rose said. 'I've had a child out of wedlock but that is only immoral, not illegal. I've been holding my breath but only a couple of journalists have taken pictures so far – and they just reported the facts about my return to the show. I'm not sure how long my luck will last.'

'They are biding their time. I think they may be preparing for opening night. We'll see what happens after your first night back on stage.'

'Yes.' Rose sighed. 'I suppose that is all we can do, Jason. I am going home now to spend the afternoon sewing some sequins on my dress and looking after my daughter.'

* * *

Luke stood outside the tall house in a quiet square. Once upon a time these large terraced houses had belonged to the rich, but those families had moved on some years ago and the buildings had been divided into flats. Although Mrs Barlow had refused to give him Rose's address, he wasn't about to give up and his agent had traced her. He crossed the street, climbed the three steps to the front door and rang one of the bells. It echoed loudly inside but there was no answer. He was about to turn away when he saw a woman walking towards the house. She hadn't seen him yet but he knew her at once, and his heart jerked to a stop and then raced on.

'Rose,' he said and stepped out to meet her. He saw shock and indecision in her eyes, as if she were on the verge of taking flight. Even as she hesitated, the front door of the house opened to reveal a young woman holding a child.

'I am sorry, sir,' she said. 'I was changing the baby and could not answer immediately.'

'It is perfectly all right. I came to see Miss Barlow – and here she is now.'

'Luke,' Rose said, and her tone was cold. 'It's all right, Jean. Take Elspeth back to her nursery. I'll be a few minutes with this gentleman and then I'll look after her and you can have a couple of hours off.'

'If you're sure, Miss Barlow. I don't mind staying a bit longer. I only wanted to do some shopping.'

'No, you deserve your free time and this business will not take long.' Rose looked directly at Luke. 'Please come into the sitting-room, Sir Luke.'

She led the way into a large room that overlooked the square. This consisted of a small central area of grass and a few trees, where people could sit on a fine day. The room itself had high ceilings and a frieze, and a chandelier hung from a ceiling rose. It was clear to Luke that the house had once been very grand, and the silk wallpaper and beautiful Adam fireplace still carried echoes of that grandeur. Above the mantel hung the painting he had done of Rose.

Luke felt his stomach clench with shock. He'd had no idea that she owned the portrait. Outside the bustle of London traffic was a muted roar, but inside the silence was deadly. Rose took off her gloves and hat and placed them on the shining surface of a Georgian side table.

'I was sorry about your father, Luke.' She turned her beautiful eyes on him. 'I know you were fond of him.' Luke's eyes went over her, taking in the small changes, drinking in the sight of her.

'Thank you. He had been ill a long time but it was still a shock.'

'Death always is.' She frowned. 'Did Sarah give you my address?'

'She gave me your mother's address. She doesn't know why I want to see you – though she may have guessed that we had a relationship.'

'Is that what you call it? I would have called it a fling,' Rose said coldly. 'How long did your promises of loving me for ever last – was it three weeks or four? I can't quite remember.'

'I know that what I did was unforgivable. Tell me, is Elspeth mine?' His expression was intent, anxious.

Rose's eyes flashed with sudden temper. 'Do you really think so little of me that you need to ask? I'd like you to leave, Luke. I don't think we have anything further to say to one another.'

'Rose – please. I wasn't sure. You went straight to Jason Brent...' Luke couldn't keep the jealousy out of his voice. 'You might have done it because you were angry.'

'I might but I didn't,' Rose said. 'Please just go, Luke. I told you that night that I wouldn't be your mistress and I meant it. Just go and leave me alone.'

'I can't do that, Rose. I love you.'

Disbelief was in every line of her body. 'If you loved me you wouldn't have asked Amanda Rawlings to marry you.'

'I was backed into a corner and couldn't get out of it. I made a wretched mistake and I can't blame you for being angry. I'm not going to marry Amanda. She decided that she preferred someone else – an American.'

'So she dumped you and you've come crawling back to me!' Rose looked at him as if he had slunk out from under a rock. 'Thank you but I'm not interested. I had my child without help from you and I can bring her up alone.' Her eyes flashed with temper and he saw the way her hands clenched at her sides. 'Jason is a good friend. I am not his mistress and I never was – and if you are still in any doubt, Elspeth is yours.'

'Are you refusing to let me see her?' Luke asked. 'She is my daughter. I would like to see her often – and I wasn't asking you to be my mistress, Rose. I was going to ask you to marry me.'

'What about your precious duty?'

'I've told you I was a damned fool. I behaved badly but I cared for my father. He was ill. I couldn't tell him I wanted to marry you – it would have killed him. He wasn't so much a snob as set in his ways, Rose. However, he is dead now and I'm free. If you will have me I want to marry you, Rose. I've been a bastard and I wouldn't blame you if you hated me – but I do love you and I want you to be my wife.'

'Thank you for the offer, but the answer is no. You hurt me, Luke. How do you think it feels to be told you are good enough for an affair but not to marry? I wanted to die when I knew you had asked that girl to marry you – but I got over it. I don't need you any longer and I don't want you.'

Luke recoiled as if she had slapped him. He stared at her, sensing the hurt pride and anger she had stored up. She had every right to be angry. He deserved this, but he had hoped that she might forgive him... Might still love him, as he loved her.

'I know I deserved that, Rose,' he said quietly. 'I wish I could go back and change what I did. I was a damned fool. I should have told my father the truth. The honest thing would have been to wait to marry you until he was dead. I was dishonest with Amanda too – which is why she fell in love with someone else. I've made a mess of things all round and I'm sorry. I love you. I shall always love you. If you change your mind you know where I am.' Rose shook her head. 'I'm going to the flat for a while. I want to try painting again.'

'Why did you sell the painting of me?' Rose demanded. It had hurt her so much when she saw it; if Luke had cared for her he could never have parted with it. 'Jason bought it for me. He knew at once it was me and didn't want anyone else to have it. How could you sell something so intimate?'

'I couldn't bear to be reminded of you – and the gallery had asked for more of my work; something different from the war paintings,' Luke admitted. 'After it was sold I regretted letting them have it, but it was too late. They wouldn't tell me who purchased it; they didn't want me to try to buy it back. I would have done, Rose.'

'Well, it is here now,' Rose said. 'I would give it to you but you might sell it again and I don't care for anyone else to have it.'

'Do you hate me, Rose? I wouldn't blame you if you did.'

'No – but I don't trust you. I may be able to forgive you in time, but I'm not sure I shall ever forget the way you hurt me.' Tears hovered in her eyes, but she blinked them away. Luke wanted to hold her, to make her smile again, but he wasn't sure she would ever let him near her again.

'Give me a chance to make it up to you. I promise I'll never hurt you again.'

'I can't. Not yet, perhaps not ever. But I won't stop you seeing Elspeth. You can visit her once a week. Jean looks after her. I am here most afternoons, but mornings and evenings I am out. You can come when I'm not here. I'll tell Jean to let you see her – but if you try to take her from me I'll fight you with every ounce of my strength.'

'I wouldn't do that to you. I swear on my honour.' Luke saw her expression and grimaced. 'I do still have some honour, you know. I love you, Rose. You may not believe it now, but one day you may learn to trust me again. I want you to be my wife.'

'It wouldn't work. You know it wouldn't, Luke. I couldn't live at Trenwith as your wife. Your mother would hate me – and everyone else would think I'd got above my station.'

'I don't give a damn what my mother or anyone else thinks. Besides, we do not have to live there. We could live anywhere you like. It would suit me to travel; I would have something to paint.'

'What about my career?'

'We could live in London while you're in a show.'

'I don't know, Luke.' Rose looked at him sadly. 'I was very much in love with you, even before we were together. I think I married Rod because he reminded me of you. Even when I worked for your mother I was attracted to you. I knew it wouldn't do and I kept a discreet distance between us, but when we met during the war...' She shook her head. 'I believed you when you told me you loved me and that you would always be faithful – then you asked someone else to marry you.' She moved away as he tried to take her in his arms. 'No, Luke. It doesn't work that way. I am sorry. I can't just let you back in.'

'No, I see you can't.' Luke felt the pain twist inside. What had he done to her? 'Please think about it, Rose. I've loved you for as long as I can remember and I shall always love you.' He picked up his hat. 'I shall come and see Elspeth on Thursdays. Perhaps we can all go out to tea somewhere as she gets older – and I want to give her presents. Just toys for now, but I'll put money aside for her as she grows up. She is my daughter too, Rose. I have a right to do what I can.'

'Yes, you do. Just don't spoil her too soon. I want her to understand that sometimes you have to wait for things.'

'I had things as a child, but I never had love, Rose. I loved my father. For a time I probably loved my mother. I believe she cared for me as much as she was able, but she doesn't know how to love. I want my daughter to have love as much as anything else.'

'My mother and Myrtle dote on Elspeth. Come on Thursdays then. I may not always be here, but if I am there is no reason why we shouldn't be civil to one another.'

'None at all,' Luke agreed. 'Thank you, Rose. Please try to forgive me.'

He walked to the door and looked back. Rose had turned her back on him and gone to the window. Her shoulders were straight, her head held proudly. He sighed but said no more as he went out.

* * *

Rose sank down into an armchair after Luke had gone. Her chest felt tight and the tears were burning behind her eyes. She blinked them away. She wasn't going to cry and she wasn't going to fall straight back into Luke's arms like a fool. He had hurt her too badly and she didn't dare trust him. If he really cared for her and Elspeth, he was going to have to prove himself before she would allow him back into her life again.

Yet she had ached for him to kiss her. It was no use pretending that she no longer felt anything for him. Just seeing him standing outside the house had made her heart race wildly. If she had let him take her in his arms she would probably have given in, but he had behaved like the gentleman he was, taken his cue from her and kept his distance. A sudden surge of anger banished her tears. Once again Luke had sworn that he loved her, and this time he had promised marriage, but why should she believe him after what he had done to her the last time? The hurt went too deep for her to forgive instantly.

She shook her head, putting the sense of loss and regret from her as she went in search of Jean and her darling Elspeth. The nanny was a good girl and she deserved her time off. In any case, Rose loved spending time with her daughter. Sometimes she wished that she hadn't promised Jason she would go back to the show. He had assured her she could return on her own terms, but he wanted her to do an afternoon show twice a week and she would have to be careful he didn't try to increase her working hours.

Despite all her reservations about him, Rose liked Jason. He was generous and a good friend. She still wasn't sure that he had told her the whole truth, but then most people had secrets they kept even from their loved ones.

She thought that she believed what he had told her about Sally, and it made her all the more determined to be careful herself. Sally had got into trouble because she'd fallen in love. She had ended by hating William Trent, and perhaps she had killed him. It might be the reason she had got into bad company and then taken her own life with an overdose of opium.

Rose hadn't made any other close friends among the cast. She knew that some of them resented the way she had just walked back into the show to be given top billing. Nevertheless, despite the envious glances that occasionally came her way, no one had been actively unfriendly, though she suspected they talked about her behind her back.

She could put up with that; it was a small price to pay for continuing to perform on stage. What really mattered, as far as her career was concerned, was the audience's reaction to her when she opened on Monday night.

9

Rose finished singing her first song of the evening. The applause was generous, but not warm or wildly approving as it had been the first time she appeared on stage. She took a deep breath as the music began for her second and last song of the evening. It was the song made popular some years earlier about a woman who was kept in riches but unhappy. When she sang the words 'She was only a bird in a gilded cage...' someone gave a catcall from the audience and there were a couple of boos and then some shushing from others. When she finished there was dead silence for a second and then a man rose to his feet and started clapping. For a moment he stood alone and then others began to follow, getting to their feet and applauding. Gradually the whole audience was on its feet and the applause echoed round the theatre. They called for her to sing again, and she looked down at the orchestra, choosing a song she had made her own in the last show. When she finished, the applause was warm and spontaneous, and only after five curtain calls did the audience finally let her go.

Jason was waiting in the wings to present her with a large bouquet of flowers, before sending her back to take one last bow.

When the lights finally went up, he followed her to her dressing-room.

'It was a close call,' he said. 'We owe a debt of gratitude to the man who stood up and applauded you. For a moment I thought you would get booed off stage. I gave you that song because it was a test, Rose. If you can get away with that you can get away with murder as far as your audience is concerned.'

'Do you really think we've got away with it?' Rose asked. She realised she was trembling. She had been more nervous than she had anticipated and the catcalls had dismayed her. 'What do you think the papers will say tomorrow?'

'You may get some stick from them. We always knew that, Rose. They left you alone while you stayed out of sight, but now you are back in the public view and I daresay some of them will turn on the moral bit. You know the saying, "Put your head above the parapet and expect to get shot at." However, if the audience had turned against you that would have been it. We'll soon know if ticket sales drop, but I don't believe they will. Some women may look down their noses at you, but, after all, you aren't going to be presented to the King or anything. I don't think we need to worry.'

'No, of course not!' Rose laughed. 'Do you know who stood up on his own? It was Luke Trenwith.'

'I thought he dumped you for the kind of girl his family wanted him to marry.'

'He did, but he isn't going to marry her. He came to see me and he wants to visit Elspeth – he wants to marry me.'

'Don't fall for that one,' Jason warned. 'I know he turned the tide this evening, but that doesn't mean you can trust everything he says.'

'No, it doesn't,' Rose agreed. 'I am grateful, however. It could have been awful tonight, but it wasn't, thanks to Luke.'

'He started the ball rolling, but there were others,' Jason said, and his eyes glinted with what looked remarkably like jealousy. 'You won't walk out on me, Rose?'

'I shall stay while the show is successful,' Rose said. 'You don't need to warn me, Jason. I'm not going to fall straight into his arms, even though I'm grateful for what he did.'

A dresser poked her head round the door. 'There are two gentlemen asking to see you, Miss Barlow: Sir Luke Trenwith and Mr Barney Hale.'

'Tell them both to come in.' Rose looked at Jason. 'I'm not going out to celebrate this evening. I know the photographers want pictures, but they can wait. I have a child and my daughter's nurse has been looking after her all day.'

'The press expect you to go to nightclubs. You're Rose Barlow, the famous singer, and you should give them something to write about.'

'I will see people tomorrow. They can come to the theatre and I'll talk to them, but this evening I am going home – alone.'

'Have it your own way.' Jason frowned and went out. Rose knew he wasn't too pleased with her, but she was following her instincts.

A moment or two later there was a knock at the door. Rose called her visitors in. She finished changing behind her dressing screen and then walked out to greet Luke and Barney, who stood together and seemed a little at odds with each other.

'Thank you for the flowers, Barney – and you too, Luke. They are all lovely.'

Luke glanced round the dressing-room. 'You seem to have almost too many.'

'It's always like that on opening night. Jason sends at least three baskets just in case no one else does. He says the papers like to know things like that, because it makes good copy. He wanted me to go to a nightclub but I refused. I have a daughter at home and Jean needs some time to herself.'

'You need more than one nurse,' Barney said. 'Marianne has three – Nanny and her two assistants. It means she hardly has to see the children at all.'

'I love spending time with Elspeth when I can, although she will be asleep when I get home. I like Jean to have some free time though. I suppose I could get her an assistant. I shall have to ask her how she feels.'

'I was going to ask you out to dinner,' Barney said. 'You were wonderful, Rose – better than ever.'

'Can I take you home, Rose?' Luke asked. 'I have a cab waiting.'

'Thank you both, but I shall go alone. I have to be a bit careful, Luke. As you know, the audience could have gone either way this evening. Thank you for what you did – you, too, Barney. I may see you on Thursday, Luke, but this evening I am going home alone. I don't want to give the papers a chance to label me as a bad mother, spending my time in nightclubs or being seen out with men when I have a baby at home.'

Luke nodded. She could see that he was disappointed, but even if she had wanted him to take her home it would not have been wise. There would be photographers waiting at the stage door as she left. She knew they would not have rested until they had discovered his name.

'Of course. I shall call on Thursday, as agreed. I just wanted to tell you how beautiful you looked on stage.' Luke took Barney's arm, steering him from the room. 'We had better leave Rose to finish whatever she has to do.'

Rose sat down and looked at herself in the dressing mirror. She was glad that Luke had not come alone. She might have been foolish enough to agree to his taking her home if Barney had not been there.

She hadn't told anyone except Jason who the father of her child was, though she suspected her mother had guessed – and Sarah probably had, too. Lady Trenwith could not know of it yet and nor could Marianne. Both of them would be outraged. Rose shuddered at the thought of the scandal that would ensue if the papers got hold of the story.

* * *

'So you've come back at last then!' Marianne said sullenly as Barney entered the bedchamber at Trenwith. She had refused to accompany him home, and so far she had only ventured as far as the garden once or twice in the early mornings. 'I suppose you've been visiting that woman again!'

'What woman?' Barney was mildly irritated by his wife's accusations. 'I do not have a mistress, as you would be aware if you ever noticed what was going on around you.'

'You want someone else. Don't lie to me!' Marianne cried petulantly. 'I've known for a long time there was someone. I've seen the bills for flowers – expensive flowers. There has to be a woman somewhere.'

Barney sighed. 'The flowers were for someone I admire. She has a beautiful voice and she has made something of her life. She has no interest in me, unfortunately. She loves someone else.'

'Who are you talking about?' Marianne's eyes narrowed in suspicion. 'You mean Rose Barlow, don't you – that little skivvy who went on the stage and got herself into trouble. The reason she's got where she is must be because she slept with that producer, whatever he's called.'

'Jason Brent.' Barney looked thoughtful. 'No, her child doesn't belong to Jason. I'm not certain but I think his tastes lie in another direction.'

'What do you mean?' Marianne stared at him. 'You don't mean

he is a queer – that is disgusting! Men like that should be locked away.'

'Don't talk about things you don't understand, Marianne. The man is entitled to his preferences. I'm not sure, anyway. It was just something I overheard the other night at the theatre when I went backstage. He was talking to someone – a young and rather pretty man.'

Marianne pulled a face. 'Well, I think the whole idea is revolting. Why did you go backstage if you aren't interested in Barlow?'

'I went to congratulate Rose on her performance. Luke was there too. We went together and we left together. Besides, I told you, she isn't interested in me.'

'You mean you would be interested if she gave you the chance?' Marianne glared at him. She put a hand to the red scar on her face. It had healed but it was unlikely that it would completely disappear, and she was bitter. 'You did this to me, Barney – and now you want someone else.'

'If I did want someone else it would be your own fault, Marianne.' Barney gave her a hard look. 'I don't care about the scar, but if you like I'll arrange for you to go somewhere to have it treated. I'm not sure I want to live with you again, but for the sake of the children we'll stay married. You can have a house wherever you like – a villa in the South of France perhaps?'

'Damn you! I hate you. I should never have married you!'

Marianne lay back on the pillows after he had gone. She had grown used to Barney following her like a little puppy, willing and eager to do whatever she asked. She didn't like the feeling that he was no longer her slave to command at will.

She was convinced that there was something between him and Rose Barlow. No man sent expensive flowers in that quantity to a woman unless he loved her. She had been suspicious for more than a year, and now she was certain. Barney had said Rose's child wasn't his, but Marianne wasn't convinced. She wanted to see the child for herself – and she wanted to know if Barney was lying to her.

Her fingers stroked the scar on her cheek. If Rose Barlow had stolen Barney from her, she was going to pay! She would make them both pay. She wasn't in love with Barney, she never had been – but he was hers and she had no intention of letting him dance attendance on a slut like Rose Barlow!

* * *

'I want to hire a private detective,' Marianne said to her mother when they met later that day. 'I know you had one once when we were children – how did you find him?'

'Why do you want to know?' Lady Trenwith looked at her hard. 'If Barney has a mistress you should let him get on with it. I found it best not to make a fuss. Men are such fools. They fall for highly unsuitable women, but in the end they come back to their wives.'

'Did you ever love Father?'

'I respected him,' Lady Trenwith said stiffly. 'We married because our parents wished it. My mother did not allow me the freedom to choose that you had, Marianne. If you are dissatisfied with your lot you have only yourself to blame.'

'I made a mistake,' Marianne said bitterly. 'I should never have jilted Troy.'

'No, you should not. No one forced you to accept Barney Hale. Had you waited for a while you might have found someone you liked better.'

'I realised on my wedding day I'd made a mistake. You knew I didn't want to go through with it, but you made me marry him.'

'You had caused enough scandal by jilting Troy Pelham. I could not allow you to cause more.' Lady Trenwith fixed her daughter with a warning look. 'I hope you are not thinking of a divorce? I shall not permit it.'

'No, I don't want a divorce. I think Barney wants one but he won't ask because of what he did to my face.'

'That was an accident,' her mother remarked. 'If you continue to blame him, Marianne, he will tire of being your whipping-boy. You should accept that you are no longer the beauty you were and settle for being a good wife and mother.'

'I don't want to settle for that,' Marianne said and touched her scar. 'If Barney is after that Barlow slut, I shall kill myself.'

'What?' Lady Trenwith's gaze narrowed; she was suddenly alert. 'Are you talking about Rose Barlow?'

'Barney has been sending her flowers again. I saw the bills. He always leaves things in his pockets and I accused him of having a mistress. He admitted the flowers were for her, but said she wasn't interested in him. He and Luke went to see her backstage after her show reopened in the West End the other night.'

'She has a child.' Lady Trenwith scowled. 'I thought it was that man's – the producer.'

'Barney says he is a queer,' Marianne said. 'If he isn't the father, I want to know who is. It could be Barney.'

'I doubt it.' Lady Trenwith looked thoughtful. She was silent for a moment. 'Leave this business to me, Marianne. You're too involved emotionally. Believe me, I'll get to the bottom of this nasty little affair.'

Marianne felt chilled as she saw the look in her mother's eyes. 'What are you going to do?'

'I haven't made up my mind yet, but I have some suspicions and if I'm right about the father, that woman is going to get the shock of her life.'

'You will tell me if it is Barney?'

'Yes, I'll tell you,' her mother said. She looked at Marianne's scar.

'Why don't you go to America and have that scar fixed? Ask Luke about it.'

'Luke is in London.'

'Well, go to London then. You aren't going to stay in your room for the rest of your life, are you?'

'People will stare.'

'Wear a hat with heavy veiling,' Lady Trenwith advised. 'And stay away from Rose Barlow. I'll have her watched and I'll tell you what is going on. Believe me, if she has got above her station she will pay for it.'

'Very well.' Marianne got up and went to the mirror. She suppressed a shudder as she looked at her face. Her mother was right; if she wore one of her pretty hats with dark veiling no one would be able to see the scar. She was sick to death of being here at Trenwith. If there was a chance of getting something done to improve her appearance, she would be mad not to try it. 'I'll go up tomorrow and speak to Luke.'

* * *

'I'm glad Mrs Hale's gone away for a while,' Emily said as she sat at the kitchen table and drank the tea Mrs Jarvis passed her. 'Driving me mad, she was. If she comes to live here permanent, I'm off. I'm telling you, I've had enough.'

'Why don't you ask your Rose to give you a job?' Mrs Jarvis suggested. 'She must be earning a lot of money these days. She's a proper star, is Rose Barlow. You could help her look after the baby, I shouldn't wonder.'

Emily looked thoughtful. 'I heard the mistress and that sulky bitch talking about Rose yesterday. I was outside the door with the tea tray and I might have heard a bit more, but Jarvis told me not to listen at doors and I had to take the tray in.'

'Jarvis is right, you shouldn't listen at doors. What people say is private.' Mrs Jarvis cut a generous slice of seed cake and passed it across the table. 'What were they saying then?'

'Something about staying away from Rose Barlow, and she – Lady Trenwith – was going to have her watched.'

'You couldn't have heard right, Emily. The mistress wouldn't do anything like that – why should she?'

'I don't know. I was hoping to hear more but Mrs Hale said she was going to town to see her brother and then Jarvis made me take the tray in.'

'As you should,' Mrs Jarvis said primly. 'Listening at doors never did anyone any good, Emily Redfern! I should like to know why she wants your Rose watched though.'

'Yes, so would I,' Emily agreed. 'I think she hates Rose. I could tell by the way she was talking. She didn't like Rose leaving to be a VAD in the war. You may be sure it puts her nose out to know Rose is doing so well for herself.'

'Yes, I wouldn't be surprised. She was bad enough when Sir James was alive, but there's no pleasing her now. By rights she should have moved into the dower house, but she'll cling on here until the last. You see if she don't.'

'Do you think he'll get married now – Mr Luke, or Sir Luke as I should say, now as he's master here? Do you think that girl broke his heart when she jilted him?'

'You don't know she did jilt him; it was by mutual agreement, the paper said,' Mrs Jarvis reminded her. 'I doubt if he broke his heart over that flighty piece. I could never see why he asked her in the first place. There are plenty more fish in the sea. It will put madam's nose out when he finally brings a wife home. She won't like it if she can't rule the roost here.'

'Well, maybe he won't get married. He's gone off to London to paint. Maybe he won't ever come back.'

'Sir Luke won't desert us completely,' Mrs Jarvis said. 'He might spend most of his time in London, but he'll make sure things are right here.'

* * *

'Marianne – this is a surprise,' Luke said as he opened the door to her later that afternoon. He smiled. 'I am glad to see you out again. That hat looks very stylish.'

'Well, at least it covers my face,' Marianne muttered. 'I've been thinking about what you said, Luke. Do you believe that surgeon in America could help me?'

'I am certain he could make the scar look better than it is. I'm not saying it would vanish completely – but I'm sure it could be improved. The surgeon who sewed you up was trying to save your life. You had other complications; he wasn't sure you would live. I have to say though, he might have made a better job of it.'

'I look ugly! I wish they had let me die. I might as well be dead as look like this!'

'That's a bit dramatic, isn't it?' Luke arched his brows. 'I think you look fine even with the scar, Marianne. Not as flawlessly beautiful as you were, but still lovely.'

'Will you come with me?' she asked. 'Please, Luke. Say you will take me to America and stay with me while I have my face done – please.'

'I'm not sure. I have other things I need to do, Marianne.'

'You don't care about me! It was always you and Sarah.'

'Of course I care,' Luke said. 'It's just that I can't leave London immediately.'

'Oh, you are as bad as Barney,' Marianne cried. 'Mother said to come and see you, but I might as well have stayed at home.'

'Barney would go with you.'

'I don't want Barney. He hates me and I hate him.'

Luke stared at her unhappily. He was just getting to know his daughter and he wanted Rose to trust him. If he went to America with Marianne she would think he was deserting her again.

'I shall have to think about it. Give me a few days, Marianne. I'll make all the arrangements, but couldn't Mother go with you?'

'She has other things to do,' Marianne said. 'I've never asked you for anything, Luke. You know this is important to me – please say you will.'

'I'll talk to people and get it set up. It's bound to take a few weeks to sort out, but I'll take you if I can manage it.'

'Thank you.' Marianne smiled her satisfaction. 'I am so grateful, Luke. I really can't bear to spend the rest of my life looking like this.'

* * *

Luke managed to resist the urge to buy every toy in the exclusive department store. Elspeth was still very young and the assistant had assured him that a teddy and a silver rattle with a coral teething drop were perfect for a young baby. He paid for his purchases and left, deciding to walk to his destination. It was warmer now and it seemed that spring was on its way. He felt better than he had since before the war. At last, the world was moving on. People now talked about other things apart from the war, and they looked happier. It was a new world; although remnants of the old one still clung on, he could see the changes happening.

There were far fewer horses on the streets, which seemed cleaner as a result. He had seen a man with a cart and a long broom sweeping gutters. The man had a fearfully scarred face and Luke guessed he had been injured while fighting for his country, but he looked pleased to have a job. The prices of food and clothing seemed to have steadied too, and there was more to buy than there had been a year ago when the war ended. Luke reflected that he had certainly seen more cars on the streets.

Jack Barlow had been right when he had predicted that the future would be all about cars and machines. Luke wondered about Rose's brother and Louise. They were prospering and life seemed good for them. He had almost made up his mind to tell Rose the truth about Jack, but he very rarely saw her.

This would be his third visit to his daughter. He looked forward to it more each time, and hoped that Rose would arrive home before he left. He wasn't sure if she was deliberately avoiding him, but she hadn't been there on the last two occasions he'd visited.

He reached the square and glanced back. He didn't know why but he had an odd feeling that someone was watching him. He had experienced the same sensation once or twice recently but had dismissed it as his imagination. He saw no one in the square now who looked familiar, so he put the thought out of his mind.

Luke knocked at the door and waited until Jean let him in. She smiled as she saw the teddy bear in his arms. 'More toys, sir? She will soon have no room to lie in her cot.'

'Have I overdone it, Jean?' he asked as he walked into the house. 'Is she awake?'

'I've just given her the bottle so she is sleeping,' the nursemaid told him. 'However, Miss Barlow is in the sitting-room. I've been told I can go out for a few hours. I expect Elspeth will wake up soon.'

'Thank you.' Luke's heart took a flying leap as he went into the front parlour. Rose was standing by the window. She was looking down at something, and as he approached he saw it was a song sheet. 'Learning something new?' he asked.

'Yes. Jason wants me to do another song at the beginning of the show as well as the two I do later. He has given me some to choose from. I'm not sure which would go down best.'

Luke studied the sheet with interest. 'This is new – jazz or blues, I think. You've never done anything like that before, have you?'

'No, I thought it might be a change.' Rose looked up as Jean tapped on the door. 'Yes, come in.'

'I'm leaving now, Miss Barlow. Elspeth is asleep. Do you want me to make the tea before I go?'

'Thank you, Jean, but I can manage. Go and have a lovely afternoon.'

'Does she often have time off?' Luke inquired as Jean went out and they heard the door close. 'If you need someone else to share the work here I could help you pay for it, Rose. After all, Elspeth is my responsibility as much as yours.'

'I am thinking of getting another girl to help,' Rose said. 'I had a letter from my cousin, Emily. She wrote to the theatre because she didn't know my address. She is thinking of leaving Trenwith and she wanted to know if I could help her find a job. I might suggest that she comes here until she finds something better.'

'I like Emily. She would be just right.'

'It would mean that everyone at Trenwith would know you visit Elspeth and me,' Rose said. 'Emily would be bound to write home, and the servants talk.'

'Don't they always?' Luke looked amused. 'You told Sarah that I was very untidy once. She told me that I ought to be more careful and pick my things up myself when I had finished with them.'

'She shouldn't have told you,' Rose said and laughed. 'Your room always took me twice as long to tidy as anyone else's – but I liked doing it. I used to look at your work, though I knew you didn't want anyone to see it.'

'I still hate anyone looking until I've finished it.' Luke glanced at the picture over the mantel. 'I'm not sure I got that quite right...'

'I've changed since then,' Rose said. 'My face was a little thinner than it is now.'

Luke's gaze centred on her face. 'Yes, you are right. I think you are even more beautiful than you were, Rose.'

'Do you?'

'Yes, I do.' Luke moved in closer. 'I love you, Rose. I could buy a house for us in town. We could be married whenever you like.'

'Luke... I'm not sure,' Rose said, but she didn't move away as he reached out for her, drawing her close. 'I want to be certain this time.'

'I swear I won't hurt you again.' Luke bent his head and kissed her. Neither of them was aware that they were standing right in front of the window, or that they were being watched from the middle of the square. 'I love you, my darling. I want us to be together always. Please give me another chance, Rose.'

'I need a bit longer,' Rose said and broke away from him. 'I think I still love you, but I need more time – and I can't leave the show yet. Jason has invested time and money in me, and I can't let him down.'

'You don't have to, my darling. I don't want to keep you hidden away from the world. You will be my wife and I am proud of the fact that you are Rose Barlow and you sing like an angel.'

'What about your mother and your sisters?'

'Sarah will be pleased. She hasn't said anything outright but I'm sure she knows. If anything, she was angry with me for asking Amanda to be my wife. I think Troy advised her not to interfere or she would have told me I was a fool to let you go. And I was, of course.' He smiled ruefully. 'You are far above me, Rose. You always were.'

'Don't put me on a pedestal,' Rose pleaded. 'I want a few weeks to think about the future. I would rather we didn't see each other alone until I make up my mind. If you're seen visiting when I'm here it will cause gossip.'

'I understand your position, but any gossip would soon die down once we announced our marriage.'

'Give me three months. By then I shall know what I want to do. That isn't too much to ask, is it?'

'No.' Luke looked at her thoughtfully. 'I told you about Marianne's accident, didn't I?'

'You said she has a nasty scar on her cheek that looks as if it won't fade.'

'She is upset about it. She wants me to take her to a surgeon in America. He does what they are calling cosmetic surgery – it is skin grafting and various techniques to repair damaged faces. Most of the poor devils they treat have had cancer or accidents – much worse than my sister's – but I think they could help her.'

'Why doesn't Barney go with her?'

'Things aren't too good between them at the moment, Rose. It wouldn't surprise me if they eventually decide to divorce.'

Rose nodded, because she knew it had never been a love match, at least on Marianne's side. 'That is a shame. I know Barney was unhappy a while ago, but I didn't realise things had got so bad.' Rose looked at him. 'Do you want to go with Marianne?'

'No, not very much,' Luke admitted. 'She asked me the other day, made a big thing about it, and I said I would see if I could get away. I was going to try to persuade Barney to take her.' He hesitated. 'But if you don't want me to visit for a while...'

'Yes.' Rose nodded. 'I think you should go with her, Luke. We will talk again when you return. Then, if you are still sure – and I feel that I want to marry you – we can buy a house in town. I may carry on singing for a year or so, but I may decide to give it up soon. I want to be with Elspeth as she grows up.'

'We could go anywhere you want. Trenwith hardly needs me these days. I'm thinking of turning the house into a hotel.'

'Luke! You wouldn't!' Rose stared at him. 'Your mother would hate that – you know she would.'

'Yes, well, maybe I'll wait for a few more years, but I don't intend to live there in the old way. She can close a part of the house when I've gone, as they did in the war – or live in the dower house. She should have done that when Father died.'

'She will not leave unless you force her.'

'No, I suppose not,' Luke said ruefully. 'I don't intend to live there with her, that is for certain. It is like a morgue sometimes. Even when Marianne is in a temper it is better than being alone with Mother. If you won't marry me I may go abroad, find a new life somewhere.'

'I haven't said I won't marry you.' Rose reached up to kiss him softly on the lips. 'It is such a big step for both of us, Luke. My mother will not approve any more than yours does. I'm too busy to see her yet, but as soon as I can get a couple of days I shall go down and talk to her.'

'You won't let her change your mind?'

'You don't know what I'm thinking yet,' Rose challenged him, a smile in her eyes.

'Yes, I do.' Luke smiled back at her. 'You wouldn't even talk like this if you weren't fairly sure you were going to say yes.'

The sound of Elspeth crying made them both look up. 'I'll fetch her down,' Rose said, 'and then you can show her the teddy bear.' She smiled at him and went out.

Luke stood at the window. He noticed a man in a raincoat standing at the other side of the square who seemed to be staring at the house. When he saw Luke looking back at him, he turned and walked away.

Luke frowned as he remembered the odd feeling he'd had of being watched recently. Had the man followed him here? And if so – why? He couldn't imagine why anyone would want to spy on him, but perhaps it was Rose the man was watching. She was gaining quite a reputation for herself as a singer, and the newspapers liked to get pictures of her when they could.

He turned as Rose came back carrying their daughter and smiled, all thought of the mysterious man in the raincoat vanishing from his mind like summer mist.

* * *

'Luke has agreed to take you?' Lady Trenwith looked at Marianne, suddenly alert. 'I must admit, I am surprised. I wouldn't have thought it... but I am pleased. I am sure the sea journey will do you good.'

'I'm not going for my health.' Marianne touched the scar on her cheek. 'I want to get rid of this disfigurement.'

'It isn't as bad as all that,' her mother told her. 'Some women would simply carry it off – but I daresay this surgeon may be able to help you.' She frowned. 'What does Barney say?'

'I haven't seen him since he left Trenwith.'

'You didn't see him when you visited Luke?'

'No. I stayed at the flat with Luke and then went to visit some friends. I don't care if I never see Barney again.'

'You are being very foolish, Marianne. It will cost money to have your face done and you like money. If Barney were to divorce you, your settlement might not be enough for your expensive tastes.'

'If it were not for this scar I would leave him,' Marianne said and scowled. 'I know he wants Rose Barlow. I think he may still be seeing her.'

'Oh, no, he definitely isn't seeing her,' Lady Trenwith said. 'I've been having her watched since we spoke. She has two male visitors. One is Jason Brent – and Barney was right about him. He is a queer. I've had him watched too. Her other visitor... You don't need to know that.' Lady Trenwith smiled in a way that chilled her daughter. 'By the time you get back from America it will all be over.'

'What do you mean?' Marianne looked at her mother curiously. 'How can you affect Rose Barlow's love life?'

'I can and I will,' Lady Trenwith affirmed. 'I shall put my plans into action once you and Luke have left on the ship. Rose Barlow is in for a fall. The little guttersnipe is too big for her boots, but she will soon discover that it is easier to fall than to climb.'

Marianne was fascinated and yet repelled at the same time. She had no idea what her mother was talking about, but she sensed the hatred. She despised Rose Barlow herself, but she didn't hate her. In fact she had felt a certain admiration for the girl when she'd seen her picture in the papers. Her mother though clearly hated her former servant. Why? Marianne wasn't sure. She had an uneasy feeling that it might be something to do with Luke. Had her mother suggested that she get Luke away so that she could do whatever she planned to do to Rose?

Marianne wondered uneasily if she should warn Luke that their mother was planning to ruin Rose, but she shied away from the trouble that might cause. Besides, he might change his mind and refuse to take her to America and then she would have to ask Barney for help. She was determined not to go to him until he came crawling back to her.

Rose Barlow could take care of herself. She'd had an illegitimate child, but she was still the darling of London audiences. Marianne didn't see what her mother could do to ruin Rose. It was just spiteful talk; she wouldn't really carry out her threats.

Marianne put the disturbing thoughts from her mind. She had never considered anyone more important than herself, and though her mother's manner had made her uneasy, her own needs were more important.

10

Luke stood at the rail of the modern liner as it left for New York. He watched the people waving and throwing streamers and sighed inwardly. Marianne had gone straight to her cabin, declaring that she would stay there until they arrived at their destination. He was aware of a feeling of unease, though he had no idea why or what was troubling him. Marianne had been giving him some strange looks, but he had never understood his sister. He thought she was feeling guilty about something, though he didn't know what it was – unless she was regretting leaving without a word to Barney.

Luke turned and went below deck. He hadn't realised until they reached the docks that Barney didn't know they were going. It might be a good idea to send him a telegram to explain and to tell him where they would be staying.

He frowned as he thought of Rose. She had imposed this three-month separation and Luke had reluctantly agreed. He couldn't wait for the time to pass and he prayed that she would feel the same way. Yet three months was nothing when only a short while ago he had believed that he might never see Rose or hold her in his arms again. He had to be patient and give his sister the attention she needed, but he would certainly send that telegram right away.

* * *

'I think I should like to stay in London for a week or two,' Sarah told Troy as they took breakfast together that morning. 'I need some clothes for myself and for the children, and I should like to visit the theatre.'

'You want to see Rose, don't you?' Troy smiled at her, his eyes teasing. 'What bee have you got in your bonnet now, my love?'

'Oh, nothing much.' Sarah hesitated, and then continued. 'It was just something Marianne said before she and Luke left for New York. She sort of hinted that Mother was planning something unpleasant, to do with Rose, but when I asked her what she meant she clammed up.'

'Why would your mother wish to do something unpleasant to Rose? I know she still thinks of her as a servant, but surely that doesn't mean she would harm her?'

'Mother's suspicions are the same as mine.' Sarah was uneasy. 'Neither Luke nor Rose has confided in me, but I believe Luke is the father of Rose's child – and I think he wants to marry her if she will have him. He held off while Father was alive, but I think he may go ahead now.'

Troy's eyebrows rose. 'Lady Trenwith would move heaven and earth to prevent that happening.'

'Yes, I am sure she would. Luke has become harder since Father died. I don't think anything Mother said or did would change his mind once it is made up – but she might get to Rose.'

'So you are going to speak to Rose yourself?'

Sarah nodded. 'I shall warn her, anyway – and tell her that I shall be proud to have her as my sister.'

'We'll give them the wedding here if they do decide to marry. But do you think it is likely? I mean, why would Luke take Marianne to America if he wants to be with Rose? It is a little odd, don't you think?'

'Marianne persuaded him, but perhaps Rose asked for time to make up her mind. She knows it wouldn't please my mother.'

'When do you want to go up to London?'

'I thought next week.'

'I have a couple of important meetings next week. If you could wait until the following week I shall be pleased to take you. We can make it a holiday; go shopping, visit the theatres and give a dinner for our friends.'

'That would be lovely,' Sarah said, and she got up to kiss him on the cheek. Troy turned his head so that their lips met. 'One week can't make much difference, I am sure.'

* * *

'Have you seen this filthy rag?' Furious, Jason pushed the newspaper in front of Rose. 'I don't know how they got hold of such intimate details. I must have been followed for weeks.'

Rose read the article, which was full of innuendo about a certain theatrical producer who made a habit of escorting beautiful women about town but who was, the reporter hinted, of a very different sexual persuasion. It went on to describe orgies with three partners in a bed, drug-taking and the abuse of under-age young men.

Shocked, she put the paper to one side. 'You can't let these lies get to you, Jason. You don't behave in the depraved way they are describing. Perhaps they mean someone else.'

'They mean me all right,' Jason said and looked angry. He walked about the dressing-room, his expression brooding and dark.

'How the hell did they get hold of this story? That is what I would like to know.'

'I swear I didn't say anything to anyone,' Rose said. Her smooth forehead wrinkled in thought. 'It's odd but I've felt that I've been followed recently. Do you think the same person has been following you?'

'I wasn't aware of it. I've always been so careful, Rose. I never meet my lover in public... Except that he came here to the theatre once and visited backstage. I warned him not to do it again, and I was careful not to say or do anything that could be noticed.'

'I've seen a man in a raincoat standing across the road from my flat a couple of times. I didn't think anything of it at first, but then I saw him again when I took Elspeth for a walk in the park.'

'Let's hope they don't start on you next. This didn't happen by accident, Rose. Someone is trying to make trouble, believe me.'

'You've had bad press reports before and it hasn't made any difference to the ticket sales,' Rose reminded him. 'People like a bad boy, especially when they are famous. You can get away with things that would sink other people, Jason. I should just put it out of your mind and forget it if I were you.'

'I threatened to sue last time,' Jason said. 'My hands are tied this time. Some of this is true – oh, forget the drugs and the orgies... Paul is seventeen. He is an adult in his thinking and feeling, but according to the law he is still a child. If the police take this up and prove it, I could end up serving a long prison sentence.'

'Oh, Jason... I am so sorry...' Rose wasn't sure what to say. Jason had told her he was of a different persuasion, but she'd never thought about the meaning of his words. If his lover was a young man – young enough to be classed as a child in the eyes of the law – it meant that he could be in serious trouble. 'What will you do?'

'I shall have to stop seeing him, at least until this all blows over.'

'That is rotten for you.'

'I love him, Rose. I know everyone thinks these affairs are just a perverse form of sex, but I really love him...' Jason's anguish was written on his face. 'People call love between two men a vice, but ours is a true love affair.'

'I'm so sorry about all this mess. I wish there were something I could do to help.'

Jason shook his head. 'Don't even try, Rose. The last thing we need is for them to start on you too. I am going to ignore this article and hope that it is the last.'

'I can't see why anyone would deliberately set out to destroy you.'

'I have made enemies. I can be ruthless, Rose. You haven't seen that side of me, but others have felt the rough edge of my tongue. I've turned down hundreds of hopefuls for my shows... and it looks as if one of them wants his or her revenge.'

'Well, I think it is disgraceful,' Rose said. 'That article is vicious. I can't imagine why anyone would hate you that much just because you turned them away from an audition.'

'Maybe it is because of something else,' Jason said. 'I suppose the only thing I can do is wait and see what happens next.'

* * *

Rose saw the headlines on a newspaper stand as she walked to her corner shop the next afternoon. This time it was the London evening paper, openly accusing Jason of having an affair with an under-age boy. The paper had decided to take a moral stand and demanded that the police investigate the producer at the heart of the scandal.

She bought the paper and took it home. The article repeated much of what had been said the previous day, but this time it used names and there was a picture of Jason speaking to a young man.

The young man's face had been blotted out, because the paper called him the innocent victim of a depraved man's sexual appetites.

How dared they print such evil lies? Rose was outraged by the accusations being levelled at Jason. Surely the press couldn't be allowed to get away with this kind of stuff? It was sufficient to ruin anyone's reputation at the very least, and it could be more serious if the police investigated.

She frowned as she read the last few lines of the article. The paper challenged Jason to sue them if he disputed their accusations – and then right at the bottom she read a few sentences that chilled her.

When a theatre producer has as his leading lady a woman who has given birth to a child out of wedlock and continues to entertain gentlemen at her flat, it brings the tone of society to a new low. What has happened to the morals of today's society when people flock to watch this scarlet woman and then give her a standing ovation?

In the opinion of this newspaper the police should investigate what may turn out to be a den of vice and iniquity.

Rose had not been named but the inference was clear. She felt faint and had to sit down quickly and take a few deep breaths until her head cleared. Now they were drawing her into the scandal – where would it stop?

She remembered the night Luke had got to his feet and applauded her alone until the rest of the audience joined in. If he hadn't been there she might have been booed off stage that night. It was a horrible thought, especially as Luke must be in New York by now. The new, faster ocean-going liners made the journey in about ten days, or so she had been told. Rose wished that Luke were here in London. She wanted him to come and take her in his arms and tell her it didn't matter – that he loved her whatever the papers had to say.

She felt nervous as she prepared to leave for the theatre that night. What would happen when she went on stage? Would the audience boo her – or, even worse, get up and leave?

As she was changing for her first appearance, Janet, one of the dancers, popped into Rose's dressing-room. 'Have you seen that awful article in the evening paper?' she asked. 'I don't believe a word of what they are saying about Jason – do you?'

'No, I don't,' Rose said staunchly, because much as she hated lying, she couldn't admit the truth to anyone. 'It is all disgusting, the lies and innuendo – making out he is involved in vice.'

'It was a bit scary reading what they said about a "den of iniquity", wasn't it?' Janet went on. 'My mother didn't want me to be a dancer in the first place. I dread to think what she will say if this gets into the nationals. She doesn't read the London evening papers, but she'll see it if it is in the dailies tomorrow.'

'Oh, surely it won't be in the national press.' Rose's nerves jumped as she realised that her mother and Myrtle might see a similar article. 'I mean, Jason will have to do something now. He can't let this continue. He has to send a denial, surely?'

'He is sure to,' Janet said and grinned. 'I bet he will sue them for every penny he can get.'

'They certainly deserve it.' Rose smiled as the dancer left, but the palms of her hands were damp with sweat. She took a deep breath as she heard the five-minute warning. She couldn't run away just because she was scared. She had to go out on stage whatever happened.

A couple of the chorus girls passed her as she approached the back of the stage. 'Good luck, Rose,' one of them said. 'They are in a funny mood out there tonight – and the theatre is only half full.'

Rose nodded, but she couldn't answer. She was feeling so

nervous her legs would hardly carry her to the stage. However, when she got the nod to go on, she lifted her head and walked proudly to the centre of the stage. There was a sprinkling of applause but the atmosphere was strange; thick with expectation.

Rose shut the worrying thoughts from her mind and began to sing a love song that had been popular with the troops in the war. As she finished there were one or two catcalls and boos but also some applause. She began her second song. 'She was only a bird in a gilded cage'. And then it started. Catcalls were coming from all around the theatre and several people were booing and shouting out insults.

'Filthy slut!'

'We don't want whores on our stage!'

'Get the alley cat off!'

Rose held her head high, ignoring the taunts, and continued to the end of the song. She finished to a deadly silence. And then someone stood up and threw a cabbage at her. It landed on the head of someone sitting in the front row. The man jumped up and yelled abuse at the person who had thrown it. That seemed to be the signal for all hell to break loose. Suddenly missiles of all kinds were being thrown, not just at the stage but at other members of the audience. A woman started to scream and there was a mad stampede as frightened members of the audience tried to leave and got caught in the fighting.

'Come off now, Rose,' Jason hissed from the side of the stage. 'You'll get hurt if you stay there.'

Rose hesitated, and then did as he told her. Something wet and smelly hit her in the back as she walked away. She was tempted to return to the stage and tell them what idiots they were for behaving like this, but the fighting and screaming were getting worse.

'I've sent for the police,' Jason said as he followed her into her dressing-room. His face was grey and he could hardly look her in the eyes. 'I should have seen it coming, Rose. This was set up. Someone is out to destroy me – and perhaps you too.'

'I'm your star.' Rose held her head high. She felt angry rather than frightened. She had probably lost her reputation and her chance of a successful career, but Jason could lose a lot more. 'You gave me a chance. I've had a good time and I've got money in the bank. I shan't blame you, Jason. It isn't your fault this has happened.'

'You know I shall have to close the show?'

'Yes, although it was me they were getting at. Couldn't you carry on if I left?'

'I don't think I want to,' Jason said. He looked defeated. 'I told you I was going to give Paul up, but he threatened to kill himself if I left him. I think we might go abroad; some place where attitudes are more tolerant of people like us – perhaps Turkey or the East...'

'Oh, Jason, your career...' Her throat felt tight. 'This has ruined you, hasn't it?'

'Pretty much, as far as my career is concerned,' he agreed. 'I have enough money put by for emergencies, Rose, and I can sell my house in London. We shall manage. Maybe I can find work. We'll travel for a while and...' He broke off and shook his head. 'It doesn't matter. Paul is right. We have to be together and be damned to what they think of us!'

'He sounds rather lovely.'

'He is.' Jason smiled wryly. 'If I could, I would have loved you, Rose. I do love you in my way. I should have married you and pretended everything was fine.'

'I would have known it wasn't real. We've been friends, Jason. We always shall be. When will you leave the country?'

'Almost immediately, I think,' Jason said. 'The sooner the better. After this there will be no hiding. The police will come calling and...' He shrugged. 'I've sent Paul to France and I'll fly there tomorrow. We shan't be so well known there and we can travel on together.'

Rose leaned towards him, kissing his cheek. 'I am so sorry this has happened, Jason. Someone must hate us both a great deal.'

'Yes, I think you are right,' Jason agreed. 'If I were braver I would have my day in court and make a stand for men like me. The way we are treated is wrong and cruel, Rose. One day we shan't have to run and hide, but I can't face the thought of years in prison simply for the way I am.'

'You go while you can,' Rose advised. 'Write to me and tell me when you're safe, please.'

'Where will you be?'

'I'm not sure.' Rose was hesitant. 'I'll stay in the flat until the end of the month. I may go to my mother then. It all depends on how much more the papers make of my having an illegitimate child. They left me pretty much alone until all this started. I had the impression that they were being fair; that they accepted I had a child but that I wasn't leading a promiscuous lifestyle. I'm not the only stage performer to have had a child out of wedlock and I haven't flaunted it or gone out every night to get drunk.' She raised her head. 'Damn them. I shan't let them get me down. If you write to my mother's home, the letter will reach me.'

'This was all very sudden.' Jason looked sad. 'I'm sorry you were caught up in it, Rose. I must have a very vindictive enemy.'

'Yes – or I have,' Rose said. 'Whoever was responsible singled me out from the rest of the cast. No one else was mentioned – just you and me.'

'But why would anyone hate you that much, Rose?' Jason was puzzled. 'I have enemies, I know that – but you've never done anyone any harm, have you?'

'Not intentionally. If I have, I don't remember,' Rose said. 'It could have been aimed at me, though. The one sure way to bring me down is to force you to take the show off. I wouldn't stand much chance of getting another job on the stage even if I wanted to – but I don't, so that is all right.'

'I still don't understand why they went to all this trouble.'

'I only know of one person who might hate me that much,' Rose said. 'I can't be sure she would do something like this – but I think she might have the power. She has money and she knows a lot of people. If she is responsible, I only wish she hadn't chosen to act in this way – because of the harm it has done to you and all the others. I'm not the only one who has lost a job.'

'Most of them will find work easily,' Jason reassured her. 'They haven't been tainted by this filth – but I still can't believe you were the target, Rose. I am sure it must have been someone who hates me.'

* * *

'Oh, no...' Sarah stared at the morning paper. 'I can't believe these dreadful things they're saying about Rose! It is disgusting...' She handed the paper to Troy, but he shook his head.

'It is in mine too. There was a riot at the theatre. Rose was booed off stage as she started to sing her second song. It seems the police were called and they have decided to investigate the private affairs of Mr Jason Brent. He was arrested and taken from his home late last night.'

'Oh, how awful it must be for the poor man. Rose will be devastated. She was doing so well... She was so successful...' Sarah stopped and read a little further. 'This paper says the whole thing was an outrage and they support a person's right to privacy. They say that Rose hasn't done anything illegal and the way she was treated was a disgrace.'

'Mine is saying that although they deplore what happened in

the theatre they still maintain that moral standards needed to be upheld.'

'Rose didn't do anything terrible.' Sarah was angry and upset. 'It was nothing I didn't do – but she wasn't as lucky...'

Troy picked up some of the other papers and glanced through them. 'There seems to be divided opinion as far as Rose is concerned, but Jason Brent is being damned by pretty well everyone.'

'I am sorry for him, but I don't know him. It is Rose I am concerned for.' She glanced at the mantel clock. 'Do you think I could catch the ten o'clock train to London?'

'You want to see her?' Troy lifted his eyebrows. 'You do realise that there will probably be several reporters camped outside her door?'

'You think I shouldn't go because of the scandal?'

'I was just warning you what it will be like. I'll come with you.'

'Don't you have a meeting this afternoon?'

'Father can take it for me. I'm not going to let you face that mess alone, Sarah. Besides, the press will probably lay off Rose a bit if we go there together. Our name stands for something.'

'Yes, it does. Father won't mind?'

'He may not like our name being in the scandal rags, but we can't let that stop us, Sarah. Rose is a friend. She needs us now – the way you needed her when you were in trouble.'

'Yes, she does,' Sarah replied. 'I do love you, Troy Pelham. I wonder why?'

'Because I am so bloody handsome,' Troy said and grinned.

'Yes, you are actually,' Sarah agreed, because she never saw the scars of his war wounds. 'But I think there may be a few other reasons...'

Sarah stood up; she knew they had to be quick if they were to catch the first train. She reached the door and then looked back. 'Troy, you don't think my mother...'

'I don't know. This is a vicious attempt to ruin more than one person's reputation, Sarah. Do you think your mother would stoop to something like this, even if she does dislike Rose?'

'If it was her, I shall never forgive her. And this time I mean it. How could anyone do such a wicked thing?'

* * *

'They are still there, Miss Barlow,' Jean said as she came in with a pile of the evening papers and some milk. 'They kept asking me if you were here and how you had taken the closing of the show, but I wouldn't answer them.'

'Thank you for braving the wolves.' Rose gave her a grateful look. 'I couldn't have faced them this morning, but I wanted to see what the papers are saying about Jason. I'm worried that he is in a lot of trouble.'

'I shouldn't read the nasty things,' Jean advised. 'People who write this sort of thing need shooting if you ask me. Making out they are as pure as the driven snow. I wonder how many of them have got secrets they wouldn't want the world to know?'

Rose laughed at her outraged look. 'Thank you for standing by me, Jean. If you wanted to leave I would pay you to the end of the month.'

'They won't drive me away with their nasty tales,' Jean said staunchly. 'I know you're not the scarlet woman they make you out to be, Miss Barlow – and I've told them so, but they won't listen.'

'I only have my reputation to lose. Jason was arrested last night when he was at home. He managed to telephone his lawyer, who rang me late last night. He is trying to get Jason released on bail, but he wasn't certain they would let him go this time. He thinks the charges will stick.'

'Well, I can't say as I hold with... you know what.' Jean's expression was prudish. 'Mr Brent was a real gentleman, though. He often gave me a guinea for myself when he came. I am sorry he's in trouble, because I liked him.'

'I like Jason too,' Rose said. 'But the way he is – homosexual – it's illegal in this country. I am not interested in anything like that personally, but I believe that everyone has the right to choose for themselves.'

'Women don't... together... do they?' Jean stared at her, astonished but obviously fascinated. She looked horrified as Rose nodded. 'Well, I never! I had no idea – I don't think I'd like anything like that, miss.'

'No, nor would I – but do we have the right to force our views on others?' Rose asked. 'There were a couple of girls like that in the first show I was with, but they kept themselves to themselves and didn't flaunt what they did. Poor Jason. He told me he couldn't face the idea of being in prison for years. He was going to leave the country, live abroad with his lover.'

'Maybe they will let him go.'

'I wish I could believe they would, but I don't think Jason will lie this time,' Rose said. 'The police have been after him for a while and now they have the evidence they need. He won't just be ruined; he will be put on trial and may serve years in prison. It seems so unfair. I just wish I knew who had done this to him.'

'He must have an enemy, miss.'

'Yes, perhaps.'

Rose went to stand just behind the curtains, gazing out at the reporters. There seemed to be a bit of a commotion going on. She caught her breath as she saw two people talking to the reporters and recognised them.

'Oh, no, why have they come?' She turned to Jean. 'You had better go to the door. Some friends of mine have just arrived. They really shouldn't have come; they will be in all the papers now. Goodness knows what Sarah has been telling the reporters...'

Jean went through to the hall and opened the front door. The photographers clicked busily, hoping for the elusive picture of Rose they had come to get, but were disappointed again.

'I thought they would never let us through,' Sarah complained as she entered the parlour and came to embrace Rose. 'I told them who I was and that you were my best friend. Let them do their worst. Troy told them to leave or he would get an injunction to make them. I think a couple went but the rest wouldn't budge.'

'Oh, Sarah,' Rose cried. 'It is wonderful to see you – but you know they will have your picture in all the papers, don't you?'

'Fame at last,' Sarah said and grinned at her. 'A couple of them recognised Troy and they started to ask him questions about various things, but nothing to do with you. He will give them a story that may satisfy them. He insisted on coming, Rose. I know he will do what he can to help you.'

'This doesn't bother me, at least not too much.' Rose glanced at Jean. 'Will you get us some tea, please, Jean?'

'Yes, of course, Miss Barlow.' The door closed behind her.

'Jean has been wonderful since this fuss began,' Rose said. 'I shan't let them drive me away. My rent is paid until the end of the month and I'm going to stick it out. It is Jason I am concerned about.'

'He was a loyal friend to you. Does he have a good lawyer? I am sure Troy could help in that department – though there isn't much else we can do for him.' Sarah looked at Rose. 'You know you are welcome to come to us, I hope? Nothing has changed as far as we are concerned. We love you and care about you, Rose.'

'I know.' Rose looked round as Troy joined them. He had stayed to talk to the reporters in his calm but authoritative manner. 'Thank you for coming with Sarah. I am glad she didn't have to face that alone.'

'I wouldn't have let her,' Troy said. 'I expected they would be here, Rose. Are you managing for everything?'

'Jean has been braving the fire for me. I am grateful to you for coming, Troy – but I'm afraid they may have taken photographs.'

'I posed for them,' Troy said. 'And I reminded them that I was a war hero.' He touched the scars on his cheek. 'Might as well make these count for something. I think you may find the tone of their reports has changed in the morning, Rose. I told them that you are the widow of a Canadian who fought for this country and who was killed doing his duty. I also said that you are secretly engaged and will shortly marry the father of your child.'

'Troy!' Rose stared at him. 'I know you meant well, but... it may not happen now.'

'I knew I was right,' Sarah said. 'If Luke doesn't come home and marry you now I'll have his guts for garters.'

'Aptly put.' Troy showed his appreciation. 'I am not sure your choice of words would meet with general approbation, my love – but we get your meaning.'

'Oh, Sarah,' Rose said sadly, 'your mother was far from approving of me as a wife for Luke before this happened. She will never allow us to marry now.'

'Mother may not be pleased but I do not think she has a choice in the matter. Luke is in love with you, Rose. I have known it for ages. He got himself entangled with that silly girl he was engaged to because Father wanted it, but he was so miserable. I am glad Amanda had the sense to break it off, because it would have been awful for them both.'

'Luke explained. He asked me to marry him before he took Marianne to New York for her operation.'

'You said yes, I hope?'

'I said I would think about it. My mother will not be pleased either, Lady Trenwith will be angry – and now, after all this stuff in the papers, it's hardly fair to Luke, is it?'

'As far as you are concerned, Rose, I think it's a storm in a teacup,' Troy said. 'I admit it is serious for Brent. I don't think anything will save him from a prison sentence.'

'He said that he didn't have the courage to have his day in court. He was going to leave the country and join his lover in France.'

'It is a pity the police didn't just let him go.' Troy looked disapproving. 'I will see if bail can be arranged, but personally I doubt it. The police have been after Brent for a while and now they have got him.'

'Are you sure you won't come home with us?' Sarah asked. She went to the window and looked out. 'Most of the reporters have gone. I can see a man in a raincoat standing at the other side of the square. I don't think he was with the reporters when we came in.'

Rose went to look. 'That is my shadow. He has been following me for weeks – since before Luke went to America.'

Troy glanced out and scowled. 'If my hunch is right that is your culprit for this wretched business. I think I shall have a word with him.'

He left the room abruptly and went out, walking across the square. The women watched from the window as the man in the raincoat took flight with Troy in pursuit. Troy managed to catch up with him when the man was forced to pause to allow a car to pass on the road. A fierce altercation took place, and then a long and involved conversation. Several minutes passed before Troy returned looking grim.

'You won't see him again,' he said with a snarl of satisfaction. 'He knows he is in trouble if he comes here even once more.'

'What did he say?' Sarah asked. 'Did he tell you who paid him to follow Rose?'

'He has been following Rose and Jason – and Luke for a while,' Troy said. 'He was paid to get all the dirt he could on Jason and on Rose. He couldn't find anything on Rose because he admitted that only two men visited here – Jason and Luke. He was rather luckier with Jason, but he had a head start, because the person who employed him pointed him in the right direction. She told him that Brent was a homosexual.'

'A woman – it was my mother! Don't deny it, Troy, I know it was her. She did this to stop Luke marrying Rose.' Hearing the little cry from Rose, she swung round. 'She is a wicked woman, Rose. You can't let her win. Luke won't allow it – and you mustn't either.'

'How can I marry him, knowing that his mother hates me so much?' Rose's face was ashen. 'She destroyed Jason's life in order to destroy me. How could she do that?'

'I don't know.' Sarah felt wretched herself. 'She was always cold and without emotion. She never loved any of us. You know the way she was, Rose – but since Father died she has got much worse. When I saw that report in the paper – no, even before then – I was sure she was up to something unpleasant. I could hardly believe she would go this far, but now I know it is true.'

'Yes, it was Lady Trenwith,' Troy admitted. 'I do not pretend to comprehend why she did such a thing, but apparently she has used that rogue's services in the past.'

'Jason has lost everything and it's my fault.'

'Of course it isn't,' Sarah retorted. 'It is *her* fault, Rose. My mother did this and I shall never speak to her again. She can rot in hell for all I care.'

'Oh, Sarah,' Rose said sadly, 'please do not say that... Please do not hate her because of me. I have caused enough trouble in your family as it is.'

'None of this is your fault,' Sarah insisted. 'Luke should have had the courage to marry you in the first place. He loves you and he should protect you from my mother's spite.'

'You mustn't tell him,' Rose begged. 'Please, Sarah – promise me you won't tell Luke what she did. He would hate her. I can't do that to him. I just can't.'

'Luke isn't stupid.' Troy had the last word. 'We shall not tell him, but I think you will find that it won't take him long to work this out for himself.'

Rose sat in silent reflection after her friends had gone. Sarah had tried hard to persuade her to go home with them, but Rose refused after thanking her for her support. In a way she was glad when they had gone, because she needed to think. It was bad enough that she had been smeared with filth by the newspapers, but the knowledge that Lady Trenwith hated her so much that she would destroy the lives of other people to bring her down was sickening. How could Rose marry Luke knowing what she did?

She knew he loved her. She was sure that he would marry her despite the scandal, because he loved her enough to ignore it – but if he did, it would end all his ties with his mother, and perhaps his elder sister too.

Did she have the right to expect him to give up so much for her sake? Rose felt the pain twist inside her and regretted that she had not given him his answer when he begged her to marry him. If she had done so they would be married by now and none of this would have happened – or did Lady Trenwith despise her so much that she would have done it anyway?

It was difficult to understand such vicious hatred. She had always found Lady Trenwith cold and harsh, but this vindictiveness had not been evident when Rose was a servant. Why had it come to the surface now? Had it always been there, waiting to raise its ugly head like the serpent in Eden?

Rose knew that she had to visit Jason at the police station. She had to tell him what had happened, why his life was in ruins – and then she would leave London, go away somewhere until this was all over.

She didn't know when Luke would return to England. She was sure that he would come looking for her when he did, which meant she couldn't go to Sarah or to her mother. She had to lose her identity, become someone else for a while, if that was possible.

Perhaps when this upset had blown over she would find Luke, but nothing would have changed. If she married him he would be forced to leave everything that was familiar and dear, because Lady Trenwith would never let go. She had brought Rose's world tumbling down – what more would she do if they defied her?

11

Luke stared at the telegram, which had just been delivered to his hotel suite. He read the cryptic message again and swore. What had his mother done now? He had no doubt that the trouble Troy described had something to do with his mother. He'd known from the beginning of their trip that Marianne was hiding something. She had known what was going on even before they left England.

He went through to the bedroom where she was recuperating from her operation. She lay with her eyes closed, her face still covered with bandages.

'I've had a telegram from Troy. I need to go home.'

'You can't leave me here alone, Luke.' Marianne's eyes registered alarm. 'You promised you would stay with me.'

'You've had the operation, everything is fine and Doctor Morris will come here to remove the bandages soon. He says you will hardly know you had a scar once the swelling goes down.'

'But I don't want to be alone.'

'Rose is in trouble. I think Mother has done something to harm her. She threatened once before that she would – and she took her chance while I was away.'

'It isn't my fault,' Marianne said. 'Please don't leave me, Luke. I can't stay here alone.'

'I'll telephone Barney at his hotel. You know he arrived in New York a few days ago.'

'Because you told him we were coming here,' Marianne accused. 'You knew I didn't want him near me. He doesn't love me.'

'Barney wouldn't be here if he didn't care. You've treated him worse than a dog, Marianne, but he still cares enough to follow you here. Now is your chance to make it up to him. If you want someone to look after you it has to be Barney, because I'm leaving as soon as I can get a berth back to England.'

'You don't care about me.' Marianne's tone was sulky.

'Should I care? You knew Mother intended something before we came. Don't even try to lie, because I know you. I am not blaming you, but you could have warned me. I am going home whatever you say. Barney is here. I shall tell him to move into my room so that he can take care of you.'

'I don't want him.'

'Do you want to end up bitter and alone like Mother?' Luke gave her a straight look.

Marianne's eyes fixed on him and he saw the fear. 'No, I don't want to be like her. I didn't know what she planned, Luke – only that she hates Rose. I couldn't tell you, because you wouldn't have come with me.'

'I would have sorted her out before we left. I'm not blaming you. She threatened to ruin Rose if I told Father I loved her and was going to marry her. I let her bully me that time, but never again. I have to repair the damage she has done and make sure she can't do any more.'

'Barney won't come,' Marianne said, and she plucked at the bedcovers. 'He doesn't love me now.'

'If he didn't, you would have only yourself to blame, but I am certain he does. He may be sick of being treated like a dog, but he cares. Make the most of this chance, Marianne. Be a bit more loving and appreciative – and then I think you will find that things will improve between you and Barney.'

'I had an affair...'

'Forget it and move on,' Luke advised. 'Don't rub his nose in it, Marianne. Tell him you miss him and you want to start again – and mean it this time!'

'I do,' she said in a small voice. 'Barney loved me. I don't want to end up unloved and like Mother...' She shivered. 'She was so vicious, Luke. I'm not like that – truly I'm not.'

'Now you're being sensible.' Luke looked approving. 'I'm going to make a couple of calls. I think you will find that Barney will be here within minutes.'

Marianne smiled. 'What will you do to Mother?'

'She has done it all to herself. She can stay in that mausoleum if she chooses, but I shall not visit her after the way she has behaved. When she finally has the sense to move into the dower house I shall pull a part of the old building down and turn the rest into a hotel.'

Marianne looked at him in awe. 'Are you going to tell her that – about the hotel?'

'That and a lot more,' Luke said. 'I am going to turn the estate into a cooperative with shares for all the workers. The Trenwith family will retain the largest block of shares and we'll have the casting vote – you, Sarah and me – but everyone who works for us will receive a share of the profits. That means I'll be opening all the gardens to visitors and the stables will become a gift shop and café. I have other ideas for attractions – perhaps a miniature train to take visitors round the estate. Trenwith has to be a business to survive in the future and that is just what it will be.'

'My God, you do mean to punish.' Marianne looked at him in awe. 'I think I'll stay here for a bit longer, until the dust settles.'

'You must do just as you like but I imagine you will enjoy New York society once the swelling goes down and you are a flawless beauty again. Why waste the trip of a lifetime?'

'I should look even better,' she said and gave a little giggle. 'The surgeon took a couple of little lines from the corners of my eyes.'

'I am certain Barney will fall in love with you all over again if you are decent to him. You are very lucky to have another chance, Marianne – don't waste it.'

'I shan't,' she said. 'I was angry when Barney followed us because I knew you had sent him a telegram – but thank you. I've been such a fool, Luke. I didn't realise what I had until I almost lost it.'

'Most of us don't.' Luke smiled ruefully. 'I've been in love with Rose since before the war. When she married I thought I had lost her for good, but then I had another chance and I let her slip through my fingers. I'm going home to find her, Marianne – and when I do I'll spend the rest of my life making her happy, because that is the only way I can be happy.'

'She is lucky – and we shall always be pleased to see you, Luke. I know I've been a snob where Rose is concerned. Sarah is so much better than me, which is why Troy loves her.'

'Were you ever in love with him? Or do you regret losing him simply because he turned to Sarah?'

'I'm not sure,' Marianne admitted. 'I suspect it was mostly hurt pride, and that was a part of the reason I was so awful to Barney – but I've learned my lesson. I'll find a way to make Barney love me again.'

Luke smiled, went out into the sitting-room and lifted the phone.

* * *

'I thought she might be here.' Luke ran his fingers through his thick blond hair. 'I went to her flat first but it has a "to let" sign in the window. The agent told me she moved out soon after the story broke.'

'We went to see her there,' Sarah told him. 'Troy came with me when all the press photographers were waiting outside. Troy talked to them and most of them left. He told them about Rose's husband being killed in the war and some of them did a more sympathetic piece the next morning. A few reported it when she visited Jason in prison a few days later, but since then I haven't seen anything at all.' She frowned. 'I think they were shocked when Jason Brent hanged himself in his cell a few days before he was due to go on trial.'

'Yes, I saw that in my newspaper when I got back,' Luke said. 'Poor devil! It was all so unnecessary.' His face darkened with anger. 'Why did Mother do it, Sarah? I know she hated the idea of my marrying Rose – but to destroy someone's life like that...'

'Rose didn't want you to know it was Mother who paid for the investigation that started it all. Troy didn't tell you?'

'No, of course not; I didn't need anyone to tell me. I am well aware what a viper she is these days. I don't understand her.'

'I've been thinking a lot about it. I believe she has lost everything her life stood for. She and Father were brought up to a life of duty and respect, Luke. She married because it was the proper thing to do, the wish of her family. She did everything she could to support Father – she was even more concerned about preserving standards than he was in the end. Now it has all gone. Her life ended when he died, and I think she may have realised how empty it all was.'

'She didn't love us, Sarah. She didn't love Father and she didn't love us – so what was it all about?'

'I think perhaps she has just realised it was all a sham,' Sarah told him. 'Money, property, the old traditions – they mean nothing without love. You know it and I know it. I'm not sure how Marianne feels, but I don't think she cares much for tradition, though she likes nice things, and they cost money.'

'I think she is beginning to realise that she has been wrong as far as Barney is concerned,' Luke said. 'I believe you may see a difference in her when they come back – though it wouldn't surprise me if they stayed in New York for some months.'

'What are you going to do about Rose? Isn't she with her mother?' Sarah looked anxious.

'I came here first,' Luke said. 'I wasn't sure Rose would go to her mother in the circumstances. She is proud and she wouldn't want to bring trouble on her family.'

'Surely they would understand?' Sarah said. 'Rose hasn't done anything wrong. She had a baby but no husband – what is so terrible about that? I know some people will look down on her, but she isn't the only one it has happened to.'

'Even that was my fault.' Luke looked anxious. 'I have to find her, Sarah. She hasn't written to you?'

'No, because she would know that I would tell you where to find her. I am sure she would tell her mother where she is though, because I suspect Mrs Barlow wouldn't tell you if she knew.'

'I'm going to see her when I leave here tomorrow.' Luke smiled grimly. 'I know Mrs Barlow doesn't trust me, but I hope to convince her that I am going to marry Rose.'

'If she will have you. She has taken it into her head that she would ruin your life and I'm sure that is why she has run away.'

'She ought to know that the only thing that can ruin my life is if I never find her – but that isn't going to happen. I don't care how long it takes, I shall find her, Sarah. I have to!'

'Troy says we'll give you the wedding here. He was really angry when he discovered the reason for all the trouble.'

'Thank Troy for all he has done,' Luke said, 'but I have other ideas.'

* * *

'Rose wrote to tell me not to worry,' Mrs Barlow told Luke two days later. 'She did not give me an address, but even if she had I would not give it to you.'

'Please believe me when I tell you that I have only Rose's happiness in mind,' Luke said. 'I asked Rose to be my wife before I took my sister to New York. She promised to think about it, and I believe that she intended to say yes when I returned. She would have married me if all this unpleasant business had not happened.'

'It was rather more than unpleasant. Someone set out to ruin Mr Brent and to bring my Rose down. Now who do you think that might be, sir? I have my suspicions and I don't like them very much.'

'Nor do I,' Luke told her. 'I intend to discover and to punish the person who did this, Mrs Barlow. Believe me, I am as angry as you are over this wicked spite. Rose must be so hurt and humiliated – and that hurts me.'

'I should think she is more upset for that poor man than for herself. I'm not saying as I hold with them sorts of goings on – but Mr Brent was good to Rose, and she was grateful. She liked him right or wrong and now he's dead, and that's a bad business in my book.'

'Yes, it is,' Luke agreed. 'I wish I could change what happened, but there's no point in looking back, is there? I want to marry Rose. I shall take her away for a few months at least. We'll travel and forget all that has happened and perhaps then we shall come back. It will be for Rose to choose.'

'Tell him what you know,' Myrtle said. 'The poor man is desperate to find her and she'll be glad to see him. It is all nonsense, hiding away because she doesn't want to ruin his life. He can't live without her and that's the truth of it.'

'Rose didn't give me her address, but I think she is in London.' Mrs Barlow handed him an envelope. 'It is the same postmark as used to be on her letters when she was living there during the war.'

'Do you think she could be staying with her old landlady?' Luke felt a rush of excitement. 'I thought she might have gone away somewhere she isn't known.'

'Rose Barlow the famous singer would be known anywhere,' Myrtle said. 'Mrs Rose Carne wearing the kind of clothes suited to her station might not be noticed in a crowd.'

'Thank you. Thank you so much!' Luke seized Myrtle and kissed her. 'You will both come to the wedding, won't you?'

'Yes, of course we shall be there.' Myrtle turned to her cousin. 'And she will come too – won't you, Lizzie?'

Mrs Barlow looked at her in annoyance and then nodded. 'If it is what Rose wants then I shan't go against her – but if you hurt my girl again I'll make you wish you had never been born!'

'I give you my word I shall never hurt Rose intentionally. I can't promise we shan't have words, because everyone does – but I love her more than my own life.'

'Then I daresay you will find her at Mrs Hall's. I've got the address somewhere...'

'I remember it. I went to tell Rose about Jack being missing during the war – do you remember?'

'Yes, I do. It was good of you.' Mrs Barlow smiled. 'You'd best get off then, for there's no telling how long she will stay there.'

* * *

'Any luck?' Mrs Hall asked as Rose walked into the kitchen. 'Your little angel has been as good as gold. It is nice to have a little one to take care of again.'

'It is only until I can find work and somewhere to live,' Rose told her. 'It was good of you to take me in just like that, Mrs Hall. Jean has gone home for a few weeks. I told her she was free to find another job but she says she wants to come back once I've sorted myself out.'

'Well, you're welcome to stay as long as you like,' Mrs Hall said. 'I don't know why you don't try for another job on the stage. The papers weren't that hard on you, lass – some of them even said there wasn't anyone to replace you in the West End at the moment.'

'I couldn't – not after what happened to Jason.' Rose shivered. 'If she could do that to someone she didn't even know, think what else she might do if she thought I was defying her. Besides, Luke would find me and I don't want that. He can't marry me after what has happened. It would mean a breach with his mother and his elder sister.'

'I shouldn't think he would want anything to do with his mother after what she did,' Mrs Hall said. 'If his sister is anything like Miss Sarah, she won't want much to do with her mother either.'

'Marianne isn't like Sarah. Anyway, it's the scandal... Luke shouldn't marry me now for his own sake. His friends might cut him and they certainly wouldn't accept me.'

'That is nonsense, my girl. His real friends will stand by him. Some will look down their noses because you used to be in service, but that was a long time ago and things have changed. People are so glad to get a maid now that they nearly lick their backsides...' Mrs Hall gave a cackle of laughter as she saw Rose's face. 'Well, it's true, lass.'

'Not Lady Trenwith. Believe me, nothing will change her.'

'Well, she'll find herself having to change afore long, you mark my words. She will get her comeuppance one of these days.'

* * *

'I think she is going bonkers.' Emily sank down into a chair in the kitchen. 'She keeps giving me orders then changing her mind.'

'What did she ask for then?'

'She told me to make up the fire and then she asked why I'd put another log on when it was too hot already – then she told me to serve tea with the best silver because Sir James was going to take tea with her in the library.'

'She never did!' Mrs Jarvis looked at her in concern.

'I heard her talking to him yesterday. She was telling him the gardeners had been neglecting their work again – and she called me Barlow twice this morning.'

'Does she think Rose is working for her again?' Mrs Jarvis frowned. 'It sounds as if she is losing her mind – but she is sharp enough with the accounts. She questioned me for an hour yesterday over the butcher's bills. She wants all the best cuts and then she grumbles because the bill is high. I'm blowed if I know what she wants these days.'

'I reckon it's being here all on her own,' Emily said. 'It was all right when Mrs Hale and Mr Luke were living here – but she gives me the creeps. If she carries on like this I shall give in my notice.'

'Don't do that, Emily love,' Mrs Jarvis begged. 'It was hard enough to get servants before but now it's impossible. I've put three adverts in *The Lady* but nothing came of it – and Maisie was saying her niece wouldn't come here if she were paid a fortune.'

'Some hope of that,' Emily said. 'I shan't leave until I see the way things go – though I should have been off like a shot if Rose had given me a chance. Ma says it's a good thing she didn't ask me to go up to London. She went off after all that business and Aunt Lizzie doesn't know where she is.'

'Well, I'm not surprised after what happened; terrible business that was and a great shame for your Rose. I daresay she will get another job, mind you – you can't keep someone like Rose Barlow down, whatever you do.'

'Well, I would still work for her whatever anyone says.' Emily grinned. 'It would be better than working here for that daft old bat upstairs.'

* * *

'See who that is, will you, love?' Mrs Hall asked as there was a knock at the front door. 'I've got me slippers off and I can't answer the door like this.'

'Yes, of course.' Rose got up and went through the hall. They did not often have visitors, but it was probably Milly from next door come to borrow a bit of butter or a cup of sugar. She unlocked the door and opened it, staring in shock as she saw who was standing there. 'Luke,' she said at last, her mouth dry. 'How did you find me?'

'Persistence and guesswork. Myrtle took pity on me and told me you might be in London. She bullied your mother into telling me she thought you might have come here.'

'She shouldn't have told you.' Rose's heart was beating like a drum. 'After what happened, Luke – it is all over between us. It has to be. You can't marry me now, it would ruin you.'

'I don't see why. I am sorry the show folded and very sorry for what happened to Brent – but it hasn't stopped me loving you or wanting you to be my wife.'

'Oh, Luke...' Rose said helplessly and stepped back into the hall. Luke took that as an invitation and followed her inside. 'You know this can't work.'

'It can if we want it to.' Luke reached for her. He pulled Rose close, bent his head and kissed her, feeling the way she melted into his body, sensing her capitulation as the kiss deepened. Their mutual hunger was such that neither of them noticed when Mrs Hall came to look, smiled, and then went back to the kitchen. 'I love you, Rose Barlow. You are my whole life. Nothing else matters, you must believe me.'

'But your mother...'

'Deserves no consideration from us,' Luke said, and the smile left his eyes. 'She blackmailed me once before by saying that she would ruin you if I asked you to marry me. I don't know how much she knew but I'm pretty sure she had me followed and discovered that I had visited you and Elspeth. She persuaded Marianne to get me to take her to America – and then she struck. She will pay the price for that, Rose. She took everything from you and now I shall take everything from her.'

'No! No, I won't have that, Luke.' Rose lifted her clear gaze to meet his. 'I don't want you to take revenge on her. She is your mother. I know what she did, and I know she hates me, but it makes no difference. I love you and we can go away somewhere. If you punish her it will come between us.'

'She doesn't deserve mercy, Rose.'

'Please, Luke, don't do anything cruel. If we do something to make her unhappy we are lowering ourselves to her level. I just want to be married quietly and go away together.'

'We could make her give us a big reception at Trenwith.' Rose shook her head. 'Sarah wants us to be married from Pelham,' Luke continued.

'I should like a quiet wedding. My mother will give us a reception at the hotel. We can ask Sarah and a few friends, but I would rather it was just a quiet wedding... Please, Luke?'

'Yes, of course. I always knew you were too good for me, Rose.' Luke reached out and touched her face. 'I am sorry I wasn't here when you needed me, my love. I promise I shall never leave you alone again while we both live.'

'Sarah and Troy stood by me. So did Jean. I shall let her know that she can come back now. Myrtle will find a room for her somehow.'

'Myrtle is quite a determined lady,' Luke said. 'I am going to take you to your mother and Myrtle and then I shall go to Trenwith. I won't turn Mother out – but I must speak to her, Rose. She thinks she has got away with this and I intend to tell her that she is mistaken. I did my duty for too long, but in future I intend to do what I think is right.'

* * *

'She is such a little darling,' Myrtle said as she nursed Elspeth on her lap. 'That man of yours will spoil her rotten. Have you seen the rocking horse he's had sent down from London? What does a little mite like Elspeth want with something like that?'

Rose laughed. 'Luke can't help buying things for her – and for me. Elspeth will grow into it, but I'm sorry if it is in your way. I don't know what we are going to do with half the stuff he has been ordering. I think it will have to go into storage while we are away. I know he is thinking of buying a house, but that won't be for ages yet.'

'You can store a few bits in your room when you leave,' Myrtle said. 'I daresay he has something in mind – though you won't want to live at Trenwith?'

'No.' Rose gave a little shudder. 'My cousin Emily told me it was like a mausoleum there now – empty and half the rooms shut.'

'It sounds as if it ought to be pulled down and a new modern place built,' Myrtle said. 'No one wants them big old houses these days. Half of them will be left to rot in the next few years. You see if I'm not right.'

'Luke says that he is going to pull the oldest wing down one day and then turn the main house into a luxury hotel and open it for conferences and things. In the meantime he is opening the gardens to the public and having the stables turned into a café and a gift shop.'

'Is that why he went back for a few days?'

'I expect it was a part of it. He has agents and managers to do all the work these days. Luke doesn't want to be tied to Trenwith the way his father was the whole of his life. He says Trenwith has claimed all the sacrifices it is going to get – he calls it a monster.'

'Sounds as if he hates the place?'

'I don't think so – he just hates the memories.' Rose looked thoughtful. A shiver went down her spine. 'He hasn't telephoned yet today. I hope everything is all right.'

'Why shouldn't it be? He is a grown man, Rose, love. He can take care of himself.'

'Yes, of course.' She hadn't told her mother or Myrtle that it was Lady Trenwith who had started the investigation that led to the show closing and then Jason's death. Her mother might have guessed but they hadn't talked about it. Mrs Barlow hadn't said a lot at all, but she had agreed to give them a wedding and she seemed happy enough to make plans for the reception. 'I shall just be glad when Luke is back here with me.'

* * *

'Your father would turn in his grave.' Lady Trenwith gave her son a look of dislike. 'I do not know how you could forget your promises to him so soon after his death.'

'Father told me not to waste my life,' Luke replied coldly. 'I told him what I planned for the café and the shop and he asked me to wait until he was dead. Enough time has passed and I want to put my plans into action before I take Rose abroad.'

Lady Trenwith's eyes shot daggers, but they passed harmlessly over his head. 'I know I cannot command your duty. You care nothing for the mother who gave you life.'

'There was a time when I cared for you. You lost all right to my respect when you behaved so despicably, Mother. If you loved me you would accept that Rose is the woman I love.'

'I shall never receive her!'

'I could force you to give a reception here if I wished, but Rose begged me not to. I shall not tell you to leave, Mother. You may stay here until you decide to retire to the dower house.'

'And then I suppose you will tear this house down? You have destroyed everything your father and I stood for.'

'Things had begun to change even before the war,' Luke told her, 'but the war accelerated the change. And you played your part. You cannot treat servants as if they were dirt beneath your feet and expect them to stay. This is the twentieth century and the world has moved on – life is going to be very different. It would be madness to cling to the past. Father wanted the estate to go on – the family to continue. I promised him it will but in a new way. I am going to tear down the oldest wing and turn the main part of the house into a modern hotel. I shall wait for another year or two, because I am going to travel and give myself time to paint, but when I return I shall expect you to move into the dower house.'

'Damn you! You think you have won, but I shall have my chance yet. You wait and see.'

Luke watched as she walked away. He had promised Rose he wouldn't take his revenge and he had given his mother time to get used to the idea – but he had made up his mind. The estate was paying at last but it would pay far more once all his changes had been implemented. The café and shop were far enough from the house not to interfere with his mother's way of life, but she would just have to get used to people walking round the gardens.

He smiled grimly as he went back to his room and collected the possessions he really wanted. He was taking the things his father had given him, everything of sentimental value that remained here. The house contained many treasures, some of which would be sold when the time came. His father had never bothered to insure them, but Luke had taken out a policy to cover their loss. With the house being run by a mere handful of servants these days anything could happen.

As he carried the last of his bags downstairs, one of the maids came up to him. He recognised her as she bobbed her head to him.

'No need for that, Emily. I don't hold with the old ways, you know that,' he said and smiled. 'Did Rose send you an invitation to the wedding?'

'Yes, sir, I shall be there. I should like to work for Rose but she says she has a nurse for Elspeth.'

'Well, I daresay we could manage two. Give your notice in and come to us when you attend the wedding. I expect Lady Trenwith can find someone to take your place.'

'Yes, sir, I suppose so. Thank you, sir.'

Luke nodded, but didn't notice her hesitation. He was in too much of a hurry to get out. As he left, he did not look back at the upper windows. He might have been shocked if he had seen the hatred in the face that looked down at him, but he was whistling as he got into the car and drove away.

* * *

'You look lovely,' Mrs Barlow cried as she saw her daughter in her simple white dress and wide-brimmed straw hat. Her shoes, gloves and tiny bag were all in the palest pink to match the silk roses under the brim of her hat. She wore a string of beautiful pink pearls that Luke had given her as a wedding gift with matching earrings that she and Myrtle had bought between them.

'I never thought I would see this day, Rose – you marrying Luke Trenwith.'

'I have to admit that I didn't either.' Rose hugged her mother. 'Be happy for me, Mum.'

'Be careful or you will crease your dress,' Mrs Barlow said. 'Of course I'm happy for you, love. Luke loves you and that's the important thing. It didn't seem right to me to begin with, but now that I've got to know him better I know he is the man for you – and you will make him happy. I think he deserves that, Rose.'

'Yes, he does,' Rose said and smiled a little sadly. 'You were strict with Jack and me, but you loved us – and so did Dad. We might have lived in a cottage, but we were luckier than Luke.'

Mrs Barlow smothered a sigh. 'It is a pity our Jack isn't here to see this day, Rose.'

'It is the one thing lacking to make it perfect,' Rose said. 'I've never really given up on him, Mum – but I know in my heart he must be dead or he would come home.'

'The money I was keeping in case he came back is yours now, Rose. Not that you will need it! You'll be spoiled rotten before you know it.'

'You keep it a bit longer. As you said, I don't need it. I've always kept the money Jack left me – just in case…'

'We're a proper pair, talking like this on your wedding day!' Mrs Barlow shook her head. 'The cars will be here any minute. You'd best finish getting ready and come downstairs.'

'Yes, Mum.' Rose heard the telephone shrilling downstairs but it was answered immediately. 'You go and I'll be down in five minutes.'

* * *

The wedding took place in church. It was a simple ceremony, attended only by a handful of family and friends. Sarah and Troy were there and Jean with Elspeth in her arms, as well as Emily Redfern, who was going to help Jean look after the child. Mrs Barlow and Myrtle were there of course, as well as two friends of Luke's from his days in the RFC, one of whom was his best man. Luke introduced him afterwards as Tony Banks. Mrs Hall had sent a telegram, which was opened at the reception, but no one else had been invited, because Barney and Marianne were still in New York.

'It wasn't much of a wedding for you, darling,' Luke said after they had cut the cake and toasted their friends and themselves. 'I should have held it at Trenwith and invited everyone from the estate. I've got a few relatives somewhere.'

'It was best this way.' Rose kissed him. 'The men you think of as friends were there and my family.' She sighed. 'I wish my father and Jack could have been here but I don't mind about anyone else.'

'Yes... I'm sorry they weren't,' Luke said, an odd expression in his eyes. 'I suppose we had better start thinking about leaving for our hotel. Jean and Emily will take Elspeth on ahead and we'll see them in the morning before we go to the airport.'

'Yes, I ought to change into something more suited to travelling.' Rose broke off as her mother came towards them. Her manner told Rose that something was wrong. 'What is it, Mum? Are you feeling ill? You look as white as a ghost.'

'I'm afraid I've got some bad news.' Mrs Barlow looked at Luke. 'The call came just before we left for the ceremony, but Myrtle didn't tell me until a moment ago. She didn't want to spoil your wedding, Rose – but you have to know.'

'Please tell us,' Luke said. 'Is it something my mother has done?'

'In a way, yes, I suppose it is. They aren't sure whether she did it on purpose – or whether it was an accident.' She paused, then continued. 'It appears that she was taken ill after you left, Luke –

wandering in her mind, Mrs Jarvis said. Last night she lit a candle and went into the old wing. There were only two servants still living in – Mrs Jarvis and her husband. He woke and smelled the smoke. He sent Mrs Jarvis out of the house and then he went to rouse Lady Trenwith, but she wasn't in her room. The old wing was already blazing and he couldn't get in. By the time the fire engines arrived and got the blaze under control it was too late. Nothing could be done. I am very sorry, Luke. Your mother died in the fire.'

'Oh, my God!' Luke clenched his fists at his side. 'She said she would have her revenge on me.'

'You think she did it on purpose?'

'Yes, I do.' Luke looked grim. 'We had another argument when I went home. I told her that she could stay at the house for a year or two, and I said I was going to pull the old wing down and refurbish the main house as a hotel. She said I would be sorry...'

'She couldn't have intended to set the house on fire, she loved it,' Rose said gently. 'She wouldn't have done it to spite you, Luke. Emily told me that she had been wandering in her mind for a while. She must have got worse. She probably took the candle with her and went looking for something or someone.'

'I daresay she was looking for the past,' Mrs Barlow said. 'She was troubled in her mind and lonely, I shouldn't wonder. Things have gone badly since the war started. Your sister is in her room getting ready to leave. Do you want to tell her yourself?'

'Yes, I must.' Luke hesitated. 'I'm sorry, Rose. I think we shall have to go to Trenwith before we leave for France – just until the funeral. There will be things to sort out that only I can do.'

'Yes, I know. I understand how you feel. I am so sorry, Luke – so very sorry.'

'I'm just glad Myrtle had the sense not to tell us until after the reception,' Luke said, and his eyes were unsmiling. 'I wouldn't put it past her to have done this in an effort to prevent the wedding.'

* * *

'Mother wouldn't have set fire to the house deliberately,' Sarah said as Luke related the story to her. 'I know what she did to Rose and I told her that I should never forgive her. She said that it did not matter because she had never forgiven me for letting the family down. She said that she only allowed me to visit Trenwith because my father asked it of her.'

'She was such a cold bitch. You think it was an accident – but I shall always think she did this on purpose. She wanted to cast a shadow over my marriage to Rose – and she has succeeded.'

'Only if you let her.' Sarah laid a hand on his arm. 'She can't win unless you let her, Luke. I don't know how bad the damage is to the house. Are you insured?'

'Yes, though I don't know if they will cover it if she did it deliberately.'

'It was an accident, Luke. Mother had had a little bit of a turn, as the doctors say. Emily says she wasn't well. She didn't know what she was doing.' Sarah frowned. 'What will you do if they refuse to pay out?'

'Pull the old wing down and save what I can. There were some valuable things in that wing. I had given orders for it to be closed and I was sending some of them to be sold.'

'Wait and see how bad it is. We shall go to Trenwith from here. If Troy can do anything for you he will.'

'Thank you. I suppose I must attend the funeral, even though I don't feel as if I want to – and I'll see what can be saved. That is all I can do.'

Rose glanced at Luke as they were driven the last few miles towards Trenwith. He had been silent for much of the time, though every now and then he made the effort to talk naturally. She understood the conflicting emotions that were going on inside him and touched his arm.

'You mustn't blame yourself for any of this, Luke. Your mother quarrelled with everyone – Marianne, Sarah and anyone else who disagreed with her.'

'I blame her,' Luke said, and his mouth was hard. 'She did this on purpose. Oh, I shall let it be thought an accident because that is best all round, but in my heart I know it was her last act of defiance. I had set changes in hand that she disapproved of and this was her way of showing me that she could still control the future.'

'You mustn't be bitter, whatever happens. We still have each other.'

'Yes, of course.' Luke leaned towards her, kissing her on the lips. 'I wish I had married you years ago,' he said. 'I can't say I am looking forward to seeing Trenwith as it is, even though Mrs Jarvis says that there is only some smoke damage in the main building – but I didn't intend for us to live there. We shall live abroad for a time, and when we do want to settle in this country we can choose a house somewhere.'

'We can think about it when you're ready. I wouldn't have wanted to live in Trenwith as it was – but the dower house is rather nice. I used to think it was a lovely place when I cleaned it sometimes.'

'Yes, it is a far more sensible size. I told Mother she would be more comfortable there but she insisted on staying in the house. If you are happy to stay at the dower house until after the funeral, that's what we'll do. I think Troy and Sarah will probably stay with some friends. Sarah said Troy was telephoning them to make arrangements.'

'I should imagine the house will stink of smoke for quite a while – and it may need to be made safe.'

'We shall know in a minute,' Luke said as they turned through the gates of the estate.

Rose felt the tension in him as the car drove towards the main house. She heard his gasp as they saw the blackened shell of the old wing. The roof had gone and the windows were open, the glass cracked or smashed by firemen trying to control the flames; the walls were black and dripping with water. A thin column of smoke still hung over the wing. In contrast, the main building still had its roof, though there was some smoke damage to the walls that had adjoined the old wing, and a couple of windows had gone.

Rose felt heartsick as the car swept by, taking them to the dower house at the far side of the estate. She glanced at Luke, seeing the nerve flicking at his temple and the way his hands had clenched. She wasn't sure if it was from anger or sorrow.

'You may be able to rescue most of the house,' she said, and he nodded, but the grim look remained on his face.

When the car came to a halt outside the dower house, the door opened. Mrs Jarvis stood there ready to welcome them.

'Welcome back, Sir Luke – Lady Trenwith. I am sorry it is such a poor homecoming, sir. Jarvis can tell you what the damage is. He walked up this morning. He and some of the other men have put the valuable things that remain into storage for safety.'

'Thank you, Mrs Jarvis,' Luke said, and he gave her a brief smile. 'I believe I owe it to Jarvis that the damage to the house was no worse.'

'He alerted the fire brigade. A lot of men from the estate got there first. They had started to douse the flames by the time the engines arrived, but the fire had got a hold.'

'Yes, I know you all worked very hard to save what you could.' Luke smiled properly this time. 'Tell Jarvis I shall want to take a look in the morning – for now, well, this is my wedding day...' He turned to Rose and then swept her up in his arms. 'This is one tradition I don't intend to neglect.'

Rose laughed, looking shyly at Mrs Jarvis, but all she saw in the older woman's eyes was approval. She clung to Luke as he carried her over the threshold and then kissed her as he set her down.

'I prepared the best rooms for you, sir,' Mrs Jarvis said, looking on with a smile. 'And there's a cold supper waiting for you upstairs. Jarvis and I have moved into one of the cottages you had done up, sir. I shall be here at half past seven in the morning. If there is nothing else you need, I shall leave the house to you and her ladyship.'

'Please,' Rose begged, 'I'm Rose – or madam if you prefer. I would rather not be called her ladyship or Lady Trenwith.'

'No, madam, I understand. We were all shocked and upset over what happened to Lady Trenwith – but it was a mercy there were only the three of us in the house.'

'Yes, it was,' Luke agreed. 'I know you did all you could. Had I realised my mother's mind was wandering I would have had a nurse in to care for her, but I didn't understand how bad things had got here.'

'I think when her ladyship's maid upped and left with only a day's notice it was the last straw,' Mrs Jarvis told him. 'Emily had gone a few days earlier and that made the situation almost impossible in a house of that size. I did what I could for her, but I couldn't manage everything – and Maisie wouldn't live in or tend her ladyship.'

'No one is blaming you or Jarvis. I should have forced Lady Trenwith to come here and closed the house. I knew the position was becoming untenable, but I allowed her to have her way.'

'Your nursemaids are here now,' Mrs Jarvis said as a second car pulled up in the courtyard. 'I'll just take a peep at the child and then I'll go.'

Rose looked at Luke as Mrs Jarvis went out. 'I don't know about you,' she said, 'but I could do with a cup of tea. I'll put the kettle on and we'll all have one before we go up.'

* * *

'Luke, come to bed,' Rose called softly. She had woken to see him standing at the window. 'It is too early to get up yet.'

Luke turned and then came back to her. He looked down at her in the light of the moon, which had filtered in through a gap in the curtains.

'The moon woke me. I've never been able to sleep if moonlight gets into the bedroom. I was trying to close the gap but I couldn't shut it out completely. I think the curtains must have shrunk at some time.'

'By the look of them they have been washed a lot,' Rose said. 'I think the house could do with some refurbishment if you want to live here.'

'I hadn't planned on it.' Luke reached out to stroke her neck beneath her hair, which tumbled loose over her shoulders. 'You are so beautiful,' he said huskily. 'It was all right for you tonight?'

'Of course, more than all right – perfect,' Rose said, and she held out her hand to him. He sat down on the edge of the bed and took it, his fingers closing over hers. 'I love you, Luke. I think I always loved you, even when I didn't know how you felt.'

'I wanted tonight to be perfect. The hotel had promised us the bridal suite and all the trimmings – and we end up here.' He pulled a wry face. 'Mrs Jarvis did her best, but it wasn't what I planned.'

'You made up for it.' Rose reached up to draw his head towards her so that they could kiss. 'I am happy, Luke. Believe me, I don't mind all this. I know you can't just go off to France with me until you've sorted this mess out.'

'I'll know more in the morning,' Luke said. 'Once we've had the funeral I shall be glad to leave the detail to others. I was hoping to sell some of the pictures from the old wing. If they are damaged beyond repair I may have to sell something else, but it doesn't matter.'

'Perhaps the insurance will pay out. Anyway, there's no sense in worrying until you know the worst. Come back to bed, Luke – this is our wedding night.'

'Yes, I know – that is why I am so upset. It may be a temporary annoyance, but it is a victory for her.'

'No, it isn't – not if we don't let it be,' Rose said, and she threw back the covers, inviting him to join her. She was naked, her night-dress having been discarded at the beginning of the evening. 'Make love to me, Luke. We can be happy together wherever we are. We love each other and no one can take that away from us.'

'You're always so sensible,' Luke said, and he lay down beside her, gathering her close. He stroked the silken arch of her back, his breath coming faster as his desire rose again. 'I love you so very much, my darling.'

'I know. I love you too.' She pressed herself closer. 'Think about us, Luke. Forget the past and make love to me...'

Luke kissed her, his tongue invading her sweetness. As he felt the way she moulded herself to him, her body seeming to become a part of him, he smiled and let go of the bitterness that had been lingering in his mind. Rose was right, as always. They had each other and their child; the rest did not matter.

* * *

The next morning Luke walked back to the dower house. Some of the paintings had been removed from the old wing prior to the fire and were in storage waiting to be sent to the saleroom; others had been lost. Most of the furniture too was either damaged by the smoke or burned. However, apart from some water damage, the main building was sound. Once the old wing had been pulled down and the ground restored, Luke reflected, the main building could be refurbished just as he'd planned. In all, the fire had probably cost something in the region of £10,000. It was a large sum, and after his first call to the insurance company, he doubted that he would recover more than a small part of the money. Despite this, he could probably manage to go ahead with his ideas, though it might mean selling some property elsewhere.

Luke wondered if he might do better to sell the estate and buy something smaller and more manageable. Yet, after the way his staff had behaved during the fire, he would feel he was letting them down. It looked as if he might be stuck with his duty towards Trenwith after all. He wouldn't need to be here all the time, and he still planned to take a few months abroad – but even if he and Rose decided to live elsewhere, the estate would require his attention from time to time.

Suddenly, he saw the funny side of things. He had struggled against the ties of duty for so long when they were imposed on him, but now that he was free to do as he pleased, his own feelings would not allow him to abandon those ties.

Seeing Rose in the garden, he quickened his step. Nothing else really mattered except the way they felt about each other. He tried to put his last remaining worry to the back of his mind. It was time he told Rose about her brother, although he had waited this long already; he would wait a bit longer, until the funeral was over and they were on their way to France.

12

'Are you sure you are ready to leave Trenwith?' Rose asked as Luke came back after a last-minute meeting with his agents. 'If you need to be here for a bit longer I can wait. I've been helping Mrs Jarvis sort out new curtains for the dower house. There were some in the storerooms at the main house. They smelled of smoke but after they were washed and hung out to dry the smell disappeared. You won't get moonlight in the room next time we sleep here.'

'You've been wonderful. You haven't complained once all the time I've been having meetings with builders and the insurance people.'

'Have they decided to pay out?'

'They say we may get help with pulling down the old wing and something towards the contents – but they are disputing the amount and I think we'll be lucky to get half.'

'They are happy enough to take the money when you insure with them but they don't like paying out.' Rose shook her head at him. 'It doesn't matter, Luke. You said we could manage.'

'Yes, we can,' he agreed. 'I shall be pleased whatever we get.'

'Then why do you look as if you have lost half a crown and found sixpence?'

Luke smiled as she put her arms about his waist. 'I'm not worried about the house or the money. I've got something else on my mind.'

'What?' Rose's gaze narrowed. 'Is it something I won't like?'

'You might be angry with me. It is something I should have told you a long time ago. I need to tell you now, Rose. I was going to tell you once we were married, and then I thought I would wait until after Mother's funeral. I've been putting it off.'

'It can't be that bad. Have you decided you don't want to be married to me – or that you don't love me?'

'No, of course I haven't. I adore you – you know that, Rose.'

She sat down on the sofa and patted the place beside her. 'Tell me, Luke. You're not ill, are you?'

'No, I'm not ill. In a way it is good news – the best. I'm not sure how you will feel though – you may be angry because I didn't tell you when it happened.'

'You had better start at the beginning.'

'You remember when my plane was shot down in the war? I came to Sarah's and you were there but you left suddenly because your father was ill.'

'Yes, I remember.'

'I would have told you then, but I couldn't because you were grieving. It concerns the man who pulled me free of the plane when it was on fire. I would have died if it hadn't been for him.'

'Are we going to visit him? I should like to thank him, whoever he is.'

'Yes, we are going to visit him and his wife. In France he is known as Monsieur Georges Marly...' Luke hesitated and Rose's eyes widened in disbelief. 'Have you guessed it? It was Jack who pulled me from that plane, Rose. He was on a special mission when he was wounded. He lost his memory and did not recover it until he saw my face properly when he got me back to the farm.'

'Jack is alive?' Rose gave a cry and folded her arms over herself. Her face was chalk white and she looked as if she might faint, but when Luke put out a hand to touch her she shook her head. 'No! Don't touch me! How could you, Luke? How could you keep such news from me all this time?'

'I should have told you long ago but it never seemed the right time. After your father died I thought you had enough to deal with. I didn't see you for so long, and then... well, you recall what happened... I wasn't sure if Jack would still want you to know. I went to visit him in Paris. His wife has a café and I think Jack was about to buy a garage.'

'Why didn't he tell me himself?' Rose asked. 'Why didn't he tell any of us? He must have known we were grieving.' She rocked back and forth in agitation. 'You have no idea how this hurts me; how much I have longed for him to come back and tell us it was all a mistake and he wasn't dead.'

'I'm sorry. I didn't want to hurt you. Jack should have made his way through the lines once his memory returned. I tried to persuade him but he didn't want to leave Louise. She is his wife now. If he came back to this country he might be sent to prison as a deserter. He could have been shot for it during the war – though to the French freedom fighters he was a hero. I know they awarded him a medal.' He hesitated then continued. 'I thought you might rather go on thinking Jack was a war hero, which he was in his own way, though the army would not agree.'

'I would always have wanted to know he was alive,' Rose said, and tears trickled down her cheeks. 'I told him to keep his head down and not to be a damned hero! I love him.'

Suddenly the tears were released and she was sobbing. Luke drew her to her feet and into his arms. She fought him for a moment and then she subsided, weeping against his shoulder as he held her and stroked her hair.

'I'm sorry, I'm sorry,' he said softly. 'I was wrong but I did it because I thought you'd had enough sorrow.'

'I know.' She took the handkerchief he offered. 'It wasn't all your fault, Luke. Jack could have told me himself. Just wait until I see him! I'll make him wish he'd never been born...' She raised her head, looking at Luke in wonder. 'I'm going to see him. I'm really going to see him. Jack is alive. He is alive.'

'Yes, we shall visit him and Louise. They have quite a story to tell, Rose. Jack was far from a coward, believe me. He saved my life and I think he did the same for others.'

'I can hardly believe it after all these years. Ma...' She stared at Luke. 'I don't know how I shall tell her. She will be angry that he didn't write to her – and she may think that he was wrong to desert his comrades.'

'Now you understand how I felt about telling you. Wait until you've talked to Jack, Rose. Let him tell you why he stayed at the farm instead of coming back through the lines with me.'

'Yes, perhaps I should,' Rose said. 'It should be for Jack to decide what to do for the best as far as Ma is concerned. I only know that this is one of the happiest days of my life.'

Luke stopped the car outside the small café. It was a warm afternoon and they could hear the sound of bees droning in the honeysuckle that wound its way over the rose-coloured walls. He looked at Rose as she sat up straight, her hands on her knees. He could feel the tension inside her.

'Shall I go in first and ask Jack to come out to you?'

Rose looked at him and then nodded. 'Yes, please – if you

would. I'm going to walk round to the back yard. It will be more private there.'

'That's a good idea,' Luke said. 'It's bound to be as emotional for Jack as it is for you.'

He got out of the car, holding the door for Rose as she slid out and walked through the small side alley to the yard at the back of the café. It was quieter away from the busy streets of the city and she was glad she had chosen it as the place to meet her brother.

The yard was a good size, with a herb garden close to the kitchen door and a few fruit trees at the bottom. In between was a patio where Louise could hang out washing on a line. A large table and some chairs had been placed in a sunny spot. It had an intimate charm and Rose could imagine sitting there in the cool of the evening with a glass of wine. Jack had found a good place for himself – but she was still angry with him. How could he leave his family to grieve when he could have put an end to their suffering with a few lines on a card?

She saw a lavender bush and bent to pull a few flowers through her hands to inhale their scent.

'You always did like lavender.'

Rose turned as she heard his voice. She stared because he was just the same – and yet not quite. His skin had a deeper tan; there was a scar at his temple and she noticed that he walked with a slight limp as he came towards her.

'Jack...' She felt as if her feet were glued to the ground. She was holding her emotions on a tight rein as anger, relief and sheer joy coursed through her body. 'Damn you, Jack! Why didn't you tell us?' Suddenly she was released. She flung herself at him, beating her fists against his chest. 'Damn you! I'm so angry with you for what you did – but I am so happy you are alive...' The tears were pouring down her cheeks as his arms went round her and he hushed her. 'I've missed you so much...'

'I've missed you, Rose. I can't tell you how often I wished I could tell you the truth.'

She raised her head, a glint in her eyes. 'You could have told me! Do you think I would have betrayed you? I would never have given you away, but it would have meant so much to know you were alive.'

'I told Luke he could tell you, but he found it difficult.' Jack looked sombre. 'It nearly killed me when the letter came to say Father was dead. I wanted to be there, but I had made my choice and there was no going back. I chose Louise, Rose. She needed me. I couldn't leave her – and I didn't want to go back to those damned trenches. We were like lambs to the slaughter – cannon fodder. I doubt I would have survived the war if I hadn't been given special duties. I was damned near killed on one mission and it was a long time before I knew who I was. By then I was in too deep. I couldn't leave Louise because I love her.'

Rose stared at him. She didn't really understand, but she was willing to forgive. 'It doesn't matter now. I was angry but it has gone. I love you, Jack. I'm so glad you're alive.'

He drew back and looked at her, smiling. 'So you're married to Sir Luke now – Lady Trenwith no less.'

'Don't call me by that name,' she said. 'Luke doesn't bother with his title and I don't either. His father died some time ago and his mother died recently in a fire at Trenwith. The old wing has gone but Luke was going to pull it down anyway. He is going to turn the main building into a hotel.'

'So the old traditions will be gone.' Jack nodded. 'Maybe it is just as well. Are you going to live on the estate?'

'We might live at the dower house in time, but we're going to spend some months in France. I want to get to know your Louise – and you need to meet Elspeth, your niece.' Jack raised his brows. 'She was born before we married... It is a long story, Jack, and it doesn't matter.'

'Well, I can't read you a lecture. It was years before we could marry. Louise was married when we first met.' He grinned at her in the old way and her heart leapt with joy. 'Come and meet her, Rose. We haven't any children yet – but Louise told me yesterday that she is pregnant. I hope everything goes well, but she will need to take care because she could lose the baby.'

Rose nodded. She understood how easy it was for some women to miscarry. 'I am looking forward to meeting Louise,' she said and took his arm. 'I like your home, Jack. Luke told me you were going to buy a garage.'

'It is up and running,' Jack told her. 'It was fire damaged and I had to rebuild it, but I am beginning to make some headway at last.'

'So you've got everything you want here? You would never think of going back to England?'

'I might end up in prison,' Jack said. 'I've thought about you a lot, and Ma – but I don't want to go back.'

'What about Ma?'

'I think she might be disappointed in me,' Jack admitted. 'I'm afraid she would not understand...'

'I think she might,' Rose said. 'I'll invite her to visit us here in France in a few weeks' time and then I'll bring her to see you and Louise.'

'Would she live with us?' Jack looked at her. 'That's if she could forgive me. I'm sure the news of my death contributed to Father's – didn't it?'

'Yes, perhaps,' Rose said. 'But she can't blame you for that, Jack. It was the war. You didn't know who you were for a long time. If I talk to Ma I think she will understand.'

'Ask her to come here. If she does we can tell her the story,' Jack said. 'I don't think she will be as understanding as you, Rose, but she might forgive me one day.'

* * *

Luke smiled at Rose as she came from the bathroom into their hotel bedroom. She was wearing one of the pretty negligées they had bought in Paris.

'Is everything all right?'

'Fine,' Rose told him. 'I'm not used to such rich food but the sickness has passed.'

'As long as you're not ill? You are happy here in Paris? I had thought we would travel for a while, but I think I could paint here, Rose. I thought we might rent or buy a small flat with a studio. There are quite a few advertised to let – but we need enough space for all of us.'

'It would certainly be better for Elspeth, and I would prefer to cook for ourselves some of the time. I like eating with Louise and Jack, but we can't impose on them too much and the hotels are too fancy for my liking.'

'Mine too,' Luke agreed. 'Are you as good a cook as your mother?'

'Not quite, but not too bad either. She taught me, so I should be able to feed us.'

'And it is what you prefer?'

'Yes, it is,' Rose said. 'I am not sure how long Jean will stay with us, because she is homesick, but Emily loves being here.'

'You do too, don't you?' Luke hesitated. 'There are plenty of theatres and cafés that hire singers to entertain the customers. Would you like to work, Rose? I wouldn't stop you if you wanted to go back to the stage.'

'I know.' Rose smiled at him. 'The answer is that I am quite content here. I enjoy walking in the sunshine, buying food and flowers in the markets. Besides, this nausea might not just be caused by the rich food.'

'What do you mean?' Luke stared and then, as he saw the gleam of laughter in her eyes, he asked, 'You mean Elspeth might be going to have a sister?'

'Or a brother,' Rose said and smiled. 'I'm not certain yet, but I've noticed that my breasts are a little tender and that was one of the signs last time.'

'You will be able to swap notes with Louise,' Luke said and grinned. 'I think she must be past the dangerous stage, don't you?'

'Yes, I think so – I hope so,' Rose said. 'I wrote to Ma this morning, asked her to come and stay for a couple of weeks.'

'Do you think she will?'

'I don't know.' Rose walked towards Luke, lifting her face for his kiss. 'Are you pleased that we may soon have another child?'

'What do you think? I missed so much last time. I am going to make it up to you, Rose. I'll look after you...'

'Please do not fuss over me the way Jack does with Louise. He had reason to make her sit down and rest, but I am feeling on top of the world, and I carried on working for a long time when I was expecting Elspeth.'

'Only because I was a damned idiot,' Luke said, putting his arms around her. 'If your mother comes she will love Louise.'

'I can't see her leaving until the baby is born.' Rose laughed, her eyes lighting from within. 'We are so lucky, Luke. Sometimes when I look in the mirror I have to pinch myself to be certain I'm not dreaming.'

'I know the feeling,' Luke said, and he bent his head to kiss her. 'Oh, yes, I know the feeling...'

'Are you sure you want to leave?' Rose asked her mother as she watched her packing her case. 'Luke would find you somewhere to live if you wanted to stay here for a while.'

'Louise has her son,' Mrs Barlow said. 'I've done my bit to help her, but she will be back at work in a day or two. They don't need me and neither do you, Rose. You've got Jean and Emily.'

'Jean is going home at the end of the month.'

'Emily can manage, and you're a good housekeeper, Rose. I always knew you would be once you got a home of your own. Besides, you could find another nursemaid if you wanted.'

'Yes, I could, but I like doing things for myself and we live simply here in Paris. It will be different when we return to Trenwith. Mrs Jarvis will take charge of the housework as usual.'

'Do you intend to live at Trenwith then?'

'We shall spend some months in Paris every year. Luke feels he can paint here and I love it – but he can't desert Trenwith altogether. He has been back once alone, just to sort something out. Next time I shall go with him.'

Mrs Barlow nodded. 'Jack has offered me a home with them, but

I shan't take it. I might visit again another year, but Myrtle needs me and she gave me a home when I was left on my own. I'm not going to desert her while she has that hotel to run. If she retired I might think again, especially if you are going to live here some of the time.'

Rose looked at her thoughtfully. 'You have forgiven Jack, Ma? I know some people would call him a deserter – but he did what he felt was right. You and Dad always told us to do what we thought was right.'

'Aye, we did,' Mrs Barlow said. 'I don't blame Jack for what he did – but he should have written as soon as he could. I think it was grief that killed his father and I can't forget that, Rose.'

'Would Father have understood?'

'He would have tried.' Mrs Barlow gave her daughter a straight look. 'Your father wouldn't have understood your marrying above your station – but he would have approved of the way you live. I've seen how happy you are, love, and I'm satisfied it was the right thing. As Luke says, the world has moved on – and so have we.'

'Yes, we have,' Rose agreed. 'Who would have thought it would one day be possible to fly to Paris, or that we would take using the telephone and electricity for granted? Luke says this is only the beginning. He says we'll have wireless broadcasts before long and even talking movies. We might even be able to fly to America one day.'

'They will put a man on the moon one of these days,' Mrs Barlow observed with a twist of her lips. 'They've opened Pandora's Box, Rose. It's too late to stop it now – though one day we may all wish we could.'

Rose smiled. Her mother spoke of moving on but her attitudes would never change. She had clung to the old ways almost as long as Lady Trenwith, but when the changes came she had accepted them while reserving judgement – that was the difference.

Rose sometimes wondered whether they would be as happy living at Trenwith as they were in Paris. It had been a halcyon time for them all, but she knew that Luke could never desert his roots altogether. He might fight against the ties that bound him to Trenwith, but in the end he would do his duty. He was that kind of a man, and perhaps that was the reason she loved him so much.

FROM THE AUTHOR

Dear readers. I hope you will enjoy these books as much as I enjoyed writing them. Best wishes, Rosie Clarke.

ABOUT THE AUTHOR

Rosie Clarke is a #1 bestselling saga writer whose books include Welcome to Harpers Emporium and The Mulberry Lane series. She has written over 100 novels under different pseudonyms and is a RNA Award winner. She lives in Cambridgeshire.

Sign up to Rosie Clarke's mailing list for news, competitions and updates on future books.

Visit Rosie's website: www.rosieclarke.co.uk

Follow Rosie on social media here:

facebook.com/Rosie-clarke-119457351778432

x.com/AnneHerries

bookbub.com/authors/rosie-clarke

ALSO BY ROSIE CLARKE

Welcome to Harpers Emporium Series

The Shop Girls of Harpers

Love and Marriage at Harpers

Rainy Days for the Harpers Girls

Harpers Heroes

Wartime Blues for the Harpers Girls

Victory Bells For The Harpers Girls

Changing Times at Harpers

Heartbreak at Harpers

The Mulberry Lane Series

A Reunion at Mulberry Lane

Stormy Days On Mulberry Lane

A New Dawn Over Mulberry Lane

Life and Love at Mulberry Lane

Last Orders at Mulberry Lane

Blackberry Farm Series

War Clouds Over Blackberry Farm

Heartache at Blackberry Farm

Love and Duty at Blackberry Farm

The Trenwith Trilogy

Sarah's Choice

Louise's War

Rose's Fight

Standalones

Nellie's Heartbreak

A Mother's Shame

A Sister's Destiny

Dangerous Times on Dressmakers' Alley

Sixpence Stories

Introducing Sixpence Stories!

Discover page-turning historical novels from your favourite authors, meet new friends and be transported back in time.

Join our book club Facebook group

https://bit.ly/SixpenceGroup

Sign up to our newsletter

https://bit.ly/SixpenceNews

Boldwood

Boldwood Books is an award-winning fiction publishing company seeking out the best stories from around the world.

Find out more at www.boldwoodbooks.com

Join our reader community for brilliant books, competitions and offers!

Follow us
@BoldwoodBooks
@TheBoldBookClub

Sign up to our weekly deals newsletter

https://bit.ly/BoldwoodBNewsletter